THE BONE KEY

THE BONE KEY

———

Sarah Monette

PRIME BOOKS

THE BONE KEY

———

Prime Books
www.prime-books.com

ISBN: 978-0-8095-5777-6

this book is dedicated to

M. R. James

(1862 - 1936)

and

H. P. Lovecraft

(1890 - 1937)

TABLE OF CONTENTS

INTRODUCTION

This book is a series of interconnected short stories, written between 2000 and 2006. Their narrator/protagonist is a museum archivist—neurotic, erudite, insomniac—and he and his world are both homages to and interrogations of the works of M. R. James and H. P. Lovecraft. They are, in other words, old-fashioned ghost stories with, at times, a modern sensibility shining through.

I came late to James and Lovecraft, but when I did discover them, in graduate school, I fell fast and hard. Here were writers who reveled in words and cherished scholarship, who at the same time were sincere and uncompromising in their desire to scare the living daylights out of their readers. "'Oh, Whistle, and I'll Come to You, My Lad'" is one of the scariest stories I have ever read, and I still can't figure out how James accomplishes it. The beginning of that story is dry and mocking, simultaneously pedantic and satirizing pedantry, making no effort at concealing its own fictionality, and yet by the end, without ever visibly shifting tone, it has reduced its reader to a quivering wreck.

I like that in a guy.

I inhaled Lovecraft and James in wholesale lots and learned a tremendous amount from them about a particular kind of horror, the old school horror of insinuation and nuance. But I also discovered that there were things about James and Lovecraft that did not satisfy me, particularly their general indifference to character development. There are *characters* in James and Lovecraft—Professor Parkins, the protagonist of "'Oh, Whistle, and I'll Come to You, My Lad,'" being a good example—but these characters generally have little or no psychological depth, and they are static. They have neither the chance nor the capacity for change. Also, of course, James and Lovecraft ignore sex and sexuality with dogged determination and, well—let us say they are not feminists and leave it at that.

None of these omissions prevents me from loving their work, but the more I read James and Lovecraft, the more I found myself wanting to take apart their story engines and put them back together with a fifth gear, as it were: the psychological and psychosexual focus of that *other* James.

The Turn of the Screw is, after all, also a magnificent work of horror.

Kyle Murchison Booth, my protagonist, emerged diffidently from the Lovecraft story "The Statement of Randolph Carter." "The Statement" has more psychological complexity than most Lovecraft stories, with the weak, unstable narrator in thrall to his brilliant, reckless friend, and while that's obviously a necessity for setting up the whammy at the end, it's also intriguing in its own right. The first Booth story, "Bringing Helena Back," essentially takes that dynamic and adds an overt homoerotic element and an unreliable narrator. I didn't go into that story intending to make a series out of it, but in working out the background details to bring Booth and Blaine's relationship to the necessary crisis point, I discovered that shy, awkward, geeky Booth had worlds within him far more vast and complex than the scope of one short story could encompass.

Booth is the most autobiographical of my protagonists. I was a shy, awkward, geeky child, and I have vivid memories of never knowing what to say, how to act, of learning to prefer being alone because it was safer than trying to interact with other children. I gave those remembered emotions to Booth, and the experience of writing him is thus both nerve-wracking and cathartic. If I'm doing it right, I bleed with him, and maybe the reader does, too.

Gentle Reader, allow me to introduce Kyle Murchison Booth. You will forgive him if he does not shake hands.

BRINGING HELENA BACK

I was contemplating the fragments of an unidentified animal's skull, late on a wet, windy Friday in March, when a voice said, "Booth? Is that you?"

My head jerked up; Augustus Blaine was leaning against my office door, as if his body were too heavy for him to support on his own any longer. I recognized him at once, although I had not seen him for ten years. He looked forty-two instead of thirty-two. I would have known his voice anywhere.

"My God, man," he said, staring, "what happened to your hair?"

My hand went up involuntarily to touch it. My hair had gone white eight years previously, over a period of about four months. It was a trait of my mother's family; all the Murchisons went white before they were twenty-five.

"Doesn't matter," Blaine said before I could do more than begin to stammer a reply. "I came here for help."

He sounded exhausted, but his eyes were feverishly bright. Carefully, I set the skull fragments down on my desk, and said, "Come in. Please, er, sit down. I think . . . there's a chair clear."

He dragged the chair across to my desk and sat, a little warily. "All your bits of pot and bone," he said, his voice somewhere between fondness and contempt. "Are you good at your job, Boothie?"

"People, er, seem to think so."

"The thing is," Blaine said, "the thing is that I think I need a spot of help."

"Anything you need, Blaine. I . . . that is, you know that."

He looked at me for a moment, his face stiff with suspicion like an African mask, and then he smiled. "By God, I think you mean

13

that. All right, then. It's this book." He set his briefcase on his lap and opened it. The lid concealed the contents of the briefcase from me, but he closed it again swiftly, left-handed, and put it back on the floor. His right hand was holding the book.

It was a slender quarto, leather-bound and badly chipped. The title had once been on the spine, but someone had carefully burned it out. "You don't want to know how much I paid for this," Blaine said, with a grin on his face that I found frightening. "It'll all be worth it, though. I'm sure. But the deuce of it is, Boothie, I can't read it."

"What do you mean?"

"It's in some kind of cipher. I've been tearing my hair out over it for weeks, trying to crack the damn thing. And then I thought of my old friend, Kyle Murchison Booth." He rolled the syllables of my name out of his mouth as if they were at once contemptible and marvelous. "This should be right up your alley, Boothie."

"What, er . . . what's the book about, Blaine?"

"Didn't I say? I think there's a way I can bring Helena back."

I was so startled—as much aghast at his matter-of-fact manner as at what he had said—that I knocked the skull fragments off my desk.

Blaine and I had met as freshmen in college. Blaine had almost immediately decided and announced that we were going to be friends. To this day, I do not know why. The things we had in common— education, wealth, the sort of genealogy that passes in America for aristocratic—did not seem to me as if they could possibly bridge the gulf between us, the gulf I had always felt between myself and people like Blaine. The only theory I had was that I offered Blaine someone with whom to discuss topics other than athletic pursuits and alcohol. He could talk to me as he could talk to no one else in his world. He was my only friend—that says, I imagine, as much about me as anyone needs to know.

Blaine was interested in everything; it was part of the way he was put together—a relentless, bright-eyed interest in everything under the sun. The action of his mind often reminded me of a lighthouse light, revolving and revolving, sending its bright, piercing beam out into the darkness in every direction, never stopping on any one thing for long, but continuing to search. He was interested in chemistry and biology and physics; he was interested in history and archaeology and anthropology; he took classes in French, German, Russian, Greek, Latin, never more than a semester or two of any of them, the beam sweeping restlessly onward. He must have taken courses in every department on campus, and he could talk for hours, scintillatingly, compellingly, about any of them.

In this, as in so many other respects, I was Blaine's opposite. Next to him I was a dull, ugly crow, without even the wit to hide myself in peacock feathers. I listened to Blaine for hours, but could find nothing of any interest to say myself. I stuck to my dry, safe work in history and archaeology, looking already toward the dim, dusty halls of the Samuel Mather Parrington Museum.

Blaine had always teased me about my love of puzzles: crosswords, acrostics, ciphers, anagrams. I solved them obsessively, as I solved the archival puzzles set by my professors; they were practice for what was to become my life's work. I am sure that Blaine remembered timing me on the ciphers I found in books of logical puzzles; I am sure that the memory is why he sought me out, and therefore my freakish skill makes me responsible for his death.

I sometimes offer myself the false comfort that Helena was even more to blame than I. Helena Pryde was the sister of Blaine's friend Tobias Pryde. Blaine met her because Tobias—good-natured, warmly gregarious, not very bright, one of the few of Blaine's friends who did not treat me like some strange pet of Blaine's—invited us both home with him for the spring vacation of our junior year. The Prydes' house ("the House of Pryde" Blaine kept calling it and snickering at his own pun) was well-proportioned and handsome, beautifully situated in an oak grove. Mr. and Mrs. Pryde were people as imperceptive and generous as their son. Helena Pryde, Tobias's younger sister, was a changeling.

She was tall and slender, with hair of an amazing dark, ruddy gold. Her hair was also unusually thick and heavy, and she habitually wore it loose, so that it hung like a cloak of fire past her hips. The effect was stunning, quite literally so; I heard Blaine's breath hitch in at his first sight of her. I suppose she was pretty—at least, everyone seemed to think so—but her mouth was small and ungenerous, and her eyes were hard. Her voice was high-pitched and always rather breathless, and she lisped just slightly. The quality of her voice was childlike, innocent, and that was a deception worthy of the Serpent in Eden.

She flirted with Blaine from the moment they were introduced. Blaine—who had dated one girl after another for the three years I had known him, an endless parade of Elizabeths, Marys, Charlottes, and Julias—responded enthusiastically in kind, and before the week was half over, he was spending more time with Helena than with either Tobias or me.

I doubt Tobias even noticed, but I was aware of it—aware of the hard, predatory light in Helena's eyes when she looked at Blaine, even more aware that his expression when he looked back at her showed that he did not see her as I did. He could not see her for what she was. Thursday at dinner, I overheard them discussing how they could meet again after this visit was over, and where and when. Friday morning, after a night spent staring sleeplessly into the darkness of my room, I had determined that I had to talk to Blaine, that it was my duty as his friend to try to make him see what sort of person Helena Pryde was.

I searched for Blaine all Friday morning, wandering in and out of the gracious, unobservant rooms of the House of Pryde. Finally, nearly at lunchtime, I thought I heard voices in the library. The Prydes' library curved in an L-shape around two sides of the house;

it was full of beautiful old books at which I doubt anyone in the family ever looked twice. They were dusted faithfully by the maids, however, and they were freely available for any guest who wished to browse. I already knew the library well, preferring its dim, serene coolness to the bright heat of the tennis court where Blaine and Tobias and Helena and a steady rotation of Helena's friends played doubles in the afternoons.

I went into the library. The lights were off, and the room was full of the cool, dreamlike, underwater glow of sunlight through oak leaves.

"Blaine?" I called. "Are you in here?"

Someone said something in a muffled voice, and there was a burst of laughter.

"Blaine?" I said, advancing until I could see into the other half of the L. "Are you . . . "

He was sitting on one of the enormous leather couches. His hair was ruffled and his tie askew. Possessively close beside him sat Helena Pryde, a little smirk on her ungenerous mouth. It took no special perspicacity to see what they had been doing. I felt my face heat.

But I had come this far. "Blaine, I, er, wanted to—"

"Go away, Boothie," Blaine said.

The one mannerism of Blaine's that I hated was that nickname, invented one night in our sophomore year when he was giddy with wine. I would not have minded so much if it had been a private nickname, although even then I thought it silly, but Blaine used it in front of other people. He did so partly to tease me, but partly to reassure his friends that he had more savoir-faire than to treat me as an equal.

I said, hating what I heard in my own voice, "Can we talk later?"

"When we get back to school, Boothie," Blaine said. "Miss Pryde has just done me the honor of consenting to our betrothal." At this they both started giggling, like schoolchildren at a smutty joke. "And I fancy I'm going to be rather occupied for the rest of our visit."

"Darling Auggie," said Miss Pryde fondly.

" . . . All right, Blaine," I said—there was nothing else I could say, no words of mine to which he would listen—and left. Just before I closed the library door, I heard them laughing again, and I knew they were laughing at me. Helena had won.

I saw the headlines when she died, of course. Helena Pryde Blaine was a society darling, always being photographed in fancy night clubs or at charity galas, her amazing hair flowing darkly, hypnotically, even in newsprint. Blaine went unremarked in the society pages, except very rarely as part of the entity "Mr. and Mrs. Augustus Blaine." That absence alone told me that the marriage was not a happy one, and I had the dour satisfaction of having been right all along. For nine years, that was all I had; Blaine, obediently following the family tradition, was not the sort of lawyer whose clients made the papers.

But the death of Helena Pryde Blaine was a lurid scandal that not even the Blaines' influence could cover up. She died of an overdose of cocaine, in the apartment of a man who was less than a husband but more than a friend. His name was Rutherford Chapin; I had gone to prep school with him and remembered him with loathing. The two of them, Rutherford Chapin and Helena Pryde Blaine, might have been made for each other, and I was only sorry, for Blaine's sake, that she had not found Chapin first.

I sent Blaine a letter of condolence; I could not bring myself to attend the funeral or to send flowers. I was not sorry that she was dead. I hoped for a while—the stupid sort of fantasy that keeps one awake at night—that Blaine might answer me with a letter or even a visit, but I received nothing more than a "thank you for your sympathy" note, clearly written by one of Blaine's sisters. Only the signature was his; I recognized it, despite the spiky scrawl into which his handwriting had degenerated. I continued stupidly to hope, but

I did not hear anything from or about Blaine for another year, until the night when he appeared in my office at the museum with his abhorrent book.

It took me a long time to get the story out of him—not because he did not want to tell me, but because he had been living alone with his obsession for so long that he had developed his own private short-hand, and he kept forgetting that he was not talking to his reflection in the mirror. He was impatient when I asked questions—and that was very like the Blaine I remembered—but I did finally piece together a narrative of the past year.

He had nearly gone crazy at first, he said (and it occurred to me that many people would question that "nearly"), looking for Helena everywhere, expecting to hear her voice every time he answered the telephone. When the truth finally sank in, the great lighthouse of Blaine's mind locked unswervingly on the idea of, as he said, "bringing Helena back." He never used the word "necromancy," or any other phrase that held an open acknowledgment of her death. A person who did not know better would imagine from his conversation that she had simply been stranded in some dangerous and barbaric part of the world, the Himalayas, perhaps, or the Sahara.

As an up-and-coming young lawyer, Blaine naturally knew nothing of the black arts, but a powerful intellect and money to burn can compensate for a remarkable number of deficiencies, and Blaine had remedied his ignorance in startlingly little time. He had read every book of dark arcana he could find, and he had found some dreadfully obscure things. He even claimed to have a copy of *The Book of Whispers*, but I suspect that the book gracing his shelves was really the elegant and convincing nineteenth-century fake by Isaiah Hope Turnbull. Even so, the collection he had amassed was astounding and disturbing.

Blaine had tried everything, everything his books suggested, and none of it had worked. "*None* of it!" he shouted at me, pounding his fist so violently on my desk that I was only just in time to keep the skull fragments from crashing to the floor again.

He had been in despair. But then the dealer who had found the other books for him (and who had gulled him so egregiously over *The Book of Whispers*) had come to him with stories of another book, even more obscure and powerful. Blaine said he would have paid any sum the man named. I was appalled, as much by his reckless credulity as by anything else. The possibility began to loom very large in my mind that the book Blaine clutched so fiercely was yet another fake, something the dealer had cobbled together to exploit this fabulous windfall still further. That being the case, there could be no harm in humoring Blaine, especially when it meant he would have to come back in a week and talk to me. I took the book home.

Here is where my guilt begins: not in humoring Blaine, but in opening that damnable book. There was nothing to prevent me from keeping the book for a week without so much as touching it, then bringing it back with an admission of defeat. I had seen Blaine's desperation; he had come to me only because he could not think of anything rational to do. He would be disappointed, but neither surprised nor suspicious. But if I did that, he would leave again. And I wanted to surprise him, to show him that I could help him. Perhaps that was the root of my folly: I wanted Blaine finally to take me seriously.

I opened the book. It was, as Blaine had said, in cipher, but it was not a terribly difficult cipher. I thought I recognized it after looking at a few lines, and my estimation of the unknown forger went up several notches. It might not have been difficult, but it was quite obscure, a cipher invented and used almost exclusively by a circle of

Flemish occultists who had flourished in the late sixteenth century. Even then, it did not occur to me that the book might be genuine, only that the forger had done his homework. I refreshed my memory of the cipher and got to work.

Within a page, I knew that the book was no fake, but by then it had trapped me.

I dare not describe it too closely, for fear that there may be another copy somewhere in existence, and that I may excite curiosity about it. If there is another copy, let it molder to dust wherever it lies.

I have dreams sometimes, in which I throw the book again on the fire, but this time it does not burn. It simply rests on top of the flames, its pages flipping randomly back and forth. I can feel my hands twitching and trembling with the need to reach into the fire and rescue it. Inevitably, I do reach. I plunge my hands into the fire, and I wake up. Although my hands are marred by neither blisters nor burns, they throb and sear for hours afterwards as if the fire in my dreams were real.

I will not give the book's true title. I have since found a few veiled references to it in the writings of those Flemish occultists, and they refer to it always as the *Mortui Liber Magistri—The Book of the Master of the Dead* or, perhaps, *The Book of the Dead Master*. I will do the same. Freed of the cipher, the *Mortui Liber Magistri* was written in perfectly straightforward Latin, with all the mesmerizing power of a cobra's inhuman gaze. Once I had read the first two sentences, I was lost. I could neither look away nor put it aside, and I finished my translation just as the sun was rising.

Then I telephoned Blaine. When Blaine answered, I wanted to say, *Blaine, this book is an abomination. I think you should burn it.* But the words that came out of my mouth, calmly and rationally, were nothing like that at all. The words I spoke were the words the *Mortui Liber Magistri* wanted spoken: "I know how to do it."

Blaine was amazed, delighted. We made our plans. We would meet that night at his house, and I would show him how to bring

Helena back. Then we would perform the ritual. "Very good," I said to Blaine, replaced the telephone receiver, and staggered to bed.

I slept until sunset, when I woke up screaming.

I will not—*cannot*—describe the ritual. If I could excise it from my brain, believe that I would. I cannot, and the ineradicability of the memory is no more than I deserve. The ritual was an evil, perverted thing, and I neither know, nor want to know, where Blaine found the materials he used—except for the human blood. That was mine.

Blaine had always been able to persuade me to do what he wanted, and he was full of good, rational reasons why it had to be my blood instead of his. Sometimes, when my insomnia is particularly sere—a vast, arid, cracking wasteland in which the dead trees do not give shelter—I wonder if perhaps that was the crux at which things began to go wrong. Blaine loved his wife enough to spend thousands of dollars and to perform this obscene ritual, but not quite enough to open a vein in his own arm and let his own blood pool on the obsidian slab in his cellar.

There is a hard, angry little voice in my head, a voice like hers, that says, *Blaine deserved his death*. That is not true, and I know it. What Blaine *deserved* was a friend good enough and strong enough to stop him, but I was not that friend.

The book had released me as soon as I had explained everything to Blaine, so I have no excuse. Where a stronger, better man would have said, *Blaine, this is madness*, I looked into his burning, haunted, driven eyes, and I rolled back the cuff of my shirt.

The ritual worked. That is the most ghastly thing. I hold no particular brief for the rationality of the world, but that this vile obscenity should actually have the power to bring back the dead seems to me a sign not merely that the world is not rational, but that it is in fact entirely insane, a murderous lunatic gibbering in the corner of a padded cell.

The ritual worked. The patterns of blood and graveyard earth, the stench of burning entrails, the repulsive Latin phrases that Blaine chanted, they combined exactly as the book said they would. A presence coalesced in the middle of Blaine's obsidian slab. It was shapeless and colorless at first, but as Blaine's incantations mounted in fervor and monstrosity, it drew itself together, taking on Helena's shape and garbing itself in her chic, severely tailored clothes. The colors were slower to come, but I remember the way her hair washed in, a torrent of blood and gold down her back. She was facing away from us.

"Helena," Blaine said, breathless with wonder and desire. "Helena, darling, it's me."

The shape did not turn.

"Helena, it's me, it's Augustus. Darling, can you hear me?"

Still she did not turn, but a voice, undeniably hers, said, "Where's Ruthie? I want Ruthie."

"Helena!"

She moved a little, restlessly, in the circle, but still she would not turn. "Ruthie loves me," she said. "He says so."

"Helena, it's Augustus!" I had an unwelcome flash of insight: that I was watching the distillation of the nine years of their marriage, Helena never looking at Blaine, always looking for something else, Blaine pleading and coaxing, talking always to her back, to the amazing sunset river of her hair.

"Why isn't Ruthie here?" Helena said petulantly, as if she had not heard Blaine at all.

Blaine stepped into the circle. I do not think he realized at that point what he was doing, for the warnings in the *Mortui Liber Magistri* against the caster crossing the circle were dire and uncompromising, and I know that he heard me when I explained them.

"Blaine!" I lunged forward, but I could not catch him in time; I had drawn too far away from the circle when Helena began to manifest.

My fingers brushed the back of his shirt with no more force than a butterfly's wing, and he was beyond help. The instant Blaine was within the circle, Helena turned. She had heard him all along, had known to a nicety—as she ever had—how to get him to do what she wanted.

Her face was ghastly. It was not simply that she was, all too clearly, still dead. It was that she was dead and yet animate. Her face was gray and stiff and bloodless, but it was filled with a monstrous vitality. Blaine had not brought Helena back to life; he had done something far, far worse.

I suppose it is possible that the thing in the circle was not Helena Pryde Blaine at all, that it was a demon or some other sort of inhuman spirit. My own belief, however, is that it was the quintessence of Helena, the thing in her that Blaine had never been able to see, and that I had been powerless to show him: the greedy selfishness of a child who can never be satisfied with her own toys if another child has a toy, no matter how shabby, that she does not. Blaine was just another toy to her, and one that bored her.

He saw the truth of her then, the insatiable, heartless greed, although he had never seen it before. He recoiled from her and tried, far too late, to back out of the circle.

"Kiss me, darling Auggie," said Helena, in her breathless, mocking way. She caught his arms and drew him toward her. Blaine stiffened and made a noise that would probably have been a scream if he could have gotten enough air into his lungs before her lips closed on his. When she let him go—five loathsome, endless seconds later—he fell down dead.

I was pressed into the corner, the cold damp bricks prodding at my back like angry fingers. My whole desire at that moment was that Helena should ignore me as she always had.

She looked at me. The face was livid and hard, but the eyes were still hers. "Boothie," she said.

I moaned, somewhere in the back of my throat. It was all the noise I could make.

She cocked her head to one side, a hideous parody of the way she had been accustomed to flirt. "I don't suppose I can talk *you* into the circle, Boothie, can I?"

My head was shaking "no," wobbling back and forth on my neck as if it belonged to someone else.

"No," she said, with a little moue of disappointment. "Auggie could have, I'll bet. But you never liked me, did you?"

"I hated you, Helena," I said, the truth croaking out of me un-willed.

She actually smiled then, and I would give anything I possess if I could stop seeing her smile in my dreams. The smile was hers, the little, gloating smirk that I had always loathed, but the dead stiffness of her face made it a rictus. "I don't hold that against you, Boothie. I always knew you were jealous." She tittered. "Boothie and Ruthie–-Auggie and I both had our little lapdogs, didn't we?"

I should have held my tongue, but my hatred of her, my crawling revulsion, was greater than my fear. "Yours killed you," I said.

"And now Auggie's has killed him. So I guess we're even."

She was starting to fade; with the death of its caster, the ritual was losing potency. She noticed it herself. "Phooey," she said. She looked at me, her eyes bright with all the malice of the living Helena Pryde Blaine. "Are you going to have a go at calling Auggie back, Booth-ie? I'm sure you could do it. He always said you were the smartest man he knew." With that, she was gone, dissolved into the stinking smoke, leaving nothing behind her but her husband's corpse.

It took me until dawn to clean the cellar, washing away the blood and dirt and other materials. I had to lift Blaine to clean under him, but after that I left him where he was. His body looked sixty-two now instead of thirty-two, and there was not a mark on him: nothing to show that he had not fallen down dead of a heart attack. He was cold and stiff, and obviously had been dead much longer than five hours, although he had died only seven minutes before two o'clock.

He had been living entirely alone, without even servants—he had dismissed them all when his interest in necromancy began to devolve into obsession—and that was my good fortune. I took away the paraphernalia of the ritual and threw all its repellant ingredients into the river on my way home.

Then I waited.

Blaine was found four days later. One of his sisters finally became worried enough about him to use her key to his house. No one, except apparently for me, had heard from him in over a week. His family had known nothing of his dabblings in necromancy. He had told no one of his latest purchase—save of course the book dealer—and no one at all of his decision to consult me. There were, as I myself had seen, no signs of violence on his body, and the coroner's judgment was that his heart had simply given out: he was awfully young for such a death, but he had been under a severe strain for a very long time, and these things did happen . . . If someone had gone exploring through Blaine's effects, they might have found evidence to suggest another possibility, but his family did not wish any further inquiry, and the Blaines are powerful. No one else asked questions, and I heard later that the book dealer who had supplied Blaine's mania had left the city unexpectedly and precipitously.

My culpability was not discovered, nor even suspected. Only I knew, and the things that came to find me in my dreams. They knew and I knew that Helena was right. I had killed Blaine, just as surely as Rutherford Chapin had killed her. The guilt and the loneliness were all but unbearable; I was as comfortless as Cain.

And all the while Helena's last question—*Are you going to have a go at calling Auggie back, Boothie?*—echoed meanly through my head. I could repeat the ritual. I had kept the book, and my notes, and I had watched Blaine. I could bring Blaine back.

I wanted to. I wanted to bring Blaine back, just as Blaine had wanted to bring Helena back. I wanted to see him again, to hear his voice. More importantly, I wanted to talk to him and to know that he was finally and forever hearing *me*, not the version of me that lived in his head. I wanted Blaine to love me as I had always loved him.

I sat by the fireplace in my living room, the book and my sheaf of notes in my lap. *It will be different,* said a voice in my head—the voice, I suppose, of Blaine's "Boothie." *Helena was greedy and loveless. Blaine is my friend. Blaine would never want to hurt me. And I won't make the mistakes that Blaine did.*

It said such wonderful, plausible things, that voice, and I wanted to believe it very badly. It was my hatred of Helena that saved me, my absolute, unassailable conviction that she would never have put any idea in my head that might have made me happy. I remembered her eyes, remembered her smirk, and with a sudden convulsive motion, flung the *Mortui Liber Magistri* and all my notes onto the fire.

The notes went up at once. For a terrible moment I thought the book was not going to burn at all, and I grabbed the poker and shoved it deeper into the fire. It was an old book, its pages dry and brittle. Once they caught, they were quickly consumed, my last link with Blaine destroyed, transformed in seconds into a pile of ashes and a bitter, noxious reek.

The sound of them burning was like the sound of Helena laughing.

I

There were fingers in the wall.

I was lifting a box when I saw them, saw the gap between the bricks where the mortar had fallen away and then the whitish-yellow gleam of bone. I lost my grip on the box; it fell and broke, sending yellowing holograph pages in all directions.

"Really, Mr. Booth!" Mr. Lucent said crossly.

"Bones," I said, still staring at that crack in the bricks. "There . . . in the wall."

"*Bones*? The dust has gone to your head."

"No, really." I wedged my fingers into the crack, cringing from the possibility of touching the bones; all the mortar was cracking and weak, and the upper brick came away easily.

"Oh!" said Mr. Lucent in a sort of gasp. "There's a *person* back there!"

There, clearly visible, were the bones of a hand, clawed into the absence of mortar as if whoever they had belonged to had died trying to dig through that brick wall with his bare hands.

"There *was*," I said.

Mr. Lucent and I were in that storeroom only because of Dr. Stark-weather's inventory, which had been eating the time and energy of the Samuel Mather Parrington Museum staff for months now. Dr. Starkweather had come in February and instituted his comprehensive reforms amid a searing barrage of contempt and invective; it was now mid-June, and there was some faint hope that we could have a preliminary, albeit woefully inadequate, catalogue ready by his six-month anniversary. We had started at the top of the museum, in its extensive attics, the ballrooms of the bats, and worked our way down with desperate, slipshod haste, aware of Dr. Starkweather smoldering in his office like an unappeasable pagan volcano-god. At the end of May, we had reached the basements.

The Parrington's basements were an empire unto themselves, a sprawling labyrinth of storage rooms and sub-basements, steam tunnels and abandoned stretches of sewer. No one knew the full extent of them now, although there were rumors that old Mr. Chastain had had maps that he had burned in a fit of pique when the previous museum director, Dr. Evans, had forced him to retire.

It had been discovered years earlier that watchmen and janitors could not be paid sufficient money to make them include the basements in their rounds. They complained of drafts and dampness and strange noises, and it was beyond argument that the electric lights in the basements—installed by the stubbornest of all the stubborn men who had headed the Parrington—burned out at twice the rate of the lights in other parts of the museum buildings. People going down to the basements told the docents at the information desk—perhaps half a joke, perhaps a little less—to send search parties if they had not returned within an hour.

This particular room—long and narrow, more like a corridor than a room—was in the second level of the basements, as near as I could reckon it beneath the Entomology Department and its horrid collection of South American cockroaches. The unfortunate junior curator who had been detailed to scout the basements had observed that this room was full of books and boxes of papers, and so its more thorough investigation had fallen to Mr. Lucent and me, as the senior archivists of the Department of Rare Books. We had been down there three hours before I saw the bones, and were hot, miserable, and thickly coated in dust.

"Wh-what should we do?" said Mr. Lucent, staring at the hole in the wall, the handkerchief he had been using to clean his glasses pressed to his mouth.

"I, er, I don't know. I suppose . . . we have to tell someone, don't we?"

"God, yes—we can't just brick him back up and leave him there, Mr. Booth!"

"I didn't mean that," I said, mostly to my shoes, as I followed Mr. Lucent back up toward the daylight. We were climbing the stairs from the first basement to the ground floor before I realized I was still carrying the brick, and at that point there seemed no sense in setting it down.

In the storeroom where the basement stairs debouched, Mr. Lucent stopped. "Who should we tell, do you think? I don't . . . I don't like to bother Dr. Starkweather."

I had no more wish than he did to disturb Dr. Starkweather with the news that we had found a skeleton in the basements. Dr. Starkweather did not like me. I said, "Major Galbraith?"

Major Galbraith was in charge of the Museum's custodial and security staff; he was a dour old veteran, no more in awe of Dr. Starkweather than he had been of Dr. Evans. And I was sure that even news of a body in the basement would not shock him.

"Yes, of course," Mr. Lucent said, beaming with relief, and we emerged from the storeroom, turned down a cross-corridor, and came to Major Galbraith's office. Mr. Lucent knocked quickly, as if to get it done before either of us could change our minds. I was strongly reminded of the nervous sensation of guilt I had felt whenever I approached a master's office at my prep school, regardless of the reason I was there.

"Come in!" called Major Galbraith. Mr. Lucent, the brick, and I entered his office.

He listened imperturbably, digging at his pipe, while Mr. Lucent explained our find. When he was in possession of what few facts we had, he sighed, put his pipe down, and said, "Suppose I'd better come have a look. Have you notified Dr. Starkweather?"

"We, um," said Mr. Lucent.

"I would, if I were you," Major Galbraith said, with a quirk in one beetling eyebrow. "You go do that, Mr. Lucent. I fancy Mr. Booth can show me what there is to see."

"Oh, yes, rather," said Mr. Lucent and left distractedly. Major Galbraith shot me a look I could not decipher and said, "All right, then, Mr. Booth. Show me your skeleton."

We made our way back to the basement room in silence. I had nothing to say, and I felt a greater and greater fool carrying that brick. It would have made more sense to take one of the finger bones, as proof that Mr. Lucent and I had not hallucinated the entire affair. I felt that Major Galbraith did not quite believe us.

But we came to the storeroom, and I pointed to the gap in the brickwork. Major Galbraith went across and took a look. "Hmmph," he said. "Finger bones, sure enough."

After a moment, I said, "What do we do now?"

"Wait for Dr. Starkweather," Major Galbraith said and pulled his pipe out again.

"Er," I said.

"Yes, Mr. Booth?" he said, his eyebrows shooting up alarmingly.

"The . . . the paper," I said apologetically.

"Oh, yes. I'll wait outside then, shall I?"

He went out. Since he had not invited me to join him, I stayed where I was. After some time—I hope that it was less than a minute, but I do not know—I pulled myself together and began collecting the contents of the box I had dropped, at last putting down that ghastly brick. The papers were letters. As I picked up the fourth one, I placed the signature as that of Jephthah Strong, a particularly obscure visionary and poet of the previous century. Another time, I might have tried to deduce the identity of his correspondent, but I was having trouble merely keeping my mind on my task. I kept catching myself looking at that unpleasant gap in the bricks, as if I were expecting the hand to reach forward, or the hand's owner to peer out at me. The latter fancy made my neck crawl, and I was relieved when Major Galbraith stuck his head in and said, "That'll be His Nibs coming now."

His warning gave me just time to put the tidied stack of letters on top of the nearest box, and then Dr. Starkweather was in the room, striding across to stare at the hole in the bricks, his expression outraged, as if someone had done this to him on purpose. Mr. Lucent came in behind him, along with Major Galbraith and Dr. Starkweather's secretary, Mr. Hornsby.

Dr. Starkweather rounded on us, demanding, "Who is it?"

"Er," I said.

"What?" said Mr. Lucent.

"Dr. Starkweather, don't you think—" began Mr. Hornsby.

"Well, clearly that's the most important question," Dr. Starkweather said. "Who is this fellow, and how did he get bricked up in our wall?"

Major Galbraith coughed. "I myself was wondering what we were going to do with him."

"I've sent a message to Dr. Ainsley," Dr. Starkweather said. Dr. Ainsley was the staff archaeologist. "He'll know what to do about extracting him."

"Should we . . . " I said and stopped under the bombardment of Dr. Starkweather's furiously blue eyes.

"Yes, Mr. Booth?" said Dr. Starkweather.

"The . . . I was only . . . that is, the police?"

"A cogent thought," said Major Galbraith.

"Nonsense," said Dr. Starkweather. "This clearly isn't a *recent* crime—if it is a crime."

"Oh, but surely—!" Mr. Lucent protested.

"*Yes*, Mr. Lucent?"

"Well, I just—I frankly don't see how this could be an accident."

"We will wait for Dr. Ainsley," Dr. Starkweather said with a ful-minating glare at all four of us.

"Yes, Dr. Starkweather," said Mr. Hornsby, whose particular gift was for placation. We waited in awkward silence. Mr. Lucent no-ticed my stack of letters and moved across to pick them up, but I could tell he was not looking at them, even though his eyes were fixed on the top page. I edged away from the hole in the wall, away from the stiff and savage figure of Dr. Starkweather, and gave myself occupation by examining the spines of a stack of books—although I was not looking at them any more than Mr. Lucent was looking at Jephthah Strong's letters.

In the end, it was not Dr. Ainsley who appeared. He was much occupied, and had been for weeks, by a box of Greek potsherds someone had found at the back of a broom cupboard on the second floor; he dispatched in his place his senior assistant, Miss Coburn. She was in her thirties, tanned from field-work, with curly, sandy-red hair that habitually escaped from its pins to hang in fine strands around her face. The common remark about her in the museum—apart from the usual, stupid calumnies about spinsters and blue-stockings—was that she knew more about Dr. Ainsley's work than he did.

"Well, Dr. Starkweather?" she said. "Dr. Ainsley said he couldn't make heads or tails of your message."

"I should think the situation would be clear to a child of five," Dr. Starkweather said and pointed. "There."

Miss Coburn investigated. "Bones," she said pleasantly. "Human phalanges. Surely you didn't need an archaeologist to tell you that."

Dr. Starkweather said through his teeth, "What. Are. We. To. Do. With. Them."

Miss Coburn straightened up, looking surprised. "I haven't the faintest idea. Who do they belong to?"

"No one seems to know, miss," Major Galbraith said. "Bit of a mystery, this lad is."

"No," said Miss Coburn, "I mean, who do they *belong* to? Are they museum property?"

"They're in our wall," Mr. Lucent said.

"We've got skeletons in our inventory." Miss Coburn's face became thoughtful. "Do you suppose . . . "

"They're all accounted for," I said—except for the miscellany of vertebrae and skull fragments still waiting patiently in my office for me, in my semi-official capacity as the museum's "puzzle man," to have time to identify them. But there was nothing that could possibly explain this.

"Drat," she said.

"I don't want him in my wall," Dr. Starkweather said. "How should we go about extracting him?"

"Oh!" said Miss Coburn, clearly meaning, Why didn't you *say* so? "I can do that for you, if you don't mind me taking the wall apart."

"Please, Miss Coburn," Dr. Starkweather said with a grotesque little bow. "Be my guest." He looked around at the stacks of books and boxes surrounding us. "Will it disturb you if Mr. Booth and Mr. Lucent get on with their work?"

"Not at all," said Miss Coburn. She glanced at the hole in the wall and added in a lower voice, "Company will be welcome."

Mr. Lucent and I worked the rest of the day around Miss Coburn, her tools, and a steadily growing rampart of loose bricks. At one o'clock, Mr. Lucent fetched down sandwiches and lemonade from the museum canteen, and we ate in a cleared space on the floor.

After the first desperate attack on the sandwiches had slowed, Mr. Lucent burst out, "Who could he *be?*"

"I don't know," Miss Coburn said. She had been dismantling the wall starting from a point about two feet above the finger bones, hoping (she said) to make a hole large enough to get a photograph of the skeleton *in situ* before she disturbed the bricks around it. "They're old bones, but they're not *terrifically* old. I shouldn't think he's been there more than fifty years."

"But why," I said and stopped. Miss Coburn raised her eyebrows at me, and I went on, "Why would you brick somebody up in the basement of the museum?"

"It seems to have been a remarkably effective hiding place," Miss Coburn said, very dryly.

"Yes, but you'd have to . . . you'd have to think of it first."

"Oh. Yes, I see what you mean."

"I don't," Mr. Lucent said.

"If you're plotting a murder," Miss Coburn said, "what kind of person do you have to be for your plan to involve bricking up your victim beneath the Samuel Mather Parrington Museum?"

"A seriously deranged one," Mr. Lucent said.

"Yes, granted, but you also have to know about the basements. You have to have access to them. And I should think you have to be fairly sure that no one's going to notice your new wall—so you have to know where to build it. When would you say was the last time anyone was in this room, Mr. Lucent?"

"Gracious," said Mr. Lucent. "We haven't come across anything more recent than eighty years ago—a little older than what you're guessing for the bones."

"Besides," I said, "it took us most of the . . . the morning to, er—"

"To reach that wall to begin with!" Mr. Lucent finished triumphantly.

"Yes, I see," Miss Coburn said. "A little judicious rearrangement of these several tons of paper, and no one can get near enough to the wall to notice there's something odd about it. How exceedingly clever."

We finished our lunch in dismal silence.

By five o'clock, Mr. Lucent and I had, after a necessarily inadequate examination, morosely divided our spoils, the books going to me and the holographs going to him. Miss Coburn had excavated a window in the wall that would allow her to use her photographic equipment and had taken several plates. She had then continued removing bricks, with a methodical neatness I could only admire. By the time we started carting our new responsibilities toward the dumb-waiter that was all the Parrington had in the way of an elevator, she had managed to extract a double row of bricks straight down to the floor without disturbing the bones (the heap at the base of the wall, and the morbid grouping of finger bones still on the brick where I had first spotted them), and was preparing her photographic equipment again.

Mr. Lucent and I flipped a coin. He got the job of going up to the mail room on the first floor and unloading everything; I would stay in the basement and ferry boxes and stacks from the storeroom to the dumb-waiter's alcove. "At least," Mr. Lucent said glumly, "we have the satisfaction of knowing that neither of us is happier than the other."

When I came back into the storeroom, Miss Coburn turned to me from where she was kneeling by the tau-shaped hole, her face white. "It's a woman."

"B-beg pardon?"

"The pelvis—that's a *woman*'s skeleton."

"Oh."

"Is that all you're going to say? 'Oh'?"

"Miss Coburn, I don't . . . I, er . . . "

"My God, he must have been mad!"

"Who?"

"The man who did this!"

"What makes you think it was a man?"

"Oh," said Miss Coburn and sat back on her heels. "Yes, of course, Mr. Booth. Let us have equal rights in all things."

"I didn't mean . . ."

"No, no—if there was anything nasty in that comment, it was directed at me. You're quite right." She pushed straying strands of hair away from her face, and her voice became abstracted, "Who was this woman, that someone had to brick her up in a wall?"

"Is there anything with her?"

"There's a thought," she said, and a distant thumping from the dumb-waiter reminded me of Mr. Lucent in the mail room. I grabbed up another stack of boxes and left.

When I returned to the storeroom, Miss Coburn said, "Hairpins, buttons, rotting cloth. And there's something else, off to the side, but I can't make it out. Some kind of bundle. That'll have to wait until I've gotten her out, and *that* will have to wait for tomorrow." She stood up, putting her hands in the small of her back and stretching her spine. "Can I give you a hand with the boxes, Mr. Booth?"

"That . . . that's very kind of you, Miss Coburn. Thank you."

With the two of us working, it took less time than I had feared to transport enough material to fill the area in the mail room set aside for the purpose. We returned to the ground floor, whereupon Mr. Lucent emerged from the mail room and said, "What *took* you so long? I was beginning to wonder if you'd died."

"Sorry," I said.

"It's my fault," Miss Coburn said. "The skeleton is a woman."

After a stunned moment, Mr. Lucent said, "Well, *that* isn't your fault."

"I distracted Mr. Booth."

Mr. Lucent waved it away. He was contemplating something else. "But who could it be? Really, you'd think she'd be the museum's great *cause célèbre*, the patron who came in and never came out."

"She doesn't seem to be," Miss Coburn said.

We stayed together, nervously and without discussion, as Mr. Lucent and I locked our offices and Miss Coburn collected her handbag. The knowledge of that skeleton, huddled in her darkness somewhere beneath our feet, was not something any of us was eager to contemplate alone in the Parrington's echoing halls. We came out the back door; I locked it behind us. Then I went one way, toward my apartment, and they went the other, to the street-car stop.

I went home, where I did not sleep, but spent the night searching my books for reasons that one might brick a human being up in a wall. There was an unpleasantly large number, testifying to the ingenuity and malice of the human mind.

When I arrived at the museum in the morning, Miss Coburn was standing at my office door, as if she had been waiting for me. "I think it must be a woman named Madeline Stanhope," she said as soon as I was within speaking distance.

"Madeline Stanhope?" I said, unlocking the door.

Miss Coburn leaned in the doorway, explaining as I went to put my morning's mail on my desk. "I went and talked to my Aunt Ferdinanda—not her fault, poor thing. My grandfather was dead-set on having a Ferdinand Truelove III, which you can't do when you only have daughters. Aunt Ferdy's memory for gossip, rumor, and scandal is unequaled. She told me all about Alderman Stanhope's wife, who was supposed to have run off with—wait for it—the Venebretti Necklace."

"Oh," I said weakly and sat down.

"You thought it was just lost? So did I. Apparently Mr. Stanhope forked over a remarkably generous contribution to several different civic institutions to get the thing hushed up. Aunt Ferdy said there was a fairly substantial minority who thought he'd murdered his wife himself, but they could never explain how the necklace was involved. And that was when Aunt Vinnie came in and said that a friend of hers had sworn herself blind that she'd seen Madeline Stanhope in San Francisco in 1905, covered in ostrich feathers and dripping with diamonds. But that seems unlikely at the moment."

"Rather," I said.

The Venebretti Necklace had been the property of Maria Vittoria Venebretti, a seventeenth-century Milanese witch and poisoner. Some stories said that she was the daughter of the Pope by a Spanish witch, others that she was the daughter of the Devil. She had been spectacularly beautiful, and as amoral as a serpent. She had married three times before she was thirty, each time to a husband wealthier than the last. When her third husband died, and clearly not of natural causes, Maria Vittoria Venebretti was tried and convicted of murdering all three of them.

The accounts of her life that I had read suggested strongly that most of Milan had known exactly what Signorina Venebretti was doing with her husbands but had feared to bring her to trial because of the influence of her father (whether papal or diabolical) and her own reputation as a witch. Even when convicted, she was not executed, but confined to a cloister, where she died three years later of unknown causes.

The Venebretti Necklace was given to her as a wedding present by her third husband, Signor Cosmo Baldessare, who would scarcely two years later die in a spectacularly grotesque fashion. The necklace was lavishly described, both by her contemporaries and by Samuel Mather Parrington in his day-book: a massive thing, made of gold and pearls and thirteen emeralds like great baleful eyes. The numerologists had, of course, worked themselves into a frenzy over those thirteen emeralds, and they were counted proof positive in some circles that Maria Vittoria Venebretti had been a witch and a devil worshipper as well as a poisoner. Others scoffed at this idea, along with the notion that Signorina Venebretti had cursed the necklace when it passed out of her hands. The necklace had been owned by five persons between Maria Vittoria Venebretti and Samuel Mather Parrington, and whether there was a curse or not, it was certainly an odd coincidence that the two of them known to have actually worn the necklace had both died by violence. Samuel Mather Parrington himself had famously been careful never to touch it with his bare hands.

"Do you think . . . you said there was a . . . a bundle . . . "

"Oh, I surely do," said Miss Coburn. "Are you and Mr. Lucent continuing your salvage operation?"

"Yes. That is, when Mr. Lucent gets in."

Mr. Lucent was notorious for his erratic time-sense. Miss Coburn grinned and said, "Will you leave him a note? I want to get to work, but I don't . . . I don't want to be down there alone with her. Or it." I could see her blush, even through her tan, but her eyes were steady and unapologetic.

"You want, er, me?"

She tilted her head a little. "You are good company, Mr. Booth. You don't *prattle*."

"Oh." Now I was blushing, and I turned away in a hurry to find a spare sheet of paper. "I'll write Mr. Lucent a note."

We walked through the morning bustle of the museum, Miss Coburn exchanging waves and greetings with her friends. I shoved my hands in my pockets and tried not to think about Madeline Stanhope. It made things no better to know the skeleton's name; it seemed somehow worse to imagine, not merely a collection of flesh and bones and hair, but a woman named Madeline Stanhope, trapped there in the stifling darkness. Had she known who had murdered her? Had she known why? I felt as if I walked inside a cold shadow, a shadow cast by bricks and mortar.

No one else was in the basements yet. "Fortifying themselves with a third cup of coffee," Miss Coburn remarked.

I opened the storeroom door. We both flinched back; then Miss Coburn caught herself and managed a laugh. "I suspect that both of us have overly morbid imaginations, Mr. Booth."

" . . . Yes," I said and followed her into the storeroom.

The empty tau in the wall looked even more horrid this morning. I could see the sad jumble of bones on the floor, the great dark emptiness of the eye-sockets.

"Yes, well," Miss Coburn said and took a deep breath. "No point in putting it off." She knelt down again among her equipment and leaned forward into the hole.

I could not help her and did not wish to watch; I began the work I would have to do in any event, jotting in my pocket-sized notebook a rough catalogue of the books still in the storeroom. As I worked, I became more and more aware of how carefully judged the collection was. Like the letters of Jephthah Strong, these books were all obscure without being rarities—collections of sermons, histories of various regions of the state, tedious genealogies of prominent local families. Someone had chosen the contents of this room with an eye to books that no one was likely to seek out.

I must have made some kind of a noise, an indrawn breath, a click of tongue against teeth; Miss Coburn said, without looking up from her collection of vertebrae, "What is it, Mr. Booth?"

"Oh, just the books."

"Anything in particular about the books?"

"It . . . it rather looks like they were chosen carefully as . . . as watchdogs."

"What do you mean?

I explained about the bracket into which the books and holograph manuscripts fell, between valuable for their rarity and discardable for their irrelevance. By the time I was done, she was staring at me, two vertebrae forgotten in her hands. "You mean this whole *storeroom* was premeditated?"

"Well, it might be, er . . . *post*meditated. That is, they mightn't have had the books and papers here first."

"But pretty damn quickly thereafter."

"Yes."

She hunched her shoulders, as if against a sudden draft. "Someone must have hated Madeline Stanhope very much indeed."

"Yes," I said, and we each went back to work.

It was about half an hour later that Mr. Lucent finally showed up. He looked ill. Miss Coburn said, "Hard night on the town, Mr. Lucent?"

"Well, I couldn't just go *home*," Mr. Lucent said. "I mean, really! Are you ready, Mr. Booth?"

"Yes," I said, and we returned to our labors; I felt rather like the Danaides, condemned forever to carry water in sieves. We had to start by clearing the mail room, which took longer than it should have because we were both clumsy with lack of sleep. Then I returned to the storeroom to carry things to the dumb-waiter, while Mr. Lucent waited in the mail room to carry things from the dumb-waiter to our respective offices.

"Thank goodness you're back," said Miss Coburn. She now had most of the skeleton—Mrs. Stanhope's skeleton, I reminded myself and looked away—laid out on the floor. "This is not a pleasant place to be by oneself."

"I'll be in and out," I said.

"Yes, I know. But if something jumps out of the wall and grabs me, at least you'll hear the scream."

" . . . Yes," I said and picked up an armload of books.

I had been in and out twice and was on my way back for the third trip when I found Miss Coburn standing outside the door, pressed up against the wall as if it were the only thing keeping her from falling down.

"Miss Coburn? Are you all right?"

"Yes," she said, although her voice was faint and breathy. "I'm fine. It's just . . . there . . . there are shackles."

" . . . Shackles?" I said, feeling my body contract as if with extreme cold.

"One of them was broken," Miss Coburn said, her voice still small but very steady. "I had been wondering, because building a wall—even a narrow one like that—it isn't the sort of thing you whip together in five minutes. It must have . . . it must have taken hours. And we know she wasn't dead, because of the hand. So I thought, maybe she was unconscious, or maybe she was tied up with ropes that have disintegrated. But she was . . . " She stopped and swallowed hard. "She was chained to the wall. I don't know how I missed them last night, except that they're old and rusty and don't . . . they don't catch the light. She must have sat there, with whatever's in that bag, and watched her murderer building that wall."

"But why?" I said helplessly. "Why would anyone do that?" My books had suggested reasons, but not the sort of reason I needed now. They did not talk about how one might nerve oneself to do such a thing, to mix the mortar and lay the bricks with one's victim watching. Had she begged for her life? Had she cursed? Wept? Screamed? Had her murderer gagged her?

"I don't know," Miss Coburn said, and she sounded as cold and helpless as I felt. "I just don't."

Our eyes met for a moment, and then we went back into the storeroom together.

Although her morbid and unwilling curiosity must have been as insistent as mine, Miss Coburn was unwaveringly methodical. She assembled the entire skeleton plus its collection of earthly detritus and then spent the rest of the morning carefully documenting that much of what she had found.

"I'm treating it as if it were a real archaeological site," she said to me at lunch, when I brought her sandwiches and a bottle of water. "Just in case Dr. Starkweather is wrong, and we ought to have notified the police yesterday, at least they'll know where everything was."

"Do you think . . . that is, will there be trouble?"

"I doubt it," she said, taking a generous swallow of water. "The Police Commissioner's sister is a docent. Come to think of it, Commissioner Harmon probably already knows. And he's probably just as glad to let the museum handle it. I shouldn't be surprised if we were asked to lose the body."

"What?"

"Scandal, darling," she said, amused. "If this gets made public, half the city is going to find itself embroiled in a very sticky and embarrassing mess. Vernon Stanhope paid once to have it all hushed up, and I imagine his heirs will do the same. And the police aren't going to want to trumpet it to the reverberate hills, either. Too many questions about how come they didn't find her fifty-five years ago. Old incompetence is incompetence still."

"But Mrs. Stanhope . . . "

"Yes, Mr. Booth?"

"I don't know. But she *was* murdered."

"You are an idealist, I see," Miss Coburn said and raised a sardonic eyebrow.

"I . . . " My nerve broke. I mumbled some disjointed excuse and fled back to the dumb-waiter to find out if Mr. Lucent was ready for the next load of boxes.

At two-thirty, Miss Coburn announced her readiness, at last, to retrieve the mysterious bundle; neither she nor I was willing to mention our speculations as to its contents. Mr. Lucent insisted that he had to be a witness, and when he arrived, it was in the company of several of his bosom friends, who also apparently had to be witnesses. Although Miss Coburn was deeply annoyed, to judge by the look she gave Mr. Lucent, in the end I think it was probably for the best.

We all watched, clumped around the storeroom like a particularly odd set of statuary, as she crawled halfway into Madeline Stanhope's *de facto* tomb. I could see now why she had refused to go after the bundle until the skeleton was properly accounted for—she put her hand in a spot initially occupied by a random assortment of ribs and vertebrae. She stretched, with a noise midway between a grunt and a gasp, and then came back out, holding a moldering linen bag, its drawstring tied shut with a knot of Gordian complexity. She produced a man's penknife from her skirt pocket and cut the bag open with the ruthlessness of a pirate.

"Oh!" said Miss Coburn, and, a moment later, "Oh!" said all of the watchers.

It was the Venebretti Necklace.

II

I went with Miss Coburn when she took the necklace to Dr. Starkweather and explained to him everything we knew about its finding place, including the hypothetical identity of its grisly keeper. I said nothing, but I saw and heard, a witness and a bulwark against Dr. Starkweather's anger. Miss Coburn had, after all, done no more than what he asked of her.

I emerged from Dr. Starkweather's office feeling rather as if I had just rounded Cape Horn in a typhoon; judging from her face, Miss Coburn felt the same.

"Well," she said. "What now?"

"Beg pardon?"

"Are you just going to leave it there? Woman, necklace, wall— how nice and pass the cucumber sandwiches?"

"Actually," I said, "I was going to the stacks."

"The stacks?" Miss Coburn echoed, then she smiled wryly. "Of course. Trust an archivist. May I come with you?"

" . . . If you like."

"'Satiable curiosity, like the Elephant Child. Come on, then."

And somehow it ended up that I followed her into the stacks, although it had been my idea.

The stacks—officially the Mathilda Rushton Parrington Memorial Library Annex, dedicated by Samuel Mather Parrington's daughters to the memory of their grandmother—were truthfully a part of the museum in which I was just as glad to have company. The Annex was a square tower, extending three stories above the ground and three below, with two levels of stacks per story, each floored with an echoing iron grill: twelve levels of dark, cramped, overpoweringly musty, and labyrinthine shelving. The electric lights were even more unpredictable here than in the basements, although the bulbs rarely burned out. It was simply that sometimes the switches worked and sometimes they did not. And sometimes, if one happened to be alone in the stacks, the lights would go on, one level above or one level below, and then after a minute, as one stood there, clammy-handed, debating whether one ought to investigate or flee, the lights would go off again—leaving one with nothing to do but return to one's researches, no matter how much one's hand-writing wobbled. Although perhaps that only happened to me, just as no one else had ever confessed to hearing footsteps not their own echoing in the empty stairwell. But the other archivists hated the stacks, even though they tried to pretend they did not.

The stacks were emphatically off-limits to the public and always kept locked. Miss Coburn had a key, as did I; there was no way to do any kind of research in the Parrington without visiting the stacks. Individual departments were strongly discouraged from keeping separate collections, although a certain amount of hoarding had always been politely overlooked by Dr. Evans. We were all dreading what would happen when Dr. Starkweather noticed.

Miss Coburn locked the door behind us, again following the museum's strict policy, and then raised her eyebrows at me. "Where to?"

"Bottom level."

"It *would* be. What's down there?"

"The, er, meta-archives."

"The what?"

I opened the door to the stairs and waved her ahead of me. "Inventories, directors' memorandum books, notes of departmental meetings . . . et cetera."

"I had no idea we *kept* things like that."

"The museum may lose things," I said, "but it never throws them away."

Our voices echoed eerily up and down the shaft. I followed Miss Coburn down the stairs, both of us gripping the handrail; the stairs twisted in a tight, steep corkscrew, and it was lethally easy to lose your footing. When I had been hired, and Mr. Spaulding had been showing me around, he had told me that ten years previously, a junior archivist had slipped and fallen down the stairs, breaking his neck along with a generous assortment of his other bones. The corpse had lain at the bottom of the stairs for two days before anyone found him. It was the sort of story that was impossible to disbelieve, whether it was true or not. Another reason I hated the Annex.

The levels were labeled with Greek letters, the lowest being the appropriate ω, rather than the correct μ. It was not a comfort. I opened the door, and Miss Coburn and I stepped into ω; I flipped the light switch. The lights went on, and I was able to breathe again.

My memory always insists that ω is dank, even though my intellect knows that the first observed drop of water would have every curator in the museum baying for blood. It is not dank, merely musty, the air stale and thick with dust.

"All the charm of the family crypt," Miss Coburn muttered, but she did not suggest retreat.

I knew what I wanted, and I knew roughly where to find it. It was Miss Coburn's turn to follow me; the aisles were too narrow for two people to walk abreast. They were almost too narrow for two people to pass each other, even if they both turned sideways. The obese and jovial Mr. Paulson from Armor and Weapons could not come into the stacks at all.

"Spend much time down here?" Miss Coburn said.

I stopped and glanced back at her. " . . . No. Why?"

"You seem to know your way around."

"Would you rather be lost?" I said waspishly, and then was appalled. "I beg your pardon, Miss Coburn. I didn't mean . . . that is, I shouldn't have . . . "

"Why not? I was asking for it." She laughed at my expression. "Clearly, Mr. Booth, you have no siblings."

"No."

"It's all right. I'm not offended. Let's get this done, though, shall we? I'm not enjoying the ambiance."

"Oh. Yes. Yes, of course."

I found what I sought two aisles further in. Samuel Mather Parrington had had a mania for documentation; he had insisted that each director of the museum should keep what he called a log—vaguely akin to a ship's log—a notation of the museum's day to day business. I had no idea what purpose Mr. Parrington had intended for his logs, but they served in practice as a kind of rough index to aid the hapless researcher in determining which of the boxes of archived material he needed. The system was far from infallible, but it was better than no system at all.

I knelt down to scan the row of ledgers, each with the director's name and the dates, inclusive, of the ledger's contents. "Fifty-five years ago?"

"Yes."

The director then had been one Havilland DeWitt, a relative nonentity in the history of the Parrington. I found the appropriate ledger, noting that the one after it was labeled "H. Catesby-Stanton." I was not exactly surprised to learn that the end of Mr. DeWitt's tenure had coincided with the loss of the Venebretti Necklace, but it sent an unpleasant frisson through me all the same.

He was probably just dismissed, I said to myself.

It took me only a brief perusal of the ledger to find the disappearance of the necklace. Mr. DeWitt had boxed that entry off with a black border, as if it were a funeral card, and it began, "A very black day for the Museum indeed." I read the entry through, frowning, then handed the ledger to Miss Coburn and said, "Does this seem . . . *overdone* to you?"

She read it. "It's certainly over-*wrought*," she said, "and there's distinctly a note of suppressed hysteria. But what do you mean by 'overdone'?"

"Nothing," I said, flipping to the last few entries, some three-quarters of the way through the ledger. There was no mention of tension, of conflict, or even of dissatisfaction. Havilland DeWitt had not, it was clear, left the museum with any kind of warning. I was liking this less and less, if such a thing were possible.

I put the ledger back and stood up. "We want his memorandum book."

"We do?" Miss Coburn said doubtfully, following me. "I suppose . . . it had occurred to me that the person most suited to the particulars of this murder would be the person running the museum. No one he would have to account to for his movements; the run of the building—and the keys; the ability to, for instance, designate that particular room to hold the collected letters of Jephthah Strong . . . "

The directors' personal memorandum books—another of Mr. Parrington's ukases—were kept in rows and rows of boxes. Some directors, I knew, disliking the idea that all of their day-to-day concerns would be preserved for posterity, kept two memorandum books, one for the museum and one for themselves. Dr. Evans had been one, but from the florid bombast of Havilland DeWitt's log, I was guessing he was not.

"Here," I said, pulling out the box labeled DeWitt. "Maybe I'm wrong, but let's start with—I'm afraid . . . that is, this may take a while."

"I asked for it," said Miss Coburn cheerfully, as she had said earlier, and settled herself on the floor.

I found the memorandum book covering the period of the necklace's disappearance and handed it to Miss Coburn. "If you'll start here, I have one other . . . " Two cases down and across the aisle were the scrapbooks of press cuttings, the first assignment of each junior curator the museum hired. I wanted to see what had made the papers when Havilland DeWitt left the Parrington.

The week after his last entry in the log, I found his obituary. I skimmed it, but was jarred to a stop by the second to last paragraph: "Mr. DeWitt was known for his tireless devotion to the museum, and his dedication is exemplified by his death. His assistant, Mr. Roland Laughton, explained that Mr. DeWitt was contemplating a 'massive reorganization and inventory,' beginning with the museum's basements. Mr. Laughton said that Mr. DeWitt must have descended to the basement after the staff had left for the day, and thus he died alone, surrounded by the artifacts to which he had devoted his life."

"Oh dear," I said.

"What?"

I read her the paragraph.

Miss Coburn ticked the salient points off on her fingers. "By himself, in the basement, after hours. I'd like to believe there's an innocent explanation for that, but I'm finding it difficult."

"It does suggest guilty knowledge, at least, if not . . . "

"Actual guilt? When did he die?"

"About a year after the necklace disappeared."

"And Madeline Stanhope."

" . . . Yes. I'm sorry. I wasn't . . . that is, I didn't mean to be callous."

"And I didn't mean to sound as if I was rebuking you. It's so much easier not to think of her that I have to keep reminding myself. This isn't really about the necklace."

"No," I said. I returned the scrapbook to its proper place and came back to where Miss Coburn was sitting with the memorandum books. I sat down, feeling even gawkier and more awkward than usual, and said, "Have you found anything?"

"This man could bore a stone to sleep?" she offered. "Other than that, nothing except some gloating remarks about the museum's good fortune in acquiring the necklace."

"Hmmm," I said. "Keep looking."

"Yes, sir," she said, just enough under her breath that I could pretend I had not heard her, although I am sure my blush betrayed me. I picked up Mr. DeWitt's last memorandum book and started reading.

He was verbose and, as Miss Coburn had remarked, monumentally dull. For some time, we both read in silence; I was straining my ears for footsteps, tapping, or the other strange noises that I sometimes heard when I was in the stacks by myself, but heard nothing.

"That's interesting," Miss Coburn said.

" . . . What?"

"He says he doesn't think the necklace is safe."

We sat for a moment, considering the implications of that. Then I said, "Does he say . . . that is, is there a . . . a reason?"

"No. It seems to come out of a clear blue sky. No recorded incidents, no comments from the trustees . . . just all at once he says he doesn't think the necklace is safe. He's worried that it's 'vulnerable to the general public,' and he's planning to assign another guard to that gallery—which can't have made him very popular."

I thought of the skirmishing between departments to get guards assigned to their particular treasures, and had to agree.

"Maybe we had it backwards," Miss Coburn said. "Maybe DeWitt is the hero in this little drama."

"Then how did Mrs. Stanhope end up . . . "

"I'll keep looking," Miss Coburn said.

The memoranda for the last months of Mr. DeWitt's life were almost oppressively normal, and relentless in their tedium. He was planning a buying trip to Europe, arguing with the trustees about the museum's budget, waging a campaign to educate the docents in the niceties of French and Italian pronunciation. The first two times I saw a reference to his "plans," I assumed it meant one of these concerns, but the third time, it was at the end of an entry full of self-congratulation over his progress on all three fronts. The "plans" had to be something else.

While I was puzzling over that, Miss Coburn said, "Oh dear."

"What?"

"He's been reading about Maria Vittoria Venebretti."

"Oh." I thought it through, and asked, "*What* was he reading?"

"My Italian isn't very good, but off-hand I'd say the word *diavolo* is a bad sign." She handed me the memorandum book, open to the relevant page.

I scanned down the list, my stomach becoming a harder, colder knot with each entry. Then I turned the page.

"He . . . he wasn't just reading *about* Maria Vittoria Venebretti. He was reading the books she would have read."

"Which positively begs the question: *why*?"

"I can't . . . "

"I fancy we can put Mr. Havilland DeWitt firmly back on the villain side of the equation."

We sat in grim, cold silence for a moment; I did not know about Miss Coburn, but my mind was full of images of Madeline Stanhope's bones, her vertebrae like gruesome counters in a children's game, that sad clump of phalanges I wished I had never seen, her skull. Hamlet had been disgusted by the solid heft of mortality; I was filled with a vast, hopeless desire to protect a woman who had died before my own birth. But I could not reach her, just as Hamlet had not been able to reach the man he had once loved.

"He must have been trying to *do* something," Miss Coburn said, jerking me back from my morbid reverie.

"Beg pardon?"

"The evidence we've got so far doesn't so much as mention Madeline Stanhope, but it has quite a lot to say about the Venebretti Necklace. If there was a plot here, it wasn't aimed against *her*. If DeWitt's our man, then this wasn't about her at all. She was just . . . inconvenient."

"Or too convenient to waste," I muttered, still transfixed by that neat, methodical, and entirely insane list of books.

"What?"

I handed the memorandum book back to her. "While you were . . . talking to your aunt last night, I was . . . that is, I have read many of the same books as Mr. DeWitt, and, er, there are . . . there could be *reasons*. If he bricked her up alive . . . "

"Which certainly appears to be the case. What sort of reasons?"

"Nothing I want to talk about here or . . . " I looked at my watch. "Oh God."

"What?" she said, scrambling to her feet as I did.

"It's six o'clock. The museum's closed."

She did not ask me why that mattered, either because my fright was infectious, or because she had heard the stories for herself. Even those employees, such as myself, who habitually worked late hours did not go into the stacks after the museum closed. We all knew that the next time it might be us lying at the bottom of the stairs for two days before we were found.

When I opened the door to the stairwell, I heard the faint, echoing tap-tap-tap of footsteps even before I reached for the stairwell's light switch. One glance at Miss Coburn's white face told me she heard them, too.

There was no way we could climb the stairs stealthily enough to avoid being heard—even if we could have done so in the stairwell's stygian blackness—and a gibbering voice in the back of my head pointed out that the slower and more cautiously we went, the more likely we were to encounter . . . it, whatever it was.

I found the light switch with fingers that felt as cold and brittle as icicles. "Run!" I said, flipping the switch, and we threw ourselves up the stairs like a pair of demented mountain goats. It was only much later that night, lying in bed staring at the patterns the moonlight made against the venetian blinds, that it occurred to me to wonder what we would have done if the light had failed to go on.

We made enough noise for an army, maybe two—the clatter of our shoes, Miss Coburn cursing breathlessly in French, the air sawing in my lungs, and the echoes clamoring and wailing and clawing at our ears. But always, underneath it, I could hear that tap-tap-tap, unhurried, unemphatic. I could not tell if it was ascending or descending; after we had scrambled around two full turns of the stairs, I could not tell if it was above or below us. With the echoes, it was equally impossible to know if it was drawing nearer or moving away. There was just that sense of menace, filling the air like choking dust.

Whatever it was, we did not encounter it. We burst through the stairwell door at ζ, both of us already fumbling for our keys. I found mine first, wrenched the lock mechanism over, every second expecting to hear the stairwell door open behind me, and shoved the door open. We both got through it somehow, and I locked the door again with feverish panic. And then we both simply sank to the floor where we were, panting for breath. I was intensely, absurdly grateful for the cold marble pressing against my knees and ankles, for the dusty, slightly sour air of the Parrington's back hallways.

When we were both breathing more normally again, Miss Coburn caught my eye and said, "Dripping water."

"Yes, of course," I said. "But . . . I'm not going back to turn the lights off."

She laughed and got to her feet with a leggy athleticism I could only envy. "Come on," she said and held a hand out to help me up. "Let's get out of here."

I do not like to be touched. I got to my feet without taking her hand; I felt her puzzled look, but did not meet her eyes.

After a moment, she let it go, and we walked together toward my office. As with Mr. Lucent the night before, we found ourselves unwilling to separate. Neither one of us spoke; anything we said would only have made more crushing the reality of the dark, deserted museum around us.

Then we turned a corner and nearly collided with Dr. Starkweather.

"Mr Booth. And Miss Coburn." His heavy eyebrows drew together into a scowl. "Were you in the Annex?"

"Er," I said. "I . . . "

"Yes," Miss Coburn said, unfazed. "Mr. Booth was helping me with some research."

Dr. Starkweather seemed to contemplate her disheveled hair, then gave me a look I could not decipher. "I would suggest you conduct your . . . research somewhere else after hours," he said finally. "Good night."

He continued on his way; Miss Coburn grabbed my arm and dragged me in the opposite direction, disregarding my reflexive attempt to shake her off. She let me go as soon as we were out of earshot and, unbelievably, started to giggle.

"What is it?" I said.

"N-noth—" But she could not get the word out. I stood and watched as her giggles deepened to whoops of laughter; she ended up leaning against the wall, snorting and panting for breath.

"Miss Coburn, please, is it something I did?"

She shook her head. "Starkweather . . . Starkweather thinks . . . oh God!" But she suppressed her giggles sternly and said, "He thinks we were necking in the stacks."

She met my eyes for a moment and then dissolved into howls. I could feel my face burning and wondered if anyone had ever gone off in an apoplexy from sheer embarrassment. Perhaps I could be the first.

"I'm sorry," Miss Coburn said, finally composing herself. "Really. I understand that it's not funny, and I'm not . . . " She fought her giggles down again. "I'm not laughing at you. I swear."

"Good night, Miss Coburn," I said stiffly.

"Good night, Mr. Booth," she said, and I felt her amusement behind me all the way down the hall.

Again, Miss Coburn was waiting at my office door in the morning. I was rather later than usual in the hopes that this craven ploy might allow me to evade Dr. Starkweather.

"I finished with the memorandum books," she said abruptly.

"You . . . went *back*?"

"Dripping water," she said impatiently. "Nothing more. We spooked ourselves."

"Yes," I said, because I did not want to argue with her. "Did you find anything?"

"No. Nothing useful. If he was up to something, he must have realized he was incriminating himself. The most specific he gets after that entry with the books is all that talk of 'plans' just before he died."

"The books must have shown him what to do."

"You still think he killed her?"

I had not meant to say that out loud. "I . . . I need to do some reading," I said, hastily unlocking the door and entering my office. "Good morning, Miss Coburn." I closed the door, locked it again, and made my way unsteadily across to my desk to sit down. I saw the outlines of what Havilland DeWitt had done, like a silhouette cast against a screen; I did not want to know more. I could not help Madeline Stanhope now, and there was no point in unearthing the details of this sordid, lunatic crime. Havilland DeWitt had gotten his comeuppance; the Venebretti Necklace had been found; and I was sure that word of Madeline Stanhope's innocence would trickle out in the same way the original scandal had.

I honorably added Havilland DeWitt's unpleasant library to the list of my obligations and made a mental note to avoid Miss Coburn as well as Dr. Starkweather for the next several weeks.

And there matters rested for quite some time.

III

Miss Coburn leaned around my office door one afternoon in early September. "Are you going to the Museum Ball, Mr. Booth?"

"Er," I said, looking up from an odd little Hellenistic statuette that no one quite knew what to make of, and felt the immediate weight of guilt across my shoulders. I had avoided Miss Coburn so successfully for two months that I had almost entirely forgotten my half-promise to follow up on Havilland DeWitt's reading. "Yes, I suppose." Dr. Starkweather had made it clear that attendance at Museum Balls was mandatory for all curators.

"Excellent." She came in and shut the door behind her. "I need an escort."

I stared at her. Her mouth quirked up, and she said in the simpering accents of a society debutante, "But, Miss Coburn, this is so sudden! Why, we hardly know each other at all!" Then, reverting to her normal voice, "You needn't look so unnerved. Think of it as a favor."

"Oh," I said. "That is . . . what sort of favor?"

She laughed. "I have just lied shamelessly to Cameron Larkin and told him that I cannot attend with him because I already have an escort. You perceive the immediate necessity of making that lie a retroactive truth."

" . . . Yes."

"And I am confident that you will neither become vulgarly drunk nor make a pass at me at two o'clock in the morning."

"Not at all," I said, probably too hastily and too vehemently.

She smiled again, but ruefully. "If you really dislike me that much—"

Oh God, worse and worse. And I could not escape the feeling that I owed her a favor. "No, I don't dislike you, Miss Coburn. Truly. I just . . . I . . . I will be happy to, er, escort you to the Museum Ball."

"You are too kind, sir," she said with a mocking curtsey.

"Miss Coburn, I meant no offense. I just . . . "

"I know. I took you by surprise. You remind me powerfully of my Aunt Ferdy's cat Fortunato. He greets any change in his routine with that exact horrified stare." She opened the door. "I will come to your apartment at eight on Friday. I believe we can walk from there?"

And somehow she knew that I did not own a car. " . . . Yes. Yes, if that's—"

"Good afternoon, Mr. Booth." She shut the door briskly behind her and was gone.

I had never had a sweetheart, never so much as escorted a young lady to a dance. My prep school was boys-only, and contact with girls, either from the nearby girls' school or from the town, was strictly forbidden. Many boys defied that prohibition, but I was not among them. In college, my friend and roommate Augustus Blaine had held sole sway over the department of romance; even if I had been brave enough to wish to attract the attentions of a young lady, I could never have done so with Blaine in the room.

This was not, of course, a date in any proper sense of the word. Miss Coburn was merely using me as a shield. But I still felt horridly like the gawky, shabby boy I had once been, too shy to say anything to my guardians' goddaughter when she was kind enough to ask me how I did.

Gawky I still was, but shabby I was not, freed from the Siddonses' parsimony; I bought Miss Coburn a corsage. It took all my courage to go into the florist's, and I nearly fled when the young woman behind the counter asked if she could help me. But I held fast and managed to explain the situation—that I needed flowers for a lady with whom I stood on amiable (I hoped) but not romantic terms, and that, no, I did not know the color of her dress—and she provided me with some delicate white flowers and attendant greenery which, she said dimpling, would do charmingly. I suspect that she found me more than slightly comical, but my determination carried me through. I did not want to be any more of an embarrassment to Miss Coburn than I had to be.

Miss Coburn arrived promptly on the stroke of eight. I had been ready and waiting since six. I opened the door to her knock. " . . . Good evening, Miss Coburn." She was wearing a black dress, long and unadorned and austere, under a plain and slightly thread-bare black coat. Instead of its usual bun at the base of her skull, her hair was arranged in a coronet of braids, as stark and becoming to her as the dress. Her only jewels were a pair of diamond earrings and an antique signet ring on her right hand.

"Oh, God, is it going to be 'Miss Coburn' and 'Mr. Booth' all evening long? My Christian name is Claudia, and I beg you will use it. And yours is . . . Karl? No."

"Kyle," I said, "but no one calls me by it."

"What do your friends call you?"

I bit back the instinctive honesty of, I have no friends, and said, "Booth, mostly."

"Then I shall call you Booth, and you will call me Claudia. All right?"

"I . . . I got you flowers," I said and dove into the kitchen to fetch them.

"Booth," she said when I reappeared, "I promise that I am not going to bite you." She smiled a little. "But I must admit the flowers are lovely." She accepted them and pinned them deftly to her bodice. I felt a great glow of relief, as if some dreadful barricade had been passed; I had been afraid she would be offended.

"We . . . we should go."

"I suppose we should."

We left my apartment building and walked together from one streetlight to the next. She made no motion that would suggest she expected me to offer my arm, and I was grateful. But after a block and a half, she said, "It is quite appalling how little I know of you, Booth. Where are you from?"

"Oh, er, here. Well, about twenty blocks north, to be accurate."

"So you *are* one of *those* Booths."

"The last one, yes."

"You certainly don't put on side about it."

"There's nothing left to be particularly proud of."

"Oh, don't be silly. You're the last scion of one of the Twenty, and I don't think anybody knows you exist."

"Considering the scandal of my mother's death, I prefer to be forgotten. Are you a . . . a native?"

"My mother was a Truelove who married beneath her. I don't know whether I ought to be counted as a 'native' or not, although I suppose I must have spent about half my childhood here, all told. My parents' marriage was rather stormy."

She did not sound as if she wished to say anything more, and we walked for some time in silence. Then she said, "You ditched me, didn't you?"

"Miss Coburn, I . . . "

"I recognize the plumage. I just want to know why."

"I, er . . . I didn't . . . "

She waited.

"I didn't want to know any more," I said.

"You?"

"I . . . " She was right. It was not like me; I was known in the museum for the terrier-like tenacity of my pursuit of facts. It was why I was the person to whom all the mysteries were sent.

"It wouldn't help to know," I said, looking away from her into the darkness. "Havilland DeWitt stole the necklace. He murdered Madeline Stanhope. Does the rest of it matter?"

"I'm an archaeologist. I don't like theories. I like proof."

"But what good does it do to prove it?"

"*You're* the one who wanted justice for Madeline Stanhope."

I did not look at her and did not answer.

We walked without speaking until we came in sight of the museum's brilliantly lit front entrance. Then Miss Coburn stopped and said, "Do you dance?"

"Beg pardon?"

"Dance. Do you?"

"No . . . that is, not—"

"Then I'll lead." She put one hand up to touch her hair, a gesture which recalled my mother to me in a painful momentary flash, and then said, with the hint of a sigh, "Well, Booth, let's do the pretty, as my Coburn grandmother would say. Give me your arm. And just to prove you can do it, will you call me Claudia? Once?"

I could not tell if she was still angry at me or not. " . . . Yes, er, Claudia," I said and offered my arm. I had braced myself and did not flinch when she took it.

"Very nice," she said. She smelt of verbena. "And now I will stop baiting you. On all fronts. You are, after all, doing me a favor, and I appreciate it."

She was not still angry; I let my breath out, relieved, and dared, "Is Mr. Larkin so very awful?"

"Horrid. I've met *cows* with more personality."

"Oh." I wondered how I compared to cows in Miss Coburn's estimation.

"There's nothing worse than a garrulous bore. Oh, look, a limousine. That'll be Reginald Dawe and his fifth wife."

"You seem to know a great deal about . . . "

"High society? You may thank my Truelove aunts. Mama was the only one of the three who got married, and so Aunt Ferdy and Aunt Vinnie have no one but me to lavish their expertise on. They don't count my brother. They say men don't notice things anyway."

She gave me a bright, sidelong look, as if daring me to respond. I said nothing. We came to the steps, proceeded up them. Miss Coburn was looking very grand, as if she did not take these same stairs two at a time when she was in a hurry. The rotunda was full of men in tuxedos and women in dresses that shimmered and swirled, the Foucault's pendulum swinging in their midst, the clock of the Titans' mother Gaia. As we crossed to the coat-check counter, I could feel the stares and whispers; in all the years I had worked at the museum, this was the first time I had escorted a woman to the annual ball. I could imagine the rumors starting and felt a cold quiver of dread in the pit of my stomach.

When Miss Coburn had surrendered her coat, she gave me a doubtful look. "You don't want to mingle, do you?"

"No," I said.

"Then I'll find you when the doors open. Just don't hide."

"I—"

"You do stand out in a crowd, you know," she said and swept away, as stately as a swan.

I knew I stood out; I was six-foot-three, and my hair had gone entirely white when I was twenty-four. The combination made me horribly visible. The best I could do was to stay back near the wall, in the shadow of one of the columns, and pray that no one noticed me.

I had been standing there for maybe five minutes when I saw her. I do not know how I recognized her as Madeline Stanhope, but I never had the least doubt of who she was. She was a small woman, wrapped toga-fashion in something long and white and trailing, like a bed-sheet or a shroud. She was standing very straight at the top of the museum's main staircase. She did not look like a ghost— she was neither transparent nor insubstantial to the eye—but she was clearly not a living woman. Her face was too white and too still, with her eyes burning like the promise of eternal damnation. She was staring straight at me.

Miss Coburn had accused me of "ditching" her; that was nothing compared to my crime in ditching Madeline Stanhope. I did not know why she had appeared here, now, but I knew I could not ignore her.

Madeline Stanhope gave me a very slight nod and turned away, walking into the long Contemporary Art gallery that ran the length of the museum. I understood; I followed her.

Three-quarters of the way up the stairs, I heard a clatter of heels behind me. I had been trying with all my might to ignore the assembled wealth and dignity of the Museum Ball, but at that noise, like Orpheus, I could not forbear to look back.

Miss Coburn, clutching her skirts carelessly in one hand to keep them out of her way, caught up to me and said, in a low hiss, "Booth, what are you *doing*?"

I kept climbing. There was nothing I could tell her that would not sound even less likely than the truth. "Following Madeline Stanhope."

"Foll—" Automatically, Miss Coburn kept pace with me. "Are you out of your *mind*?"

"I don't know," I said. "Maybe."

We reached the top of the stairs; Madeline Stanhope was halfway down the gallery. She moved with neither hurry nor hesitation, not drifting but walking with firm, even steps, although her feet made no sound. When she looked back and saw that I was following, her smile revealed small sharp teeth—certainly not teeth belonging to a living woman, nor like the teeth I had seen in Mrs. Stanhope's skull.

"Can you see her?" I whispered to Miss Coburn.

"No." She looked up at me. "You lead."

My spine was being replaced, vertebra by vertebra, with cubes of ice, but I followed Madeline Stanhope into the Contemporary Art gallery.

Halfway down the gallery, Miss Coburn whispered to me, "Where do you think she's going?"

" . . . I'm afraid she wants to show me something."

There was a pause. "Oh," said Miss Coburn, "I see what you mean."

Madeline Stanhope turned from Contemporary Art into Medieval, walked through Medieval into Renaissance, and from there into Decorative Arts. She came to a halt in front of the case containing the Venebretti Necklace.

I heard Miss Coburn's breath hiss in. Then she whispered, "I can see her now."

The revenant of Madeline Stanhope walked slowly around the case, as if inspecting the necklace from all angles. Then she turned to us, placed her hand on top of the case, and stared at us with the dark conflagration of her eyes.

Miss Coburn caught at my elbow. "Look!"

I could not help my flinch, but I followed the direction of her pointing finger. Clearly visible on Madeline Stanhope's wrist, dark and ugly against the glass case, was a shackle. I felt faint and queasy and cold. Together, Miss Coburn and I backed away until we could sit down on the nearest bench. Madeline Stanhope's burning eyes marked our progress, but she made no movement either to stop us or to follow us.

"Booth," said Miss Coburn, very quietly and calmly, "I think perhaps now would be a good time for you to tell me what Havilland DeWitt did."

"I, er . . . yes, I suppose so." I glanced uneasily at Madeline Stanhope.

"She'll wait," Miss Coburn said. "She'll wait until the end of time if she has to. *Talk.*"

"It was the curse," I said, because everything was fitting into place in my head, all the pieces lining up as I had known they would as soon as I let myself think about it. "At least, part of it was the curse."

"Go on."

"He wanted the necklace. You could see it, couldn't you? In his memorandum book? It's no very large step from wanting the necklace kept safe from museum patrons to . . . to wanting the necklace kept safe from *everyone*."

"No, but you haven't proved he took that step."

"That's the books. That list of books."

"Wasn't he trying to break the curse?"

"No. Not with those books. Maybe he started there, but the books in Latin—those were all necromantic texts, and the necromancers of that time had some—"

"Booth. Spare me the lecture on Renaissance necromancy, and tell me what he did."

"Havilland DeWitt had a plan, and . . . and I think I know what it was. He wanted the necklace for himself, because that's how the curse works. But he was the museum director—important man, important friends, reputation to maintain. He needed a . . . he needed someone else to take the blame."

"All right," Miss Coburn said, although she still looked dubious.

Madeline Stanhope stood by the case, watching us, her eyes full of hunger and rage. I was grateful that she was not coming any closer.

I went on: "And I believe he was quite sincere about wanting to keep the necklace safe. After all, he was planning to keep it in his own house—"

"How—"

"Wait. Let me finish. It was going to be vulnerable to burglars, inquisitive servants, prying house-guests. I guess that what happened . . . that he asked himself how Maria Vittoria Venebretti would have solved his, er, problem—"

"And thus the works on her and on Renaissance magic."

"Yes. He found his answer in the *Imperium Orbis* of Carolus Albinus. Albinus talks about how to command all sorts of things: Hebrew golems, spirits of fire and air—"

"Booth."

"Sorry. Right. Albinus also talks about how to command the dead."

"*Merde*," said Miss Coburn.

" . . . Yes. Mr. DeWitt found that the two halves of his problem solved each other. He needed a . . . a suspect who would never show up to prove his—or in this case her—guilt, and he needed . . . " I realized I was staring at Madeline Stanhope and looked away. "He needed a dead body."

"But chaining her to the wall?"

"I haven't read a great deal . . . that is, I don't like this kind of spell. But this sort of . . . of guardian needs to be . . . it's an avatar of fury, is how I understand it."

We were both looking at Madeline Stanhope now. She was staring back at us, her lips pulled away from her sharp teeth. One hand was resting on the glass case, and I could see the tension of the fingers, yearning to reach through the glass to touch the necklace itself.

"And it worked," I said, distantly amazed at how level my voice was when most of my mind was screaming. "She was bound to the necklace just as he desired, and the hue and cry went up after her—all the way to San Francisco according to your aunt."

"Yes."

"And then Mr. DeWitt was hoist by his own petard."

"What do you mean?"

"He waited a year. Then he offered a perfectly innocent explanation for wandering around in the basements at all hours and went down to take the necklace back. But he was a stupid man, and he didn't understand . . . that is, he forgot to tell her not to guard it from *him*."

"So the heart attack . . . "

"I don't think it was coincidence."

"But why—nothing happened to us!"

"Philip Burney—who is also on Mr. DeWitt's list—says that the dead see only by moonlight. And I think she must be limited . . . she must have a radius of influence, with the necklace as its focus. Or else why wouldn't she . . . that is, I'm often in the museum after moonrise. But people just aren't in the galleries at this time of night."

"The watchman's supposed to be," Miss Coburn muttered.

"Yes, well . . . "

The revenant was still standing, still staring.

"Miss Coburn," I said, "what happened to Madeline Stanhope's bones?"

"I don't know. Why does it matter? Shouldn't we be figuring out what she wants?"

"Oh, I know what she wants. I'm just afraid to give it to her."

I felt Miss Coburn's swift glance, but I could not take my eyes off Madeline Stanhope; I was too frightened.

"She wants the necklace," I said.

"Are you sure?"

"Yes. Quite sure."

"We can't give it to her. Starkweather will *slay* us."

"She wants it," I said, looking at the predatory teeth, the strong angry hands. "It's *hers* now. And I can't help thinking Maria Vittoria Venebretti would be pleased."

"What are we going to do?"

"What choice do you think we have?"

"Oh," said Miss Coburn in a very small voice.

As a senior archivist, I had the master key for the display cases. I took out my key ring and got to my feet. I could feel my hands shaking, but I advanced to the case. Madeline Stanhope watched me come, her eyes like the pits of Gehenna. I unlocked the case, opened the door. I could not bring myself to touch the necklace. Madeline Stanhope's white hand snaked in past me, seizing the necklace in a grip like a vulture's claw. As she pulled it out, her arm brushed mine; even through my coat and shirt, I could feel the burning cold of her flesh, like dry ice. She smiled at me, a terrible smile, full of teeth, and fastened the necklace around her throat. As I watched, sick and petrified, her eyes slowly filled with an unearthly green light, the same color as the emeralds that now gleamed on her chest and shoulders. I lurched back a step, unable to stay near her, consumed with terror that she might touch me again.

Then my eyes clouded, or the room darkened, for she was gone, and I did not see which way she went. Mechanically, I reached into the case and flipped over the placard, so that the side reading, RE-MOVED FOR CLEANING, was uppermost. I closed the case again and locked it.

I turned back to Miss Coburn as I returned my keys to my pocket and found her sitting with a white-knuckled grip on the edge of the bench. "My God, Booth," she said faintly. "Did you see her leave?"

"No. Did you?"

"No." She shuddered convulsively, ending with a shake of her head as if it were something she wished to dislodge from her spine. "I understand now why you didn't want to open this particular Pandora's box."

"Come on. I don't want to stay here."

"No," she agreed, getting to her feet. "We'd better sneak back and look normal."

"Normal?" The reality of the Museum Ball crashed back in on me. "How can we . . . we . . . the staircase . . . "

Miss Coburn grinned at me. "They'll just think we've been necking."

"Oh, God, no."

"If we go back right now, they won't think we've done anything worse."

I stared at her for a moment before I realized that she was not joking. "Then, please, let's go."

We went, hastily, furtively, both of us glancing back nervously over our shoulders.

"Where do you think she went?" Miss Coburn asked.

"Where have they put her bones?"

"Oh. Oh dear. Do you think . . . "

"Yes," I said.

"God help me, I do, too."

"She has the necklace," I said, trying to comfort us both.

"Yes," said Miss Coburn, "but what worries me is what she may do to *keep* it."

And to that I had no reply.

The loss of the Venebretti necklace was not realized until nearly six months later. Neither Miss Coburn nor I fell under suspicion, since the two persons with the legitimate authority to remove the necklace—Dr. Starkweather and Mr. Browne, the head of Restoration and Repairs—hated each other with a passion that would have made the daughters of King Lear proud. Each assumed that the other had taken it, and when it came out that no one in the museum knew where the necklace was, Dr. Starkweather insisted furiously that Mr. Browne had squirreled it away, and Mr. Browne maintained, apoplectically, that Dr. Starkweather must have damaged it—Dr. Starkweather's rough and clumsy hands were the bane of Restoration and Repairs—and then hidden it rather than confessing to his crime like an honorable man. In the miasma of their mutual venom, no one thought to ask any of the simple questions, such as when the necklace had last been seen and who had the keys to its case, and the idea that the necklace might be genuinely lost never arose. The new inventory pleased Dr. Starkweather, but it did not change the fact that many things lost in the Parrington are never found again.

And so all was serene, although I confess that to this day, when my mind turns to Madeline Stanhope and the Venebretti Necklace, I cannot help imagining her, somewhere in the darkness of the museum basements, stroking the emeralds with her cold white fingers and smiling, smiling.

THE BONE KEY

I had been in the paper when the Parrington opened its new fossil exhibit, an ugly, gawky presence half-hidden behind a diplodocus skull. That was why the letter came to me at work; the envelope, hand-written in a spidery copperplate with velvet-black ink, was addressed to Mr. Kyle Murchison Booth, c/o the Samuel Mather Parrington Museum. The return address was the Belfontaine Hotel.

The letter was from someone who signed himself L. M. Ogilvy, Esq. He was a semi-retired lawyer, he said, and he was writing on behalf of a client who had been dead for twenty years. His client, Regina Murchison, had wished to leave a legacy to her granddaughter, Thekla Murchison, and Mr. Ogilvy had been instructed to institute a search, armed with only the knowledge that Thekla had married a man named Grimbold Booth and moved to this part of the country; being in the city on another client's business, he had observed my picture in the newspaper and noted the unusual conjunction of my names. Therefore (he wrote), he wondered if I might be the son of the woman he sought. If I was, and could produce proof of my identity, he thought we might have a very profitable little chat. As well, there was a daguerreotype of Thekla Murchison which I might be interested in seeing.

The names were right; difficult though it was for me to believe, this lawyer seemed truly to be a representative of my mother's family. I had only been twelve when my parents died, and they had never talked to me about their pasts. I knew my father had no family and had always assumed the same was true of my mother. By the time I was old enough that I might have found better answers among their effects, their belongings had all been sold, stolen, or destroyed by my guardians, the Siddonses. Even my memories of my parents were faded, crumpled, stained. A picture of my mother, a chance to rebuild her face around the wide dark eyes that were all I remembered . . .

I wrote to Mr. Ogilvy. My letter was stiff and cautious; I knew that as I was writing it, but I could not help it. I wrote merely that I had been orphaned young and knew nothing of my parents, further that I would be pleased to meet with Mr. Ogilvy, if a mutually convenient time could be found, and signed myself, sincerely, Kyle Murchison Booth. It was a dreadful letter, and posting it felt like the worst mistake I had ever made.

Mr. Ogilvy wrote back promptly, suggesting that I should come to his room in the Belfontaine that Friday evening. And since I could not find any excuse not to, I wrote back to say that would be convenient.

The great edifice of the Belfontaine Hotel loomed up out of the darkness and spitting snow and swallowed me whole, like a giant in a fairytale swallowing a fool. The hotel was a blazing citadel, a palace of electricity in the city's cold gloom. Inside, it was warm, red velvet and brass, an echoing clamor of the elite and the demimonde. I asked at the desk for Mr. Ogilvy and was directed to Room 334. I took the stairs.

The third floor was the same red velvet and brass as the lobby, the numbers gleaming on the dark-paneled doors. I found 334 and knocked. After a pause that seemed interminable but lasted probably no more than five seconds, I heard the chain being released and the bolt drawn back.

The door swung open, and I was confronting L. M. Ogilvy. I am generally very slow in forming impressions of people, but I disliked Mr. Ogilvy from the moment I laid eyes on him. He was probably seventy or so, a small, shriveled, dried-up man with a sour, twisted mouth. He wore an ugly brown suit with an even uglier burgundy bow-tie, and his sparse white hair was neatly combed. His eyes were brown, the same mud-brown as his suit, and slightly pop, giving him a strong resemblance to a desiccated toad. I had ample time to remark the likeness, for he stared at me in silence for some moments before saying, "You must be Kyle Booth." His voice was bull-frog deep, but as dry as the rest of him.

"Yes."

"Come in, please," he said and stood aside.

The desire to refuse wrenched at me like an undertow, but since I had admitted to my identity, I could not commit the atrocious rudeness of running away. It was beyond my capacity. I entered the hotel room.

"Sit down," said Mr. Ogilvy. I sat, in an uncomfortable armchair; he took the other, so close that we were almost knee to knee. He smelled overwhelmingly of pipe tobacco, a scent I have always found unpleasant.

"Make yourself comfortable. Do you smoke?"

"No, er, thank you," I said.

"Well, I do," he said, with a croaking noise that he probably meant to be a laugh. He pulled out a meerschaum pipe and a tobacco pouch. I watched, repelled and fascinated, as he stuffed the bowl of the pipe with tobacco and then expended an amazing quantity of matches in getting it lit. Finally, though, he said, "So then, you're Thekla Murchison's son."

"Yes, sir," I said.

"Did you bring any proof of your identity?"

I did, in fact, have my birth certificate in the inside pocket of my suit coat, but my dislike of Mr. Ogilvy had been growing steadily, and his tobacco smoke was making me light-headed. I said, "Is my hair not proof enough?"

My answer seemed to please him, for he croaked out another laugh and said, "So you know about the Murchison hair, do you?"

"My mother told me before she died."

"Ah, yes. And that was when?"

"Twenty-three years ago. I was twelve."

"I see. Why did the executors not get in touch with your mother's family?"

"I don't know. I was only a child."

"Yes, yes, of course." He waved that away in a cloud of pipe smoke. "Well, you certainly *look* like a Murchison, but I'm afraid we lawyers can't proceed by appearances alone." He laughed again.

"Of course not," I said. My birth certificate sat like a dead mouse in my pocket, but I did not want, for no reason that I could explain, to give it to Mr. Ogilvy. "What sort of proof would satisfy you?"

I fully expected him to ask for documents—at which point my foolishness would be rebuked and I would produce my birth certificate like any normal person—but instead, he asked, "How did your mother die?"

"Beg pardon?"

"If she died twenty-three years ago, she must have been what? About thirty-five?"

"Thirty-four," I said.

"Then how did she die?"

"How will this constitute proof of my identity?"

"Just answer the question, Mr. Booth," Mr. Ogilvy said. For a moment, he looked to me less like a toad than like a crocodile.

"She committed suicide the night of my father's death." I remembered sitting on the stairs, alone and unregarded, listening to the harsh, terrible sound of her crying. She had come out of my father's room and looked at me without seeing me. She had gone up the stairs, leaving me there on the landing, half-formed words dying in my mouth. Less than a minute later, I had heard the crash as she threw herself out the attic window.

"I see, I see. And your father? What did he die of?"

"I . . . I don't know exactly. He had been ill for months, but the doctors couldn't agree on a diagnosis."

"Yes," said Mr. Ogilvy. I thought he was about to start rubbing his hands with glee. "Thekla thought she could outrun her blood, but it can't be done. Can't be done!"

"I beg your pardon. Did you know my mother?"

"*Know* her? Dear boy, I almost *married* her!" He began to laugh again, a croaking, rasping, vile sound that made me want to stop my ears with my fingers. "Murchisons can only marry each other," said Mr. Ogilvy. "That's our curse. Thekla thought true love could carry the weight of death, but she was wrong. Wrong!"

"Mr. Ogilvy," I said, and I was astonished to hear how level and even my voice was, "I believe you have not been honest with me."

"I've lied only by omission. I *was* Regina's lawyer, and I most certainly *did* search for twenty years without finding a trace of Thekla. 'Course, I didn't know she'd been dead for three years when I started. The only thing I didn't tell you, Kyle my lad, is that the M in my name stands for Murchison, just like in yours."

I felt as if I was drowning in his pipe smoke and his hideous revelations. It was just as well he did not wait for a response from me, for there was no response I could imagine making.

"There's even a legacy, though I don't imagine it's going to do you much good." He grinned, revealing an array of yellow, crooked, corroded teeth. "The truth. The curse of the Murchisons. Did your dear departed mama ever tell you stories about her family?"

"No."

"Poor stupid Thekla." He sighed, but it was as fake as the tears of a crocodile. "So, then, you need some family history."

"Mr. Ogilvy, I really don't think—"

"*Sit down.*" Involuntarily, I sat.

"An ancestor of yours, Geoffrey Murchison, married a woman named Alabaster Whalen. Mary Anna and Claudine always maintained that Alabaster was from Salem, but they were a pair of romantic ninnies, and I say it as their cousin. In any event, there seems to have been a good deal of coercion involved, and their only child, your five times great-grandfather, John Whalen Murchison, was conceived by rape."

He paused, giving me a sly look to see how I was taking all of this. I do not know what he saw on my face, but it must have satisfied him, for he continued: "Alabaster Whalen Murchison died in childbirth with her only son—whom she had never wanted—and she cursed both son and father with her dying breath. Regardless of Alabaster's origins—Salem witch or some other kind—her curse was effective, and it has transmitted itself to all of her descendants, including," and he gestured with his pipe at my hair, "you."

He stopped there, waiting, his eyes like a crocodile's judging the strength of a drowning man. I wanted to walk out on him, to deny him the satisfaction he sought, but the story had hold of me, and I could not.

"What was the curse?"

"Murchison men kill their wives; Murchison women kill their husbands. If your hair goes white before you're twenty-five, your spouse will be dead before you're thirty-five. And they all die like your father did, Kyle: a mysterious ailment that slowly saps the vitality. No doctor can understand it or halt its progress. Geoffrey Murchison survived his wife by about six months. John Whalen Murchison's first wife died when he was thirty four. His second, third, and fourth wives each lasted about five years. Divorce can't save you, and the absence of children is an iffy protection at best—and don't think that immorality will save you, either. It's been tried. Your great-great-grandparents were second cousins who each had the white hair when they got married; they lasted well into their sixties. That's the only effective counter-measure we've ever found: bad blood balancing bad blood. But then we found, in our generation, that there weren't enough Murchisons to go around."

He blew another enormous cloud of smoke and peered out of it at me like the cruel dragon in a fairy tale. "Thekla thought that if she cut all her ties with the family and married a man whom she loved beyond words—as she put it in a letter to Claudine—then Alabaster's curse would miss its grip. Guess she was wrong, wasn't she, Kyle?"

"Did he know?" I said, my mouth numb and ashy.

"Of course he knew. Perfect love means perfect honesty, that was what Thekla thought. She told him the whole thing before she consented to the engagement."

"And he married her anyway."

"He was a fool," Mr. Ogilvy said, his mouth twisting further with contempt. "Just like Thekla."

I remembered my father well enough to know that he had never been foolish. He had simply loved my mother enough to make the gamble. But perhaps, in Mr. Ogilvy's lexicon, that was the same as being a fool.

"We're almost all dead now," he continued in a quieter voice. "Thekla was right enough about that. Three generations of marrying your cousins, and most of the vitality goes out of the stock. There's me, and there's Mary Anna—she's in a convent in Ohio—and there's Claudine's kids, but the boy's half-witted, and poor Mavis is as barren as salt. Planning on getting married, Kyle?"

No one calls me Kyle, and I hated hearing my given name from this mummified toad, but telling him so would only please him. Mr. Ogilvy did not like me any better than I liked him; I wondered if it was on my mother's account.

"No," I said. My voice was rusty, shrill, little more than breath. I could feel Alabaster Whalen Murchison's hate, and I suspected I would go on feeling it for a very long time, perhaps forever. But there was no love left in my life which she could kill, no happiness which she could blight.

His eyebrows went up, but he said, "Well, no matter. Now, since it seems that you are indeed Thekla's son, Mavis would like to meet you, and give you that daguerreotype of Thekla I mentioned in my letter."

"Mavis?"

"Your cousin, Mavis Murchison Davenant."

"Oh. I, er . . . " I wanted to run, to bolt out of the smothering red velvet warmth of the Belfontaine like a fox who hears the baying of hounds. But I also, painfully, wanted to see my mother's image. "Yes, very well."

"She's down in one of the lounges," Mr. Ogilvy said, getting up. "Come on."

I am a fool, I thought despairingly. But I followed him.

I felt my cousin as we came out of the elevator, before I saw her, a pocket of black stillness in the midst of the bright jubilation. I turned my head and there she was, standing beneath the lobby's enormous clock. Mrs. Davenant was easily a half-foot taller than Mr. Ogilvy, her white head rising from the black collar of her dress like a funeral lily. As we crossed the lobby toward her, I saw that she was near my own age; she wore her hair unfashionably long, seeming almost to flaunt its whiteness with the heavy braids that crowned her skull. She had a narrow, high-cheekboned face, very medieval, and her dark eyes were myopic and dreamy. She looked like Julian of Norwich, as painted by Millais.

Mr. Ogilvy said, with unwholesome chirpiness, "Mavis, my dear, this is your cousin Kyle. Kyle, this is Mavis."

We shook hands. Her grip was firmer than I had expected, although her long, narrow hand was as cold as it was pale. "How do you do?" she murmured.

I bit the inside of my lower lip and managed a perfectly unexceptionable, "I am pleased to meet you."

"You are troubled," she said gently, not quite a reprimand but definitely a correction. "You did not wish to come. You are angry at Cousin Luther, and frightened."

I looked involuntarily at Mr. Ogilvy; he shrugged and smirked, deliberately unhelpful.

"Mrs. Davenant, I—"

"Please, call me Mavis. The spirits have told me so much about you that I feel almost as if we were children together." Her smile was lovely, dreamy, and did absolutely nothing to quell the cold shivers of dread along my spine. "Come. Let us go someplace that we can sit down and talk."

I could not have claimed that I wished to stay in the lobby; the crowding and the noise were already increasing the tension in my neck and shoulders. I followed Mrs. Davenant and Mr. Ogilvy into a small lounge off the main lobby, deserted except for a dark, heavy-set young woman who was seated in the exact middle of the plum-colored Chesterfield, her feet planted squarely on the floor, knitting. She looked up at our approach, and her muddy hazel eyes, fixing on Mrs. Davenant, lit like bonfires. She put her knitting aside and rose.

"Edith, darling, this is my cousin Kyle. Cousin Kyle, may I introduce you to my dear friend, Miss Edith Locksley?" The muddy hazel eyes fixed on me, and Miss Locksley produced a wholly unconvincing simper.

I shook hands with Miss Locksley because this ghastly *contretemps* was not her fault. But my unease was growing stronger, my sense of being a fox pursued by ardent hounds; I said, "I beg your pardon, Mrs. Davenant, Mr. Ogilvy, Miss Locksley, but I'm afraid I cannot stay. I have—"

"Cousin Kyle," Mrs. Davenant said reprovingly. "We have traveled a great distance in order to speak to you, and at great inconvenience to ourselves. Please, sit down. A quarter hour of your time is surely not too much to ask."

My skin scalded with mortification; I found myself sitting on the couch between Mrs. Davenant and Miss Locksley, while Mr. Ogilvy claimed an armchair. Miss Locksley picked up her knitting again, and I tore my gaze away from the needles, shuddering. They reminded me too much of Mrs. Siddons.

"Mrs. Davenant," I said, "please—"

"Cousin Kyle," she said, smiling and placing her hand on my knee, "do tell me about yourself."

I gritted my teeth and did not tell her that I hate to be touched. She smelled strongly of incense. "I, er, I work in a museum. With old books. I . . . er, I . . . that is—"

"Are you married?"

I felt myself tense, and I knew she could, too. "No," I said in barely more than a mumble, "I am not."

"Have you objections to the married state?" she pressed, and the solicitude in her voice might have been mockery or might not, and I could not tell which was the more unpleasant thought.

"Considering what Mr. Ogilvy has told me, I am amazed that you can ask."

"Cousin Luther?" she said past me, cold and stern.

"Seems I forgot to tell Kyle the most important part." My head turned, unwillingly, stiffly, and he gave me a small smug smirk. "The curse wasn't the only thing Alabaster passed on to her descendants. You don't have it. Neither do I. But your daughter would."

It took me a moment to realize what he was saying, to understand why the Murchison line had not died out over a century ago. "Oh God," I said, my voice strange and hoarse and hollow in my ears. "Oh God, no."

"Squeamish, Kyle?" said Mr. Ogilvy and leered repellently. "You shouldn't be. It's the power that matters. Your daughter could drink demon's blood. She could call on darker gods than yours, and they would hearken to her call. She could unbraid the future, feel death in her hands. She could hear the voices in the earth."

"No," I said. I was on my feet somehow, shaking. "Never."

His eyebrows went up. Not a toad, but a serpent, the serpent who knows that Eve lies when she says she has never wondered about the forbidden fruit. "Never?"

"I will not . . . I *cannot*—"

"Don't turn your back on your family so quickly, Kyle."

"And you should not be so hasty to dismiss marriage." Mavis Davenant's cold hand on my arm, pulling me back down onto the sofa. "For the spirits tell me it is your destiny."

Then either she or her "spirits" lied, for if I know anything about myself, it is that I was not designed—by nature or benevolent Providence or any other force—for the matrimonial bed. "Mrs. Davenant," I said, "please remove your hand from my person."

In the shocked little silence that followed, Mr. Ogilvy started laughing, hard enough that he seemed likely to choke.

"Cousin Luther, please," Mrs. Davenant said in genteel exasperation. Her hand was still on my arm.

"Mrs. Davenant," I said, "I was quite—"

Now there was a hand on my knee on the other side. I turned my head, my flesh crawling, and saw that Miss Locksley had set down her knitting to place one plump hand on my knee, the other splayed starfish-like on her bosom. "I can tell that you are not a believer, Mr. Booth," she said, and her voice was low and unpleasantly throaty, "but do you not feel it?"

"Feel what?" I could hardly help feeling her hand; it was heavy and, even through my trouser-leg, hot. I suspected it was also damp.

"The connection between us!" she said in accents more suited to one of Mrs. Radcliffe's heroines.

"I, er . . . that is . . . No."

"You will," she said, the muddy hazel eyes boring into mine. "The spirits have shown me. Oh, they do not speak to me as clearly as they do to dearest Mavis, but I could not be mistaken in this!"

"Miss Locksley," I said desperately, "I assure you that you could." I wanted to rise, but Miss Locksley seemed to be leaning more and more of her weight on the hand that rested on my leg and Mrs Davenant had a remarkably strong grip for such a frail-looking woman. "Ladies—Mrs. Davenant, please. I have told you that I—"

"You are very noble, Cousin Kyle, but Edith is aware of the danger and is entirely prepared to face it."

"The *danger*?" I said, my voice rising into a squawk; the understatement was too much to be borne.

"The curse," said Miss Locksley, her expression uplifted.

"It would be murder!"

"Edith is a distant cousin, and we think she might—"

"Doesn't have the hair," Mr. Ogilvy struck in.

Mrs. Davenant ignored him loftily, and I wondered how many times they'd argued the point already. "We think she might have sufficient Murchison blood to withstand the dark energies."

"And, in any event," Miss Locksley chimed in, "I don't mind."

I could not help staring at her. "You don't *mind*?"

She was looking very pure and noble and reverent, and I was conscious of a desire to slap her, an urge which I had never felt toward anyone before in my life. "My daughter will bear the power of the Murchison women. She will be a Queen of the Unseen Realms. And I know that Mavis will care for her as she would for a daughter of her own. Truly, I cannot complain if I lay down my life, so long as it is in the service of my destiny."

"Miss Locksley, this is *not* your destiny!"

Both women looked at me reproachfully, and I shrank back, feeling my face heat.

"Cousin Kyle, you shouldn't argue with the spirits. Much is revealed to them that we on this plane cannot see."

"Mrs. Davenant—"

"Family, Cousin Kyle. This formality is very sweet, but really not necessary."

No matter what powers Mrs. Davenant controlled, she was not

going to make me call Mr. Ogilvy "Cousin Luther." "Cousin Mavis, I don't at all wish to be rude, but . . . "

"This comes to you as a shock. I understand that. And no one's asking you to get married *today*." She and Miss Locksley both laughed, a celestina of bones underscored by the cries of swamp frogs.

"No, it isn't—"

"*Today* we are asking for something much simpler."

Oh, dear God. *We need a human heart for our rites, Cousin Kyle. You won't miss it, I promise.* I licked my lips. "What?"

Mrs. Davenant smiled, and I saw the hate and power and madness of Alabaster Whalen shining in her eyes. "The bone key. Where is it?"

For a moment, I truly believed she had lapsed into some other language, Chinese perhaps or ancient Sanskrit; I could make no sense of what she said. Even when, fighting panic, I replayed her words in my head, they were meaningless. "I . . . I beg your pardon?"

"The bone key, Cousin Kyle. I want it back."

"Mrs. Davenant—er, Cousin Mavis, I'm afraid you must—"

"Don't bother with the protestations of innocence, Cousin Kyle. We know Aunt Thekla took it. And it doesn't belong to you. It has always been the talisman of the Murchison *women*."

"Made from Alabaster Whalen's own arm bone," Miss Locksley said dreamily.

Dear God, I thought, no wonder we are cursed.

Mrs. Davenant gave Miss Locksley a *yes, dear, but not NOW*, look, and said to me, "It will do you no good. Aunt Thekla should not have taken it."

"I have nothing of my parents', as I think you know very well. Does the daguerreotype Mr. Ogilvy mentioned even exist?"

She allowed herself just the barest hint of a martyred sigh as she opened her handbag and produced a small, flat, rectangular object wrapped in black velvet.

"Thank you." I unwrapped it only long enough to be certain that it was a daguerreotype and that the girl portrayed was not inconsistent with my memories of my mother, then rewrapped the velvet and tucked it into my inner breast-pocket.

Mrs. Davenant said, "The bone key, Cousin Kyle."

"I wasn't *negotiating*," I said, incredulous and indignant. "I honestly don't have any idea of what you're talking about."

"A rod about two inches long—it would look like scrimshaw if you didn't know what it was."

She saw the recognition on my face before I could school my features. "You *have* seen it. Where? When?"

"The last time was at my mother's funeral. In her coffin."

Mrs Davenant's mouth thinned. "And where is Aunt Thekla buried?"

I stared at her in horror. "You can't . . . "

"The bone key is mine by rights, and I have no intention of leaving this city without it. Where?"

"No. I will not help you desecrate my mother's grave."

"But you already have, Cousin Kyle." She smiled at me sweetly. "The spirits are urging you to speak. Listen to them."

"I told you because I thought . . . I never imagined you would . . . have you no shred of decency?"

Mr. Ogilvy said, "Murchisons mostly don't."

"Cousin Luther," said Mrs. Davenant warningly, and then turned back to me. "Cousin Kyle, I mean no disrespect to Aunt Thekla. But you must know, all that lies in her coffin is the remains of her mortal shell, the shackles she has cast off. Listen, Cousin Kyle, and you will hear her say so!"

"I will hear nothing of the sort." I found myself on my feet, shaking with a mixture of emotions I could not even name. "Mrs. Davenant, I have already heard more than I wish to. I will bid you good night."

I turned to go, and Mr. Ogilvy said, "We can find the cemetery without your help, Kyle, but are you *quite* sure you want to wash your hands of us entirely?"

I froze. I knew what he meant; the sly, slow emphasis of "quite" was enough to convey his threat. Clearly, Mrs. Davenant was prepared to violate my mother's grave; it was not such a large step to wonder what else she might be prepared to do. I was not naïve enough to imagine that Mr. Ogilvy would have made any push to stop her, even if he and I had not taken each other in instant and mutual antipathy. And the thought of Miss Locksley standing in Mavis Murchison Davenant's way was merely ludicrous.

I turned back slowly. "I could go to the police," I said, but even in my own ears, my voice was not convincing.

Mr. Ogilvy snorted. "And you think they'd believe you?" He waved a hand from himself to Mrs. Davenant to Miss Locksley: an unlikely trio of grave-robbers.

"I will not help you," I said.

"Come," said Mrs. Davenant, smiling again. "Sit with us, and we will ask the spirits for guidance."

Feeling as culpably helpless as I had the night of my father's death, my mother's suicide, I sat.

To my horror, it was true that something spoke to Mrs. Davenant—something she called "the spirits." I myself would have been far more cautious about giving it a name or assuming I understood its essence. I could think of candidates other than the benevolent dead.

But whatever the true nature of her informant, it was accurate. I cursed myself for my ineffectuality as we emerged from the taxi-cab at the corner of Callum Street, cursed myself for my inability either to deter them from their purpose or simply to walk away. My mother had abandoned me when I was twelve; why should I not abandon her now?

But I could not. I could not do her that great dishonor. I knew I would not be able to live with the dreams that would follow.

Mr. Ogilvy had placed a telephone call before we left the hotel, and the results were awaiting us in front of the cemetery gates.

"Cousin Dominic!" Mrs. Davenant said, moving ahead regally, as if the cloak she affected—which made her look even more pre-Raphaelite—were coronation robes.

"We never lose track of the Murchison blood," Mr. Ogilvy whispered, his breath nauseatingly hot in my ear. "Ever asked yourself why Thekla gave you that middle name, Kyle? *She wanted us to find you.*" My shudder was slight but comprehensive, and he laughed—a low, loathsome chuckle—as he moved away again to say something inaudible to Miss Locksley.

Mrs. Davenant finished her conference with "Cousin Dominic." The small group of men approached the cemetery gates; Mrs. Davenant returned to where Mr. Ogilvy, Miss Locksley, and I stood. I was not watching, and therefore I cannot say exactly what those men—"Murchison men," Mr. Ogilvy would call them—did, but in a moment, one of them beckoned, and I could see the gates standing slightly ajar.

Mrs. Davenant produced a flash-light from beneath her cloak; by its light her smile was ghastly. "Come, Cousin Kyle," she said, as merrily as if she were proposing a picnic.

I could not extricate myself from this nightmare; I followed Mrs. Davenant into the Resurrection Hill Cemetery, Mr. Ogilvy and Miss Locksley padding at my heels.

Apparently, Mrs. Davenant's "spirits" had not deserted her, for she found her way unerringly to my parents' graves. "Here," she said to the assembled sheep-like cousins. "Dig *here*."

Obediently, they dug.

Lit only by Mrs. Davenant's flash-light and by two small lanterns the cousins had brought, the scene looked like a Goya portrait of Burke and Hare. I never knew, then or later, whether the cousins had brought their own spades or had appropriated the caretaker's; if it was the latter, I could only be grateful that the caretaker did not appear in search of his property. I felt certain that Mrs. Davenant would have ordered the cousins to beat his brains in with his own shovel.

They dug lower and lower and I found myself flinching in anticipation of the moment when their spades would strike wood. And still, when it came, it shocked me. Mrs. Davenant was immediately there, standing on the edge of the grave. A muffled voice said something about "breaking open the casket." It was like a horrible parody of my parents' funeral, lacking only the presence of the Siddonses to complete the effect. I had to fight the impulse to search among the cousins for my twelve-year-old self.

I said to Mrs. Davenant, "She is your own kin."

"But the fate of the body does not matter," she said earnestly. "Truly, Cousin Kyle, this is nothing but clay."

"*This*," I said, gesturing wildly at the grave, "was my *mother*. I cannot stop you from desecrating her body, but I ask you at least to go about it decently."

There was an uneasy murmur among the cousins at the word "desecrate."

In Mrs. Davenant's frown, I saw the spoiled little girl she must once have been. But she, too, was aware of our audience, for she grudgingly acquiesced, and we both fell back as the cousins levered the coffin out of the grave.

There was no difficulty in opening it—my mother's coffin had been hastily and cheaply purchased by the Siddonses and the only wonder was that it had not broken of its own accord. Mrs. Davenant darted forward; I turned away, unwilling to have my memories of my mother, dim and troubled though they were, be replaced by an image of her as she looked after nearly twenty-four years in her grave.

I heard Mrs. Davenant's cry of triumph and turned back to see her brandishing the bone key aloft, the only ornament beside her wedding ring my mother had ever worn.

My mother had strung the key on a black silk cord around her neck, an ivory rod the same length as her index finger, with stubby, almost vestigial wards. She had told me wonderful stories about it when I asked what it was and what it unlocked; it had been a kind of game between us, back in the days when my father had been well and my mother's affection had overflowed like a fountain. She had never told me the truth.

I could see the broken ends of the cord trailing from Mrs. Davenant's fist.

There was no bravery in what I did then, no thought, for if I had thought at all, I would surely have thought better of such rashness. I lunged forward—for once grateful for my gawky height—tore the key from Mrs. Davenant's grasp, and before any of us realized that I meant to do it, broke the key in half.

It broke with a brittle snap, an absurdly small noise. For a moment, it seemed the only noise in the entire night-bedecked world, and then Mrs. Davenant screamed, a skull-piercing banshee wail, her hands stretching like claws indiscriminately between me and the pieces of bone I held, and the cloud-louring sky.

"Gone!" she shrieked, in a voice I would not have described as human had I not known it issued from a human mouth. "*Gone!*"

The cousins shuffled and murmured. Mr. Ogilvy and I looked at each other. After a moment, he said, very cautiously, "What's gone, Mavis?"

"The power," she wailed, sinking to her knees. "The power . . . the darkness . . . "

"The curse?" said a cousin.

"The birthright?" said Miss Locksley.

"All of it," moaned Mrs. Davenant, folding forward, her hands covering her face. "All of it gone." Her voice spiraled up again into a howl, "*Gone!*"

"There, there, Mavis," Mr. Ogilvy said uselessly.

I put the broken pieces of the key in my pocket; it would not do to leave them where Mrs. Davenant could get her hands on them again. The key's magic might be gone, but that did not mean it could not be put to other uses by a determined enough witch; I had a mortar and pestle, and I had thrown viler things than a handful of bone dust into the river that ran through the city like its mortal blood. After a moment, I took the velvet-wrapped daguerreotype out of my coat and tossed it into the coffin on top of the moldered, rotting remains of Thekla Murchison Booth.

The cousins stared at me dumbly. Mrs. Davenant keened, a crumpled heap of darkness, Miss Locksley and Mr. Ogilvy hovering over her like ineffective asylum-nurses.

"Put her back," I said, with a weary gesture at the coffin, turning my back on my mother's family, starting toward the cemetery gates. "Let her rest."

I returned to Resurrection Hill Cemetery a week later. Alone. The streetcar's tracks ran through the neighborhood in which I had grown up. From the streetcar, I could just make out the scalloped shingles of the roof that had been ours, a distant glance rendered antiseptic by the dirty glass through which I stared and by the ladies' hats which framed my view.

I extricated myself from the streetcar at Callum Street and began walking, eastward and uphill, the sharp, bitter December wind blowing my coat out behind me.

I had never made a regular habit of visiting my parents' graves. Mrs. Siddons had forbidden it, stigmatizing my desire to do so as morbid and self-indulgent. I had always been afraid in college that my friend and roommate Augustus Blaine would agree with Mrs. Siddons and mock me for it. And then it had seemed too far and the journey too painful.

I turned up the cemetery's broad driveway, past the tiny chapel, and began picking my way through the tombstones and obelisks. I had come here once in the summer, and the trees that stood around my parents' graves had been covered in tiny, sweet, white flowers whose petals wept like snow across the graves lying beneath.

My parents had been buried side by side beneath a single tombstone. Its austerity had been my father's choice: nothing more than their names and dates. He might have loved my mother to the point of madness and beyond, but it was not a love he had chosen to show to the rest of the world. Such had been his nature, secretive and ascetic, holding even his passions at arm's length. It had been my mother who had filled the house with her easy affection; even now I could remember the warmth of her hugs, the gentle touch of her hand on my hair.

But the truth, the burning core, of her love had been revealed in her death. If I closed my eyes, I knew, I would see her face again, as she had looked when she walked past me on the way to her death. I did not want to remember her like that, but I could not help it, that terrible ruthlessness that had looked at me and only seen that I was not him.

She had loved in the same way that Alabaster Whalen Murchison had hated. Like John Whalen Murchison, I had been to my mother only a token of my father. And when that love was gone, when my father was dead, the token was useless to her. I could not . . . even if I had been able to face the idea of murdering a woman by marrying her, I could not abide the thought of inflicting that fate on another child, a child such as I had been.

I stood for a long time. The cousins had done a good job of repairing the damage they had done, and I thought I would not hurt myself by choosing to believe it was a gesture of respect, of apology. The graves lay silently before me. The sleepers within the quiet earth did not rise up to speak to me, and I was grateful. This was my family now, and they made no demands I could not meet.

WAIT FOR ME

I have never been quite sure how it happened that I ended up with Mildred Truelove Stapleton's diaries. I remember having a long, distracted conversation with Mr. Lucent, after our return from the Stapleton house, about how we should "divvy up our loot," as he persisted in phrasing it. And it made sense that I should have the sad collection of children's books, just as he rightly and properly took the poet's working manuscripts and correspondence. But when I try to remember why he did not also take her diaries, I rack my brains to no avail. My suspicion is that we were both too unnerved to know what we were doing.

Somehow, though, the box of diaries ended up in the corner of my office, along with the complete set of Lefevre first editions with the extra plates hand-colored by the author; Muriel Wilderhith's six-volume biography of her uncle—*Sir Cuthbert Wilderhith: A Life Spent Dreaming*—inscribed by Miss Wilderhith to Samuel Mather Parrington; and a herd of rather battered file-boxes in which reposed the entire, explicit, and scandalous correspondence between the poet Gillian Mowbray Thorne and Dorothea, Viscountess Sainver, including the notorious account of the even more notorious funeral of Judge Lemarys.

Although I fully intended to examine the Stapleton diaries, catalogue them, and send them into the stacks which housed the rest of the Parrington's collection of diaries, a sudden spate of acquisitions in the Department of Rare Books, and certain affairs of my own, left me with neither time nor energy to spare. And since the box of Stapleton diaries looked very much like the boxes containing the

Thorne-Sainver correspondence, giving it the protective coloration of an Arctic fox against snow, and since I had developed a slight aversion to Mildred Truelove Stapleton after the unpleasant things which had happened in her house, I am afraid I would have entirely forgotten about the diaries if it had not been for a small and unsettling coincidence.

It was one of the nights when my insomnia was particularly abysmal, and rather than drift comfortlessly from room to room of my apartment, I had come down to the Parrington in hopes of removing at least a few of the papers, books, and other assorted objects which stood between me and the surface of my desk.

I had dealt with a job lot of routine paperwork, cleared up a thorny question of provenance and dating which had entangled three of the junior archivists, and was peacefully sorting through a miscellany of bound pamphlets which Mr. Sullivan had bought for five cents in a thrift shop, "just in case it turned out to be interesting." Mr. Sullivan was young, but eager, and he had a good eye. These seemed to be mostly seventeenth century English religious tracts and printed sermons, none of them already among the museum's collection. I was noting the usual fiery denunciations of the atheistical, the disobedient, and those swollen with the sin of unrighteous pride—for the pamphlets were all staunchly Laudian, itself an interesting characteristic—when my eye was caught by a marginal gloss, "*Of Spirits and mirrours.*"

Instantly, and with a force like being hit by a bolt of lightning, I remembered Miss Stapleton, lying on the floor of that bedroom saying, *The girl in the mirror. The girl with no eyes.*

Mechanically, my eyes moved to the text before my protesting brain could articulate the objection that I did not want to know anything about Caroline beliefs concerning ghosts and mirrors. It was already too late.

I read:

As the Eyes are the Mirrours of the *soul*, so it is that Spirits have none, for their *soules* being departed it is but a husk that remaineth, like mindless *Ecchoe* in the pagan tale. And yet it is not true that Spirits are frighted by mirrors or that they do shun them. They appeare to the living in mirrors, and in a forme of their own chusing, so that one who was a wicked Sinner in life may appear a fair young man and thus cosen the Unwary. Truly, as *Pride* is the snare of the *devil*, so again do mirrours perform the Behests of the Ungodly and provide a Conduit for the *devil* to afflict Man and lead him from the path of *Belief*.

And then the author, like a hound abandoning a false scent, was off and running again, baying the necessity of obeying king, church, and priest, and the troubling matter of ghosts and mirrors was left behind.

Except that for me it had awakened those memories: that small, stifling room on the third floor of the Stapleton house, the dust, the brooding vanity, those battered books . . . and the sound of Miss Stapleton's screams.

Mr. Lucent and I, the senior archivists of the Department of Rare Books, had been sent to the Stapleton house to take possession of the bequest which Mildred Truelove Stapleton, the eminent poet, had left to the Samuel Mather Parrington Museum upon her death the previous winter. There had been a good deal of dissent and contention among Mrs. Stapleton's four adult children about every clause of her will, and thus Dr. Starkweather had felt it better not to take any chances with the Museum's new property, namely Mildred Truelove Stapleton's library and papers.

The process of transferral had taken several days and had been, on that Thursday, almost complete. All that remained were what Miss Amelia Stapleton, the eldest of the four children, referred to as "Mother's junk," being the poet's diaries, her working manuscripts, and that portion of her library which in her last, frail years she had insisted on keeping in her bedroom.

Miss Stapleton was a tall, bony spinster with an unfortunate predilection for ruffles, floral prints, and soft colors suited to schoolgirls. Her voice was high, childlike, and yet unforgivingly hard; it had become clear on the first day that she considered Mr. Lucent and myself personally to blame for the "desecration" of her mother's belongings. We had both developed the habit of avoiding her, and so my heart had sunk when I rang the bell on that last morning and was answered by her shrill demand to know who I was and what I wanted.

But she had let me in, and even agreed to conduct me to the spare room in which the last oddments were kept. I climbed the stairs in her wake, one set, then a second. Two doors down the third floor hallway, she stopped and said, "This, Mr. Booth, is the haunted room."

"The, er, what?" I said.

"Oh, that's what we call it. My mother insisted it was haunted and never used it. I don't believe in ghosts. We've been using it for storage, and Mother's junk is in there. I *will* warn you to wedge the door. It locks itself if you're not careful."

"Oh," I said. "Thank you."

The room revealed when Miss Stapleton opened the door did not look haunted. It was dusty and cluttered; clearly no one had lived in this room for many years. The appurtenances of a girl's bedroom were bundled into one corner: a lace-swagged canopy for the disassembled four-poster, a vanity with a dried and withered posy still stuck in the frame, attesting, like the pale flowered wallpaper, to the life this room had once held. In another corner, following Miss Stapleton's pointing finger, I found the last of what was to become the Mildred Truelove Stapleton Collection.

I understood immediately why the poet had not left her books and papers to her children. The papers were at least in boxes, although they looked as if they had merely been dumped in by the armful; the books, including her diaries, had been thrown into the corner, a careless heap like a child's discarded playthings. It seemed horrible to me that a poet's children could take out their anger at their mother on her innocent and helpless books.

"That's funny," said Miss Stapleton. "We didn't leave them like that." But there was no outrage, or even concern, in her voice, and I felt no compulsion to believe her.

I said, "When my colleague gets here, could you . . . that is, I would be grateful if you would show him up." Mr. Lucent, dilatory as always, was now nearly an hour late.

"Of course," said Miss Stapleton without warmth. "Don't forget about the door." And she left.

I wedged the door firmly open and settled in to work.

Cataloguing the books took very little time; there were only twenty-three of them. Oddly, for a woman whose tastes in literature, as represented by the rest of her library, were both catholic and sophisticated, the books Mildred Truelove Stapleton had clung to in her last years were all cheap popular editions of children's books: the Lambs' *Tales from Shakespeare*, *Robinson Crusoe*, *Pilgrim's Progress*, Marigold's *Prayers for the Young*, *Gulliver's Travels*, collections of fairy tales and poems. All of them were inscribed on the flyleaf *Georgiana Beatrice Truelove* in a schoolgirl's copperplate. Clearly, from the printing dates of the books, Mrs. Stapleton's sister, but why had Mildred ended up with Georgiana's books? I made a note to give these books to Mr. Forsythe, who was embroiled in a massive and quixotic study of children's books of the previous century, and moved on to the manuscripts and diaries which were properly Mr. Lucent's domain, except that Mr. Lucent was not here.

Aside from being thick with dust, the room was unpleasantly stuffy even with the door open; I was aware of sweat trickling down my collar and dampening my shirt. A cursory glance was enough to show that the situation pertaining among the manuscripts, diaries, and correspondence was vastly more complicated than that among the books. I groaned in spirit, loosened my tie slightly, and stood up, knowing that if I did not stretch at least occasionally, my joints would stiffen and I would have to be helped to my feet—and once I got involved in the labyrinth of Mrs. Stapleton's papers, I would very likely forget to move at all.

I paced back and forth in the narrow aisle of clear space, which brought me face to face with the old vanity at the end of each circuit. After the third or fourth time, I realized that I was avoiding my reflection and stopped, puzzled. It is true that I am homely and do not care to spend hours admiring myself in all convenient reflective surfaces, but I am not the Elephant Man or the Hunchback of Nôtre Dame, to shun my reflection as abhorrent and monstrous.

I looked at the mirror. It was dusty, of course, and the glass was old and wavery. It was not a noticeably nice vanity—not a good example of any school of furniture and a little spindly for my taste—but it was not loathsome, and there was absolutely nothing wrong with the mirror . . . except that there was. There was something about the way the room was reflected which set my teeth on edge. I realized I was staring at my reflection and had to make a conscious effort to look away from the mirror, as if I were pulling a piece of iron away from a magnet.

Do *try* to control your imagination, Mr. Booth, said the voice of one of my prep-school teachers, long dead, in my mind. I shook myself away from contemplation of the vanity, sat down again, and addressed myself to the task of creating order among Mrs. Stapleton's papers.

I began by sorting into categories: correspondence, manuscripts, diaries (which were at least easily identifiable by virtue of being in bound volumes). I was working on the chronology of the letters when Mr. Lucent waltzed in.

"You're late," I said without looking up.

"Yes, I know. *So* sorry. I was just on the way out the door when—"

"Don't bother."

"I beg your pardon?"

"Don't bother. I'm not interested in your excuses."

"Are you all right, Mr. Booth? You don't—" Then his voice sharpened. "What are you doing?"

"Your job," I said, securing together, with a paper-clip from my vest pocket, the three pages of a letter from the novelist Clemence Bradstreet.

"You have no right."

I stood up to face him. "I had no assurance that you would make an appearance today, and if you recall, we promised the Stapleton heirs not to take more than a week. What else was I supposed to do?"

Mr. Lucent had gone beet-red with indignation. "Let me remind you, Mr. Booth, that you are *not* my superior and you have *no* right to tell me how to do my job."

"Someone ought to."

"Well, it's not going to be you, you pinch-faced stick!"

A voice said mildly from the doorway, "Excuse me."

Mr. Lucent and I whipped around like stags at bay, and the oppressive, resentful anger in the room shattered into sticky fragments like a dropped egg.

It was Martin Stapleton, Mildred Truelove Stapleton's principal heir and only son. He was a quiet, decisive man, far gentler and more thoughtful than his sisters. "Is anything wrong?"

Mr. Lucent and I looked at each other. "No," Mr. Lucent said doubtfully. "We were just . . . " And then he trailed off, clearly no more certain of what had just happened than I was.

I made a desperate effort to pull myself together. "It's the, er, the heat. Can we do something for you, Mr. Stapleton?"

"Shoe's on the other foot. I was just looking in to see if there was anything you needed."

"No, thank you," I said.

"We're quite all right," chimed in Mr. Lucent.

"Although," I said because I did not want Mr. Stapleton to think we were getting rid of him in order to continue our quarrel in peace, "there was one thing ... I noticed, I was wondering, er ... that is, can you tell me who Georgiana Truelove was?"

"Mother's younger sister. She died when they were girls. Why?"

"Oh, these books," I said and waved at them. "They were hers."

"Ah," he said. "So was this room. Mother disliked it very deeply, and I am not sure I care for it myself. In any event, if you need anything, just let one of us know. We should be around most of the day."

He left.

Mr. Lucent and I stared at each other in dismal, appalled silence.

Finally, I said, "I'm sorry. I didn't—"

"No, honestly, I don't know what got *into* me. You're far more qualified than I am any day of the week."

"Mr. Lucent, please, don't say that. I oughtn't to have ... "

"Well, anyway, I'm sorry I called you a pinch-faced stick." Then, with a gesture of putting the past behind him, he said briskly, "Now tell me how far you've gotten."

Gratefully, I introduced Mr. Lucent to my three unwieldy groupings, and he got to work on the manuscripts while I continued with the correspondence. All the while, as part of my mind mechanically noted dates and authors, I wondered miserably what had happened, why I had been so vicious to Mr. Lucent, who was always courteous and kind—and good at his job, even if unpunctual. Except for my lame spur-of-the-moment explanation to Mr. Stapleton—"the heat"—I had no solution to the puzzle of what had possessed me to say such terrible things. I wondered if this might be the first warning sign of schizophrenia. In the depths of my mortification, that seemed almost more appealing than the idea that there was no reason at all, that I had said those cruel, officious things simply because, somewhere in the depths of my psyche, I *wanted* to.

With the two of us working, the organizational phase of our endeavor did not take long. Mr. Lucent pulled out his notebook and said diffidently, "If you'd like to . . . take a break or something, Mr. Booth . . . You've been at work for quite a while. It might do you good to stretch your legs a little."

He wanted to be rid of me; I did not blame him.

"Thank you, Mr. Lucent," I said and got stiffly to my feet. "I appreciate your, er . . . that is, thank you."

I went downstairs, intending to go out into the garden, but walked straight into a low-voiced, venomous argument between Mr. Stapleton and his second sister, Mrs. Hilliard.

"*Father* would have!" Mrs. Hilliard was saying as I came into earshot.

"But this isn't Father's will, and Mother made it per—"

They became aware of my presence before I could retreat and stared at me like two cats.

"I beg your pardon," I said, feeling my face heat.

"Do you need something, Mr. Booth?" said Mr. Stapleton—politely but clearly in exasperation.

"I, er . . . that is . . . fresh air?"

The look on Mrs. Hilliard's face indicated that she was wondering if the museum had deliberately insulted her mother's memory by sending a mental deficient to take charge of the library. Mr. Stapleton merely stepped aside and politely waved me to the front door.

I felt their eyes on me every step of the way, and the silence in the front hall would have done justice to a mausoleum. They were arguing again before the door had latched behind me.

A great, grimed weight seemed to fall off my shoulders as I crossed the porch, and I felt myself grow lighter and cleaner with every step I took away from the house, as if the air were water washing away the black, sticky residue of that silly, spiteful, pointless quarrel. The gardens were beautiful, benevolently peaceful in the May sunshine, and the light breeze cooled my face, caressed my hands. For a quarter of an hour, I was able not to think about myself.

But then I had to return to the house. It was not, I must make clear, an ugly house: smart white clapboard with green trim, built by Mrs. Stapleton's father on the occasion of his marriage and conscientiously maintained ever since. It was not Otranto or Dracula's castle or some other Gothic splendor. But I dreaded it all the same. The shade of the porch had the chill of deep water, and stepping into the front hall was like stepping into an opium den, except that the noxious miasma of the Stapleton house was not tangible to eyes or nose or lungs.

At this point I caught up with my runaway imagination. First the vanity, now this. I had lost my temper, I told myself; there was no need to blame the house for my shortcomings. I went resolutely up the stairs, determined to shake off my morbid self-absorption and get our task completed.

Mr. Lucent was in the hallway outside the room in which we had been working. He burst into speech at the sight of me, as if he was afraid I would accuse him of shirking: "It's Miss Stapleton. She said she needed to look for something in her mother's armoire, and she wanted privacy for her search."

"Oh," I said. Sure enough, the door was shut, and I could hear movement from within the room. "What do you think she's looking for?"

"No idea," Mr. Lucent said and made a face. He lowered his voice. "I'm not even sure there *is* anything. I think she just—"

That was when Miss Stapleton screamed.

Mr. Lucent spun round and tried to open the door, but it had locked itself, as Miss Stapleton had warned me it would. Mr. Lucent rattled the knob ferociously, but to no avail. Miss Stapleton screamed again, and we heard a terrible creaking noise; the brutal percussion of a piece of furniture hitting the floor; and the sharp prolonged scatter of glass breaking.

Miss Stapleton was still screaming.

Mr. Lucent and I threw ourselves at the door. It gave way, sending us stumbling into the room, just as Martin Stapleton came racing up the stairs, closely followed by his two married sisters, Mrs. Hilliard and Mrs. Crosby.

"What happened?" he cried. "Was that Amelia—"

And then he came to the doorway and could see for himself.

Amelia Stapleton lay pinned beneath the vanity, which had toppled forward over its own weight in a way I would have been tempted to dismiss as impossible if it had not so clearly happened. She could not have done it herself.

She must have made a last-minute effort to save herself; only one leg was pinned by the vanity's full weight. The mirror frame lay awkwardly across her hips, but was too light to have done any serious damage. She was bleeding from a number of cuts caused by the broken glass that sparkled everywhere underfoot.

She had stopped screaming as the door gave way, but now she was moaning, and not from pain.

Her forearms were crossed over her face, and I could just make out her words: "her eyes . . . her eyes . . . her eyes . . . " over and over again with the shrill monotony of a talking doll.

Mr. Stapleton took control of the situation immediately. He sent his youngest sister, Mrs. Crosby, scurrying to telephone for a doctor, and his second sister, Mrs. Hilliard, to fetch water and smelling salts and bandages. Then he looked at Mr. Lucent and me and said, "I don't think we'd better move her, but would you help me lift this damn vanity?"

Between us, Mr. Lucent, Mr. Stapleton, and I succeeded in lifting the vanity and restoring it to its former position. It was not terribly heavy, nor was it (as I had subliminally expected) unpleasant to the touch, but it was astonishingly awkward, and even when we had gotten it upright, it seemed unsteady on its base, rocking back to pinch Mr. Lucent's fingers against the wall, trying to rock forward to fall on Miss Stapleton again.

Mr. Stapleton sighed. "My mother hated this thing, but she would never get rid of it." He knelt down beside his sister, catching her hands and drawing them away from her face, and began talking to her in a low, gentle voice. To avoid looking at Miss Stapleton's dull, glazed eyes, Mr. Lucent and I looked at the vanity. Without the mirror to define its purpose as the appointment of a well-to-do young woman's room, it looked like the altar of some dark and blood-hungry god.

"How do you suppose it happened?" Mr. Lucent whispered to me.

"I don't know. It doesn't look like it could."

"She pushed it," Miss Stapleton said, quite clearly.

"Who, Amelia?" said her brother.

"The girl in the mirror. The girl with no eyes. She said, 'Wait for me, Melly,' and the vanity tipped over." Miss Stapleton clutched at her brother's hands, and her tone grew pleading. "How did she know my name? Martin, *how did she know my name?*"

Mr. Stapleton looked helplessly at us, but we could not answer his sister's question either. We waited in oppressed silence until the doctor arrived.

With Mrs. Hilliard and Mrs. Crosby in anxious attendance, the doctor bore Miss Stapleton off to bed. Mr. Lucent and I assisted Mr. Stapleton in clearing up the broken glass; in return, he assisted us in carrying the boxes of his mother's books and papers down to Mr. Lucent's automobile. We did not want to stay in that room, that house, any more than he wanted our continued presence. Standing by the automobile, Mr. Stapleton assured us that if we found anything to be missing, he would bring it to the museum himself, and we offered awkward wishes for Miss Stapleton's swift recovery.

Suddenly, Mr. Lucent, who was facing the house, cried, "What is that?"

Mr. Stapleton and I turned hastily, but saw nothing.

"What is what?" said Mr. Stapleton.

"Nothing," said Mr. Lucent, although he was frowning. "I thought I saw someone in the window of the . . . of that room. But there's no one there."

"I locked the door before I followed you down," said Mr. Stapleton. "But the window's open. You must have seen the curtains moving."

"Yes, of course. I'm sorry," Mr. Lucent said. We exchanged formal, stilted good-byes, and Mr. Stapleton returned to the house. Mr. Lucent and I watched him go.

"Who did you think you saw?" I asked when Mr. Stapleton had disappeared into the house and the door had closed behind him.

"A girl. Fair-haired, wearing a pale blue dress. Very, um, shadowy about the eyes."

". . . And do you think it was the curtains?"

Mr. Lucent said nothing for a long moment, struggling with it. Then he said simply, "No."

We returned to the museum in uneasy silence.

I had dumped the diaries in the corner of my office and forgotten about them. But that passage, that cheap superstitious rubbish about ghosts and mirrors, had reawakened the memories and with them an unhappy curiosity. I put the facts in order, oppressed with fatigue and that faint, peculiar, sourceless fear that wells up after midnight when one is entirely alone. Mildred Truelove Stapleton, her children asserted, had hated the vanity and believed the room in which it stood to be haunted. The vanity had almost killed Miss Stapleton, and both she and Mr. Lucent had seen *something*, something which they both described as a girl. Mildred Truelove Stapleton had had a sister who had died, and whose books she had kept until the end of her own life. My insomnia insisted there was a connection; my rational mind talked unconvincingly about coincidence and suggestibility. I wished, futilely but fiercely, that Mr. Lucent had taken the diaries himself.

I finished with the bound miscellany and looked at my watch. It was quarter past one. If there had been the slightest hope that I could have slept, I would have gone home and gladly. But, despite my fatigue, I was incontrovertibly awake; if I left, I knew I would only sit in my apartment and think about the diaries until I returned. Moreover, by that point in my reasoning, my conscience as an archivist had calculated how long those diaries had been sitting in that corner unheeded, and even in the midst of my dread and indecision, I was appalled.

I cleared off my desk by the simple expedient of adding everything on top of it to one or another of the piles that rendered my office floor all but impassable. I brought the box across to my desk, set it down on the floor, and opened it, taking the diaries out and placing them one by one on the desk. We had never, I remembered, properly inventoried the diaries; Mr. Lucent had only just begun to penetrate past the dates neatly written on their spines when Miss Stapleton had ousted him. That was something I could do—legitimate, purposeful. I got the necessary paraphernalia out of my desk drawer and began.

Mildred Truelove Stapleton had not kept a diary her entire life. The stroke she had suffered at age sixty-five had left her hands too palsied to write. She had continued to dictate poems, to her secretary, to her son, until her second stroke at seventy-three had made even that too taxing. But her diary writing came to an end with her ability to bend her hands to their appointed labor.

There were also long stretches of time (I discovered as I worked) when she had either made no entries or made entries so short that they were clearly token gestures. It would be a good project for one of the younger archivists (I thought and made a note of) to correlate those gaps with her working manuscripts and what else we knew of her life—the births of her children, her periodic separations from her husband and his eventual death—and see what pattern, if any, emerged. They might even get a monograph out of it. But at the moment, I was looking for something else.

Mildred Truelove Stapleton had begun her diary when she was thirteen; that first diary, bound in worn blue calfskin with DIARY stamped on the cover in flaking gilt, was inscribed on its inside cover, *Mildred Caroline Truelove*, in a tremendously ornamental hand which mercifully did not extend into the diary entries themselves.

She wrote in the diary at first as if she were writing letters to a girl of her own age, recording in a breathless gush details about her family, her friends, her schoolwork. She even explained how her godmother had given her the diary for her thirteenth birthday and exhorted her to write in it *every day* (carefully underlined in thirteen-year-old Mildred's careful copperplate), which Mildred had promised faithfully to do. *Father says that since they know I am a Budding Authoress, he and Mother will look forward to discovering what I feel worthy to be written down.* And that, I thought, explains the gush.

That bright, impenetrable surface was maintained for a little less than a year, until (I gathered) both Mildred and her parents had grown rather bored with her diary. There was a hiatus of four months, and when Mildred resumed, it was in a very different mood.

I have read in books (she wrote, almost broodingly) *of diaries which people keep and do* not *show to anyone else. I think I should like this to be that sort of diary. I shall have to hide it from Georgy, because she will read it and tattle, but I know a place she won't think to look.*

From that point on, the diary became a more honest and helpful vehicle. Tentatively at first, then with greater confidence, Mildred Truelove began to write about herself without censoring her real opinions. The differences at first were minimal; I could see that the sunny enthusiasm of her first entries had not been hypocrisy or even conscious deceit, simply, through anxiety to please, an exaggeration of those qualities in her which her parents found most acceptable. She wrote sadly about her growing realization that Georgiana was their father's favorite, crossly about her wish that her parents would not insist on reading every play, story, and poem she wrote. As she became more honest with herself, her writing matured, so that one could catch glimpses of what would emerge from its chrysalis as a poet's genius.

Knowing that Georgiana had died young and was thus the prime contender for Miss Stapleton's "girl without eyes," I paid particular attention to Mildred's remarks concerning her sister. Before her death, Georgiana featured in Mildred's diary mostly as an irritant. She was three years younger than Mildred, blonde and charming and pretty. Their father spoiled her, their mother cosseted her "delicate sensibilities" and took an inventive joy in dressing her which she had never displayed toward Mildred. Georgiana was adept at getting Mildred to do what she wanted, either by pretty pleading, threats to bear tales to their father, or deploying their parents with the cunning of a Machiavel. And her tantrums were the terror of the household. The picture that emerged from Mildred's entries was of a pretty, charming, willful child, who was accustomed to get her own way with the confidence of an empress.

Georgiana died on June ninth of the year she was fourteen and Mildred seventeen (recorded in small, lifeless handwriting: *Today my sister Georgiana died*). For many months after that, Mildred made no entries in her diary at all, and when she resumed, it was at first without reference to the tragedy. I waded through several weeks' worth of long, chatty entries that reminded me forcibly and sadly of thirteen-year-old Mildred's diamond-plated gush. And then, on May third of the year following Georgiana's death, the entry consisted solely of the sentence: *I saw Georgiana again this afternoon.*

There were no entries for a week after that, and when she next wrote, on the eleventh, her writing was very even, very calm, and filled with a desperate anguish that echoed chillingly for me with the sonnet sequence she would write when she was in her forties, called *Prayers for the Trapped*.

> I know that I see Georgiana [she wrote]. I am not dreaming, not hallucinating, not indulging in flights of fancy. This morning as I was pinning up my hair, she was standing behind me in the mirror, looking exactly as she did on the day she died, except that now her eyes are nothing more than hollow sockets.
>
> She smiled at me—although it was not her true smile, only the charming fake which served her purpose most of the time—and said, very softly and very clearly, "Wait for me, Milly." When I turned around, there was no one there, as I knew there would not be.
>
> I cannot tell my parents. And I am afraid that anyone else in whom I confided—if they believed me at all—would say it is a judgment, that it proves my guilt in Georgiana's death.
>
> Maybe they would be right.

After reading that entry, I had to leave my office and walk up and down the corridors until the crawling gooseflesh on my arms and back subsided. There was the girl Miss Stapleton had seen, complete—or incomplete—in every detail. Even the same words. And somehow it did not surprise me that the girl who had smiled a fake smile at Mildred Truelove fifty-nine years ago would try to kill Mildred's daughter now. But I still did not know why Georgiana was hostile, nor where Mildred's alleged guilt lay, and in the end it was my infernal curiosity, my overmastering need to resolve conundrums and mysteries into logic and truth, that drove me back to the diaries.

After May eleventh, Mildred's calm, despairing prose recorded a series of encounters with Georgiana in mirrors and incidents of hearing her voice in the hall outside her room—which had been left unchanged since her death—crying, *Wait for me, Milly.* There was no escalation at first, merely this relentless haunting. On May twenty-ninth, Mildred recorded with grim amusement one of her friends asking her why she avoided her reflection in shop windows. *I did not tell her that it was not my reflection I sought to avoid,* although she admitted that she had never seen or heard Georgiana outside the Truelove house.

Then on June ninth, the anniversary of Georgiana's death, the haunting burst into bloom like a upas-tree. To please her parents, Mildred had agreed to spend some time alone in Georgiana's room, as if it were a meditation chapel. My distaste grew for the Trueloves *père* and *mère*. I could not tell what Mildred's feelings were; she merely recorded their request and her obedience, her attention being focused somewhere else.

She had gone into Georgiana's room and sat down on the bed. The maids dusted and changed the sheets once a week, so the room was, as Mildred put it, *dead, but not corrupted, like an Egyptian pharaoh.*

> I sat there for I suppose ten minutes [she wrote], and I was just wondering if that was enough to please Father when I heard Georgiana, much more loudly than I had ever heard her before, though she said nothing different.
>
> I got up to leave, no longer caring whether I pleased Father or not. If I had thought about what I was doing for even a moment, I swear I would have crawled out of that room on my hands and knees. Standing, as I started toward the door, I passed directly in front of Georgiana's vanity, and my peripheral vision caught her shape in the mirror.
>
> I cannot explain why I turned to face her, except that she was my sister and it was I whom she wanted. I looked in the mirror; she stood just to one side and slightly behind me as

she always did, wearing the dress she had died in, her fair hair gleaming, and her eyes an abysm.

"I'm here, Georgy," I said.

I do not know if she heard me; I do not know if she perceives anything of the living present of this house. She said, "Wait for me, Milly," as always, and her face wore its same simpering mask.

It was worse somehow in the vanity mirror—perhaps because it had been Georgy's mirror, and I had seen her living reflection in it so many times. Or perhaps, now that I think about it, it was her mirror in some other sense.

As I stood there, staring, the vanity began to rock.

It had always been unstable, and I still think that was why she fell as she did. But now it was rocking, like the table at one of my mother's horrid séances, and when Georgiana said again, "Wait for me, Milly," it hit me all at once what she meant, what she *wanted*, and what she was about to do. I ran from the room like a rabbit, kicking the doorstop aside in my panic. I heard the door shut and lock behind me, as it always does now that Georgiana is dead. But I did not hear the vanity crash to the floor, so I shall be spared attempting an explanation to my parents. I locked myself in my own room, where I have cried now for an hour and a half. I had not realized before that she wants me to be dead, too. I will not go in her room again.

Here the writing changed, becoming wobbly, hesitant, fully of blots, although the prose remained as stately and clear as ever. The contrast was worse than a babble of unfinished and unconnected sentences would have been.

Later—I underestimated Georgiana's cunning, as I always did. Or perhaps she simply had a tantrum; she could never bear to be thwarted.

Father has just been in, and I have been accused of every sin in the calendar, right up to the edge of murder. I knew he thought I had as good as pushed Georgiana out that window, because he could not face blaming himself—or her. But I did not understand before that he thinks I *would* have pushed her if I'd had the chance. Father and I have never been truly amiable, but now I am afraid we are beginning to hate each other.

He had been in Georgiana's room and found it in chaos. Her books had been dragged off the shelves and thrown across the room; her bed had been violently unmade; every bottle and knickknack which had stood on her vanity had been knocked to the floor and broken. He had heard me, he said, run out of the room and slam the door behind me, and since only he, Mother, and I have keys (had, I should say, for he made me give him mine), he knew none of the servants was to blame.

And then he stood and looked at me in that vile way of his, more in sorrow than in anger, a man more sinned against than sinning, and waited for me to explain myself.

There was nothing I could say. He would not believe any protestation of innocence, and the macabre impulse to say, "Georgy did it," as I had said so many times in the past, I luckily recognized as incipient hysteria and did not yield to. In the end, I said only, "I am sorry," which was true, and Father shook his head sadly and left, saying that he would have to discuss with Mother and Rev. Braithwaite what was the best course of action. I am left feeling very much like a Christian martyr awaiting the lions—assuming that the martyrs were angry and guilty and nauseated with fright.

I wonder what he would do to me if I broke my mirror.

After this bleak and frightening entry, there was another, longer hiatus; in fact, that diary volume had been abandoned altogether. When Mildred resumed her diary nearly three years later, it was as a junior at Radcliffe, and her entries concerned themselves with her classwork, her poetry, her circle of friends. She recorded her dreams carefully. But she did not write about her sister or her parents or the house she clearly no longer lived in. Nor did she write about what had happened in the intervening years. I thought that she was laboring to recreate herself, and I, who had never managed to do as much, admired her for it.

I skimmed rapidly through the next several years; it was almost four o'clock, and at six I would have to go home and shower and shave in order to be presentable for the museum staff. Mildred began to publish her poems, graduated from Radcliffe, met and married Vincent Stapleton. She mentioned her mother's death in passing, with no details—although, to be fair, she gave scarcely more space to the birth of her first child, Amelia.

When Amelia was three, and Mildred's second child, Martin, an infant, Mr. Truelove died, leaving Mildred sole heir to his estate. She wrote sardonically that although her father had become more friendly toward her after the birth of his first grandchild, she believed that the will was intended primarily to spite her Uncle John, who had been assuming odiously and loudly for years that the estate would go to his son, Mildred's cousin Frederick Truelove.

The Stapleton family fortunes were at that point fairly rocky, as Vincent Stapleton was proving himself to have no head for finance; thus they were profoundly grateful both for the money and for a house large enough to contain their growing family. Mildred had a long, anxious, conflicted entry about the house, in the course of which it transpired that she now, some ten years after her encounter with Georgiana's ghost, believed—or was trying very hard to believe—that she had suffered a nervous breakdown and that this was somehow vaguely all right, because it was the sort of thing one expected of poets. It was unusually woolly thinking from Mildred, although she ended the entry by saying clearly and firmly, although without antecedents: *I shall not put anyone in her room.*

They moved into the Truelove house, and it began its long metamorphosis into the Stapleton house. There were no incidents. Mildred remained adamant about not using Georgiana's room, and as I skimmed years of entries about poetry and children and finances, I wondered if Amelia Stapleton had simply had the bad luck to be the first person to look in that mirror since Mildred had fifty-nine years previously.

Martha was born, and then Charlotte; Mildred's poetry began to attract critical attention; she quarreled with Vincent, forgave him, quarreled with him again. *Such* stupid *arguments,* she wrote drearily at one point, and I thought of Mr. Lucent and myself arguing in the bedroom, Mr. Stapleton and Mrs. Hilliard arguing in the front hall, the constant bickering and spite we had witnessed all that week between the Stapleton heirs. I had assumed the bad feeling had been caused by the fight over the will, but now I was not so sure.

But there was no mention of Georgiana (as I skimmed more and more rapidly, knowing I would have to leave soon and that if I put the diaries aside now I would never find the nerve to come back to them) until a day in mid-April the year that Amelia was thirteen. Then Mildred wrote, veering abruptly out of a dreamy essay on her garden greeting the dawn:

> At breakfast, Amelia was complaining about her little sisters [Martha being at that time eight and Charlotte six]. I wasn't paying a great deal of attention—Amelia is always complaining about *something,* poor lamb—until she said emphatically that she was tired of waiting for them to finish buttoning their boots, and she wasn't going to wait for them any more, no matter how loudly they screeched down the hall after her.

"But we didn't!" Martha said indignantly, and Charlotte shook her head so vigorously that her curls momentarily resembled the aureole of a dandelion.

"You little liars! I *heard* you!" And she mimicked viciously, "Wait for me, Melly! Wait for me, Melly!"

I intervened then—much too sharply, I am afraid—and made them talk about something else. I don't think I finished my breakfast, although I may have; I simply have no memory of it. After the children were safely in Miss Underwood's care, I went and stood in the hallway outside that bedroom and listened for a long time, but heard nothing. Maybe Martha was lying; maybe it is just a coincidence. I hope so. But no power on Earth could make me open that door.

I stared at that entry for a long cold moment, and then had a sudden moment of insight, almost an epiphany. I knew that if Mildred had ever written frankly about Georgiana, there was only one date worth checking. I flipped ahead to June ninth:

She died of being locked in a room.

That is melodramatic and not strictly accurate, but it is what comes to me when I think of Georgiana's death. There are all sorts of other causes and explanations, but for me, in the end, she died because that door was locked.

It was the day of the annual Episcopalian Youth Circle picnic, as young people from all the parishes in the diocese gathered together to flirt, and to play croquet, and to paddle on the river if they were so inclined. Georgiana had been excited about it for weeks because it meant a whole new crop of boys for her to flirt with. She had been particularly bumptious all morning—"bumptious" was Nanny's word and Nanny had been the only person who could deal with

Georgiana when she was like that. Mother murmured ineffectually; Father all but encouraged her. She and I fought like cats and dogs.

But that June 9th she provoked Father at lunch. I can't remember what she said; I have merely this shatteringly clear memory of the expression on her face, that bright, sparkling look she got when she knew she was being naughty and was going to get away with it—because she *always* got away with it.

Except that time she didn't. She must have said something that Father felt threatened his authority—I wish I could remember what she said, but I just *can't*. He became towering in his wrath—a pose he was fond of but usually only got to exercise on me—and forbade Georgiana to go to the Youth Circle picnic.

Georgiana was almost never punished or scolded, and she was *never* forbidden things. She went white with shock, and then she exploded. She pitched the worst tantrum she'd ever pitched, but Father was practically in a tantrum himself, and the upshot of it all was Father locking her in her room "to think about her behavior." By the time I came upstairs to change my dress, she had quit screaming.

As I passed her bedroom door, she said, "Milly?"

"What?"

"Don't go yet. If you wait an hour, Father will change his mind."

She spoke with absolute confidence, and although I wish I didn't, I still remember how angry it made me. "And let you wiggle out of a richly deserved punishment *again*?" I said. "I'm not waiting."

As I went into my own room, I could hear her calling after me, "Milly, wait for me! You have to! Milly, please, wait for me!"

She tried again when I went back downstairs to leave, but that time I didn't even answer. I drew on my gloves in the front hall, collected my sunshade, and went out to the pony-trap, feeling a spiteful, self-righteous satisfaction that this time Georgiana would not get what she wanted.

Patrick had clucked the pony into motion when we heard Georgiana shriek, "Wait for me, Milly!"

I turned around and saw her halfway out her window. I think it was something she had done before; she did not seem the least bit awkward, and she even had her petticoats under control. I remember wondering, outraged, what she had been sneaking out of the house to do. We never found out.

Patrick and I were both staring as if we had been turned to stone. I have tried and tried to think of something we could have done, some way I could have saved her. But I know that the only thing I could have done was wait for her when she asked me to. The accident was beyond my power to stop, governed only by the simple brutality of physics. All at once, Georgiana's body tipped outward. I think she must have been balanced on her vanity while she worked her skirts through the aperture, and it simply shifted like a seesaw. She scrabbled for a moment, but it was already too late. She fell.

My poet's brain wants to say she fell like Icarus, fell like Lucifer, both of whom fell because of their pride. But the truth is simply that she fell like a fourteen-year-old girl. She broke her neck and died.

I have never forgiven my father for saying I should have waited as she wanted me to—for admitting, in effect, that she was right and the erection of his wrath would simply have collapsed in another hour. But maybe he was right.

Perhaps my resentment of his words is nothing more than spite and selfishness. Maybe that is why Georgiana haunted me. Maybe that is why she is still in the house, why she is now haunting Amelia.

I cannot delude myself any longer. The voice Amelia complains of belongs to neither of her sisters. And I am terribly afraid she mishears it. Georgiana isn't saying, "Wait for me, Melly." She is still, all these years later, saying, "Wait for me, Milly." But she no longer recognizes me as her sister, I suppose because I did *not* wait for her. I am a grown woman now and Georgiana is still and immutably fourteen, left behind for all eternity.

I have all three keys to Georgiana's room, and I have hidden them where I used to hide my diary from Georgiana. She never found it, although I know she looked, so I feel reasonably confident that if Amelia ever takes it into her head to look, she will not find the keys. She is safe from the vanity.

But Georgiana is not confined to the vanity. I remember her appearing in my bedroom mirror. How am I to answer when Amelia tells me there is a blonde girl with no eyes smiling at her in her mirror?

And then there is this newest development.

I have not slept tonight; I have felt feverishly, painfully alert since dinner this evening, when Amelia demanded indignantly that I make Martha and Charlotte stay out of her room. They denied the allegation, and I feel sure that they are telling the truth, because when I asked Amelia why she thought they had been trespassing, she said, with that withering scorn she has such a gift for: "They left *this* on my bed," and gave me Georgiana's copy of *Robinson Crusoe*, which has been on her bookshelf for twenty years, in her room, behind her locked door.

I cannot sacrifice Amelia to Georgiana's haunting persecution. And there are Martha and Charlotte; I *cannot* wait passively for them to cross Georgiana's personal Rubicon. I think that I should sell the house, but I cannot do it. We cannot afford a new house of the necessary size. And I could never explain to Vincent and the children why I want to leave a house which they all love. And what would I say to the buyers?

I am making excuses. The truth is that Georgiana is my sister, and I bear responsibility for her death. I must protect my daughters from her, but I cannot abandon her. Mirelle Forbes sends her daughters to a boarding school with which she is very pleased. Tomorrow—later this morning—I will ask her for its address. Martin can bear me company; she will not care about him, either.

And maybe if I am very patient, Georgy will speak to me again, and I can tell her I am sorry I did not wait.

⚯

I put Mildred Truelove Stapleton's diaries carefully back in their box, carefully put the box back in the corner, and walked home in a daze of sleeplessness and nerves.

I showered, shaved, forced down a piece of dry toast I did not want, and drank two cups of strong tea. Then I walked back to the Parrington, and in the intervals of trying to conduct the museum's business properly, I drafted a letter to Martin Stapleton.

⚯

Mr. Stapleton's reply to my letter was prompt and courteous, and two weeks after I stayed up all night with his mother's diaries, we were seated together in the library of the Stapleton house.

He offered me a drink, which I declined, and said, "I'm afraid I don't quite understand your purpose here, Mr. Booth. You said you found something in my mother's diaries?"

"Yes. Er, are you using that room for anything?"

"The room where Amelia . . . No. I find that I have inherited my mother's antipathy to it."

"Good. I think it would be simplest . . . that is, would you read the marked entry?" I handed him his mother's diary, with the last entry I had read marked by an old index card.

His quizzical expression said that he was humoring me, but he opened the diary and began to read.

After the first few lines, he looked up at me.

"Go on," I said.

He did, frowning, and read the rest of the entry in silence. Then he closed the diary gently and handed it back to me.

"That's very interesting," he said, with only the slightest hint of shrillness in his voice.

"Do you believe it?"

"Amelia is still in a rest home in Vermont. She is in many ways a silly woman, but she has always had nerves of steel and no imagination to speak of. She has not altered her story. So, yes, I am prepared—if not quite willing—to believe that this house is haunted."

"There's an earlier entry . . . your mother describes the same thing happening to her except . . . that is, she ran out of the room before it, er—"

"Toppled?"

"Yes. But . . . your mother seemed positive that the ghost only noticed girls of a certain age. So it's odd that your sister . . . "

"Ah, yes," said Mr. Stapleton with a twisted smile. "Amelia Stapleton, the Girl who Never Grew Up."

"Oh," I said, thinking of Miss Stapleton's hair and clothes and demeanor. "So you think . . . ?"

"Amelia never really recovered from being sent away to school—and so suddenly, although now at least I understand why Mother did it. Martha and Charlotte were no trouble—they loved that school—but Amelia . . . Amelia seems to have viewed being sent to school as a tragedy comparable to the expulsion from Eden, and she has spent most of her life trying to reinvoke her prelapsarian state. In her own mind, Amelia *is* a teenage girl. I told you she was a silly woman."

I thought I understood. Amelia Stapleton had frozen herself in a kind of artificial girlhood which apparently resonated with the ghost of Georgiana Truelove. In fact, I saw a dreadful symmetry between the two: both of them unable to grow up, both of them preserved like insects in amber at this point of trauma, where their lives ended—Miss Stapleton's only metaphorically, but Georgiana Truelove's with a most dreadful literality.

"In any event," Mr. Stapleton said, shaking me out of this unsettling reverie, "all that sordid arguing over the will started because Amelia was infuriated that Mother didn't leave her the house. I wonder if Mother guessed."

"Surely she would have . . . "

"Said something? Mother was in her right mind up until the end, but after her first stroke, she became increasingly secretive, poor woman, and after her second stroke, it became very difficult for her to talk. But she'd kept that secret so long, I don't think there's a power on Earth that could have made her confess it."

I heard an echo of his mother in his speech. "What do you want to do?"

"Refuse entry to all teenage girls," he said promptly.

"Hardly practicable as, er, a long-term solution."

"No," he said and quoted his mother softly, "'What would I tell the buyers?'"

I did not know how to answer him and so remained awkwardly silent.

Mr. Stapleton sighed and ran his hand through his hair. "May I keep this diary a while? I shall have to tell Martha and Charlotte, and I very much fear that they will not accept my unsupported word."

I thought of Mrs. Hilliard and Mr. Stapleton arguing in the front hall. "Yes, of course."

"And I think . . . Mr. Booth, will you help me do something?"

"Of course."

"I have been thinking for months that I ought to get rid of that vanity, but I haven't been able to think of anyone who would take it off my hands. But suddenly I find that has ceased to be a consideration. I would not pass this monstrosity on even to my worst enemy. I'll need some help getting it down the stairs."

"It would, er, be my pleasure," I said, and he laughed at my feeble joke.

He took the keys to the bedroom out of his desk drawer—I noticed that like his mother he had collected all three of them—and we went upstairs.

Maybe it was only because now I knew, but I still believe I felt Georgiana in the hallway. That fretful anger, that smoldering resentment—that was what was left of Georgiana Truelove.

"I'm glad you're with me," said Mr. Stapleton, and unlocked the door.

The atmosphere in the room was much worse, stifling with dust and rage. By mutual consent, achieved in a glance, Mr. Stapleton and I did not speak, knowing that if we opened our mouths, it would only be to quarrel.

As I had remembered, the vanity was not terribly heavy, only tremendously awkward. It pinched our fingers and barked our shins. It took us nearly fifteen minutes to get it through the doorway, and we were both bruised and exasperated by the time we managed it. And although I am and admit myself to be clumsy, this time it was not my fault.

We wrestled the vanity down the hall, banging against the walls and rucking up the rug. We stopped a moment at the top of the stairs to catch our breath, then hefted the vanity again and started down.

The first set of stairs posed no particular problem, although the vanity showed a perverse genius for catching its legs in the posts of the bannister. We were about a third of the way down the stairs from the second to first floors, trying to get the vanity around the curve of the staircase, when it simply wallowed out of our hands, slamming me against the wall so hard that I saw stars, and Mr. Stapleton against the bannister hard enough to knock the wind out of him. We watched helplessly as it careened down the stairs, caroming off the bannister and denting the walls, and smashed itself to kindling on the floor of the front hall. I thought how lucky we were that it had not taken either of us with it.

There was a long silence, in which we waited for something to happen and nothing did.

"Flimsy," Mr. Stapleton gasped.

"Yes." I rubbed the back of my head. "I fancy your mother was right about the, er—"

"Yes. I think so, too."

Slowly, like veterans of some obscure and arcane war, we hobbled down the stairs and stood looking at the splintered wreckage of Georgiana Truelove's vanity.

"I shall do as my mother did and keep that room locked."

"I think that would be wise."

"And I shall be very careful of my nieces when they come to visit. Martha and Charlotte will help—they are . . . nicer than your exposure to them may have led you to believe."

"I'm glad," I said before I could stop myself, and he laughed ruefully.

"I will talk with them about Amelia. And the family has kept up my grandmother's spiritualist connections. We will work things out."

"I, er . . . that is, I'm sure you will."

We stood for a moment; I hoped that the Stapletons would find a way to lay their spoiled, sad, angry ghost to rest.

Then Mr. Stapleton said, "Would you care to help me celebrate, Mr. Booth?"

"Celebrate?"

"A bonfire."

"Oh, yes, of course. But celebrate *what* exactly?"

"November fifth," said Mr. Stapleton gravely. "Guy Fawkes Day."

It was November twentieth. I helped him carry the remains of the vanity out of the house, and we stood together and watched it burn. And if he felt the prickling sensation on the back of his neck, as I did, that there was something in the house behind us that did not love us, he did not speak of it, and the silence around us was as thick as the dust in Georgiana's room.

DROWING PALMER

I had made the mistake of admitting I had been at school with John Pelham Ratcliffe. Ratcliffe was now an archaeologist of considerable repute—although I remembered him as a pensive, unpleasant boy given to picking his nose in public—and Dr. Starkweather, in consequence of a number of Ratcliffe's recent publications, had become determined to lure him away from the Midwestern museum which currently funded his excavations in Greece and the Levant. Our Persian collection was (Dr. Starkweather felt and said, often and loudly) criminally inadequate, and Ratcliffe was just the man to redress the imbalance. Also, I believe there was a long-standing rivalry with the director of that Midwestern museum, but that was not a matter into which I cared to inquire.

Dr. Starkweather seized on the fact that I had known Ratcliffe fifteen years before, ignoring all my protests, caveats, and disclaimers, and insisted that I was the perfect person to approach Ratcliffe on the Parrington's behalf. I said (truthfully) that I was sure Ratcliffe would not remember me; Dr. Starkweather countered with the blood-chillingly logical proposal that I should reintroduce myself to him in a context that would remind him naturally of my identity. When I objected that I did not think any such context existed, he glared at me for several unnerving moments and said, "You knew him at school. Which school?"

"Brockstone."

"Private school, isn't it? Wealthy, upper-crust?"

"Er, fairly, I suppose."

"Then you have reunions, don't you?"

"Er, yes . . . that is, I've never been to one—"

"When's the next one?"

"I don't know."

"Can you find out?"

" . . . Yes."

"Well, then!" he said triumphantly.

"But what if . . . what if Ratcliffe isn't there?"

"Then you write and say how sorry you are to have missed him at the reunion and so on."

"Can't I . . . can't I do that *without* going?"

His glare became alarmingly thoughtful. "Mr. Booth, sometimes I wonder if you are as dedicated to your work as you say you are."

"Dr. Starkweather, I . . . I assure you . . . "

"Well, then," he said with sinister emphasis, and I said, "Yes, Dr. Starkweather," as if he had been Brockstone School's formidable headmaster, Dr. Grisamore.

And that was how I came to attend the fifteen-year reunion of my class of Brockstone Scholars.

Brockstone School was founded in the mid-nineteenth century by a group of well-to-do English recusants who wished their sons to be educated as proper gentlemen. I do not know why they chose to come to America, nor why they chose to settle in this part of the country, but I have always suspected the influence of *The Dial* and the more impassioned writings of Emerson.

The school itself was never Catholic, and it quickly attracted those families in the surrounding area—such as my father's—who did not wish to demean themselves by competing with the Boston Brahmins. Within a generation, Brockstone had become the school of the Twenty—the city's elite—and their satellites and clients; some of the boys with whom I was at school had grandfathers who had been in the first graduating class.

Especially since the war, Brockstone had taken to having its re-unions in batches, to try to mitigate the melancholy sparsity of its alumni population. Therefore, my fifteen-year reunion was being held concurrently with twelve-, thirteen-, fourteen-, and sixteen-year reunions. The train to Bourne was full of men about my age, all peering nervously into each others' faces, trying to determine whether this gentleman in coat and tie was a former dearest friend or someone with whom they had sworn undying enmity. I barricad-ed myself behind my research and prayed not to be noticed at all.

The reunion was an all-weekend affair, beginning on Friday and ending Sunday. I had suggested to Dr. Starkweather that surely I needed go down only for one day—an afternoon perhaps—and had been withered by his incredulous reaction. Thus I was doomed to follow the ordained schedule: a reminder in its own right of the past, when every aspect of my existence at school had been regimented by bells, dictated by the schedule written out in Mrs. Grisamore's beau-tiful copperplate. The schedule of events for the reunion was typed, on a sheet of paper that had been crisp and white before my nervous fidgeting had crumpled it, smearing the ink and creasing the lines.

Friday's schedule began with a Welcome Dinner. Saturday was full of ceremonies and speeches, while the highlight of Sunday seemed to be the baseball game between the graduating class and the alumni. I would let Dr. Starkweather fire me before I partici-pated in that event. But the rest of it was drearily inescapable. I won-dered, with a fresh chill, if the sports master, Mr. North, was still there to accuse me of lacking "spirit."

I am thirty-three, I said to myself. But somehow fifteen seemed closer and more real.

The station at Bourne did not help, being crowded and sooty and horrendously loud, just as I remembered it being. The fact that the people jostling me were grown men instead of adolescent boys helped less than one might expect. Some of them were reverting to adolescence there on the platform, bawling each others' school nicknames and obsolete shibboleths across the crowd. I wished I had had the wit to fall down the Parrington's main staircase and break my leg. Or my neck.

The school omnibus at least was new, a motorized vehicle instead of the old horse-drawn wagon. I boarded reluctantly; each passing moment, each step I took toward Brockstone School, made it increasingly likely that one of my fellow alumni would, in the manner of Sherlock Holmes, deduce my identity. And the barricade of books and papers which worked so well on a train was not feasible on an omnibus. I sat and suffered and waited for discovery.

It did not come, although I was aware of the puzzled glances of my fellow passengers. I recognized several of them: Horace Webster, Charles Cressingham, Albert Vanbeek, Robert Claudel. But I had had no friends at Brockstone School, and none of my cautiously non-hostile acquaintances were on the omnibus. I did not feel brave enough to make overtures to men who had called me half-wit, coward, freak, twenty years ago. I was afraid their opinions would not have changed.

The typed schedule also informed us alumni of where we were to sleep. We were being housed in the student dormitories, which seemed in my current overwrought state an unnecessary piece of cruelty. I was only grateful I had not been given my own old room, but I supposed that refinement was beyond even Brockstone's institutional sadism.

I found—and was filled by the discovery with something akin to despair—that I remembered the route to the dormitories with perfect clarity. Leaving my increasingly raucous fellow alumni in the vast formal entry-hall of the main building, known always and forever as the School, I started up the stairs, wondering in some remote corner of my mind if this was what it felt like to cross the Bridge of Sighs on the way to one's execution.

The only mercy was that we were not housed in the juniors' dormitories—although I learned later that groups of alumni could and did request them—but were extended the same privilege we had been extended as upperclassmen. Each of us was granted a separate room. The room I had been assigned for this purgatorial weekend was not even on the same hallway as the room I had occupied as a student. So much of my attention was consumed with being grateful for that, and in the remembered relief of acquiring a private room in the first place, that I had the door of my temporary sanctuary open before I fully took in what I had seen on the card of the door next to mine.

I froze, like one of the victims of the Gorgon Medusa, then slowly, stiffly, forced myself to step back for another look. Neatly typed, the name JOHN PELHAM RATCLIFFE stared me blandly in the face.

For a wild moment, it seemed to me as if the authorities of Brockstone School must have entered into some dark-purposed conspiracy with Dr. Starkweather. But rationality returned with the realization that, while I would put nothing past Brockstone itself, Dr. Starkweather was the last man in the world one could plausibly cast as a Machiavel; his idea of subtlety was to send me to talk to Ratcliffe. This was merely the malignant hand of coincidence.

And just when, by these reflections, I had succeeded in calming my pounding heart and was on the point of retreating into my assigned room, the door at which I was staring opened, and John Pelham Ratcliffe emerged, so abruptly and with such velocity that we only narrowly averted a collision.

He had changed remarkably. Where I remembered a weedy, sniffling rat of a boy, here was a small, spare, dry man, with fierce bright round eyes like those of a hunting hawk. Even if it had not been necessary, I suspect I would have gone back a pace.

"I beg your pardon," he said, and even his voice did not match my memories, although that was more a matter of his decisively brisk speech than of the inevitable shift in timbre. "Mr. . . . " He frowned up at me—nearly a foot, for I am six-three, and he could not have been more than five-five.

" . . . Booth," I said. "Kyle Murchison Booth. We, er . . . we were the same year."

"Ah, yes," he said, without enthusiasm. His memories of me were clearly no kinder than were my memories of him.

I should have left it there. I knew it, and yet, as if in a bad dream, I heard my voice continuing, "I, er, I work for the Parrington now."

"The museum?"

"Yes. And the director, Dr. Starkweather . . . he wanted me to ask you . . . "

"Yes?" Ratcliffe said, one eyebrow sardonically raised. He knew what I was going to say, and we both knew what his answer was going to be, and still I bleated on, "Ask you if perhaps you, er, you might be interested in . . . that is, he admires your work very much and . . . "

Ratcliffe stood there, watching me twist and thrash; I had not hated him when we were boys, but for a moment I hated him then, and from the depths of that hatred managed finally to spit it out: "If you would care to be funded by the Parrington on your next expedition?"

"No, thank you," said Ratcliffe, turned on his heel, and walked away.

I stood and watched him go, my face burning, my hands clenching and unclenching uselessly at my sides.

If there had been an evening train back from Bourne, I would have taken it. There was not, and the sordid, brute fact of the matter was that I was hungry. *Ergo*, I attended the Welcome Dinner.

It was three hours of unrelieved misery. I saw one person I knew—aside from Ratcliffe and his slight sardonic smirk—and that was Barnabas Wilcox, a bully I had feared and loathed. He was an overweight, inarticulate businessman now. He mumbled some vague greeting and thereafter left me strictly alone. Otherwise, it was a sea of half-familiar faces, voices whose adult timbres I could not retranspose into their childish ranges. The men to either side of me were two years younger than myself and close friends; they talked across me all through dinner. I kept my eyes on my plate and said nothing to no one, escaping upstairs to bed at the earliest possible opportunity. It was all too vividly like my memories of my first day at Brockstone, except that then I had been in a room with five other boys, and had not even had the dubious solace of solitude.

I was exhausted; I changed into my pajamas and lay down on the bed—narrow and not quite long enough, so that I ended up curled awkwardly, like one of the strange creatures drawn in the margins of medieval manuscripts. And yet, despite the discomfort, I fell asleep almost before I could wonder whether I would be woken by a muscle cramp in the small, dark hours of the morning.

I was not surprised to find myself dreaming about the school. I was a little surprised, at first, to find myself dreaming about the swimming pool, which I had always avoided to the greatest extent possible, but then I realized that in my dream I was not myself, and dismissed the matter from my consideration.

In the dream, in which I was not myself, I was running through the pavilion which housed the swimming pool, a monstrous mid-Victorian edifice like the spawn of a cathedral and a greenhouse and having the worst characteristics of both. Behind me, there were voices yelling, and I knew they were the voices of the boys chasing me. At first I thought they were yelling, "Pelham! We're gonna getcha, Pelham!" and almost woke myself with my frantic assertions that I was *not* Ratcliffe, and would not be for love, money, or ten pounds of tea. But before I succeeded in disrupting the dream sufficiently to escape it, I realized they were yelling "Palmer!" not "Pelham!" and I ceased struggling. It was, after all, only a dream, and I did not care if I was someone else, as long as it was someone I did not know.

And a moment later, it was too late; running, as Palmer, I glanced over my shoulder, a quick terrified glimpse of the boys following, dark horrible figures like demons, and looked back barely in time to prevent myself running straight into the water.

For a moment I teetered on the edge of the pool, arms windmilling, and then a pair of hands shoved suddenly and hard against my shoulder blades, and I fell.

The water was tepid, brackish; I surfaced, gasping, and instinctively thrashed away from the boys now standing in a solemn row along the side of the pool. There were six of them; the only names I knew were those of the two largest, the ringleaders: Grimes and Carleton. I hated and feared them both.

The light was thick, slow, syrupy with late afternoon. It was a Sunday, the one day when the swimming pool was not in use for lessons or coaching or races between years to build "spirit." There would be no one in earshot, except the six boys standing and watching.

I know how to swim. I am as ungainly and awkward in the water as I am on land, but I can swim. But in the dream, as Palmer, I could not. I splashed and floundered; the pool was a uniform ten feet deep from end to end, the bottom far below the reach of my heavy schoolboy shoes. I begged the boys to help me; they stood and watched, and the looks on their faces were terrible: solemn and exalted and inhuman, as perfectly inhuman as the faces of owls. Not one of them moved.

I tired rapidly. My clothes were heavy; I had already been near exhaustion from the blind, terrified run that had ended with me in this dark pool. And I was panicking, thrashing more and more frantically, going under and getting great mouthfuls of water in my open, screaming mouth.

And the boys on the side of the pool stood and watched. Once they laughed, and their laughter was as cruel and remote as their faces; it might have been the laughter of hyenas. Their laughter rang in my ears, even after they stopped. It was still echoing when I went under for the last time, felt mouth and throat and lungs and body fill with water, and sank slowly toward the bottom of the pool, still staring upwards at the dim, dusty light and the black wavering shapes of the boys.

I woke myself by the brutal expedient of falling out of bed, tangled in sheets and blanket and catching myself a tremendous crack on the hip as I hit the floor. I did not even notice for several minutes; hyperventilating, half-hysterical, I curled myself into an awkward knot, both hands clenched in my hair and my face pressed into my knees, every atom of control I possessed channeled into the fierce and frantic effort not to make a noise loud enough to be heard from the hall or the next room. I do not know how long I stayed that way; when I finally calmed enough to notice my throbbing hip, to raise my head, the sun was rising.

Slowly, grimly, one shattered piece at a time, I assembled my armor to face the day. More than ever, I wished I could simply leave, but now, entirely regardless of Dr. Starkweather, I could not. That scene in the pavilion had been real. I knew that as clearly as I knew my own name, as profoundly as I felt the throbbing pain in my hip. That boy Palmer had truly drowned, and his death had truly been watched by six of his so-called peers. I discovered that I remembered two names and paused, knowing the ephemerality of dreams, to write them in my pocket notebook: Grimes, Carleton.

I bathed, shaved, dressed. The bathroom mirror told me I was bloodlessly pale, and there was a jitter in my hands that I could not quell, but I did not expect anyone at Brockstone School would look at me too carefully. They never had before.

But on the way back to my room, for the second time in as many days, I came within an inch of colliding with Ratcliffe, and this time when he frowned up at me, he said, "You look dreadful. What's wrong?"

"Nothing," I said and tried to sidestep, but he sidestepped with me.

"You look like you've been dragged through Hell's own bramble bushes backwards. Is it the reunion? I know it's a bit of a pain, but—"

"No, nothing like that. Please."

I sidestepped again, and he sidestepped with me; for a moment I wavered perilously between laughter—even John Pelham Ratcliffe was not at his most formidable in a ratty old bathrobe, armed with a sponge bag and toiletries kit—and tears of pure frustration. Then he said, "Look. I came by car. Let me get washed up, and I'll drive you into Bourne where we can get decent coffee, and you can tell me about it."

"But we can't," I said. "The . . . the schedule . . . "

"To hell with the schedule. What are they going to do? Expel us?"

This time I did laugh, although the noise was choked and strange.

"Will you wait?" Ratcliffe said.

"Yes. But . . . why?"

His mouth quirked sardonically. "In celebration of the fact that we are no longer fourteen." And with that, he stepped neatly around me and headed for the bathrooms.

Ratcliffe knew, he said cheerfully, exactly where we ought to go. He guided his car—as sleek, stream-lined, and impressive as he was himself, if considerably larger—to Bourne's only hotel, a rickety old monster called the St. James which had seen the temporary housing of the families of Brockstone scholars for three generations now. The St. James's restaurant was open for breakfast, and the smell of coffee was entirely ambrosial, even to me. I do not normally drink coffee, but Ratcliffe said firmly that I needed it, and I was past the point of arguing with him.

I startled myself by being ravenously hungry, and Ratcliffe let me eat in peace, himself absently consuming a vast quantity of food while discoursing, freely, learnedly, and frequently scurrilously on his excavations in Asia Minor. But when we were both replete, he beckoned the waitress over to refill our coffee cups and said, "Now. Tell me why you were in the hall this morning at six a.m., fully dressed and looking like Banquo's ghost after a hard night's haunting."

I had had the whole meal to work out my answer. "I am sorry to have disturbed you, but it was just a nightmare. I am prone to them."

"Are you?" He gave me a strange look. "What was your nightmare about?"

"Why do you care?" The next moment I was apologizing in a welter of mortification, but he waved me to silence much as he had waved the waitress over to refill our coffee cups.

"Call it guilt," he said and then laughed at the expression on my face. "The fact that I would no more work for a Napoleonic egomaniac like Emerson Starkweather than I would paint my face bright green and propose marriage to a Bactrian camel is no reason to be rude to you. It's just that, for a moment—" He spread his hands in a gesture of rueful helplessness. "For a moment, I was fourteen again. I want to make amends."

"But, Dr. Ratcliffe—"

"Please. 'Ratcliffe' is fine. Or my friends call me Ratty, if you can bring yourself to it."

"It was just a dream," I said doggedly.

"Not by the expression on your face this morning. And I've never quite understood dismissing things as 'just' dreams. Why should that make them any less important?" He paused, then asked in a voice unexpectedly warm with sympathy, "Was it about the school?"

I found myself telling him the whole thing, with details and names and even, because he listened with such attention and concern, my belief that I had dreamed about something that had really happened. I did not mention my falling out of bed.

He was silent for a long time when I had finished, and I finally asked timidly, "You do . . . you do believe me, don't you?"

"Oh, yes," he said, as if the matter hardly warranted discussion. I must have looked startled, for he said, "Archaeology is a strange field, and Asia Minor an even stranger place. I have a colleague who has dreamed of the fall of Troy once a year for the past thirty years. Always on the same date and always the same dream. He doesn't excavate in Troy—never has—and says there isn't a power on Earth that could make him. He dreams, you see, that he is one of the women."

We were silent for a moment, watching the bright play of sunlight on the tableware; then Ratcliffe said briskly, "So I don't see any inherent implausibility in the idea that you dreamed about a real murder."

"Murder?" I said, although that was how I characterized it to myself.

"They pushed him in, and they didn't drag him out. Murder by omission is murder nonetheless. It was the swimming pool, for goodness sakes! It isn't as if there's an undertow."

"Yes," I said. "I mean, no."

"You know," said Ratcliffe, "there's a master at the school named Carleton."

"There is?"

"He wasn't there in our time. But they needed a new Mathematics master a few years ago, and he took the position. My friends who are active in the Alumni Council tell me that Old Boys often do."

"He was a student?"

"Forty years ago, yes. You didn't know about him, did you?"

"No. I don't . . . that is, I haven't been . . . "

"And that makes this a very interesting coincidence. I think we might proceed with forging our own agenda by calling to have a small chat with Mr. Carleton."

I followed helplessly in Ratcliffe's wake, like a sailboat caught by an ocean-liner—or perhaps, given the disparity in our heights, an ocean-liner caught by a sailboat. It was a little after nine when we returned to the school. Ratcliffe marched briskly and decisively through the grounds and the buildings and the carefully organized schedule, waving aside all efforts to intercept or deflect him, until he found the office of Mr. Frederick Carleton, M.A., Brockstone's Master of Mathematics.

The odds were extremely good that Mr. Carleton, like Ratcliffe and I, was supposed to be out somewhere participating in the reunion festivities, but when Ratcliffe rapped smartly on the door, an irritable voice from within demanded, "What in the name of God is it now?"

Ratcliffe chose to interpret that as meaning "Come in," and opened the door. "Mr. Carleton," he said, "we were wondering if you could spare us a few minutes of your time."

Frederick Carleton was a short, owl-like man, stocky body, round eyes, upstanding tufts of hair, and all. He was seated on the floor amid a jumbled confusion of file boxes, folders, textbooks, and papers; either he was genuinely in the middle of a massive organizational endeavor, or he had hit upon that as the most inarguable excuse he could provide for avoiding the reunion.

He looked from Ratcliffe to me, clearly trying to deduce a context in which we might both fit. He said, "If this is about the baseball game—"

Heroically, Ratcliffe turned a laugh into a cough. "No, nothing of the sort. We wanted to ask you about a boy named Palmer."

"No Palmer in any of my classes. If you're concerned about his progress, I suggest you go talk to—"

"Not one of your students," Ratcliffe interrupted, mild but inexorable. "One of your classmates."

Carleton stared at him blankly, as if Ratcliffe were some strange beast he had never before seen or imagined. "One of my *classmates* . . . Here! What is this all about?" Truculently, he came to his feet.

Ratcliffe glanced at me; clearly his ingenuity had not extended to concocting a plausible reason for our query. And I saw unspoken in his face: *After all, it was* your *dream.*

"Er," I said. I could think of no convincing lie, and I could tell that the truth would not help us; I said, "You needn't talk to us if you don't want to."

Ratcliffe's glare became positively agonized, but Carleton, deprived of an adversary, deflated like a collapsing tent. "No, no," he said, and now that he did not sound pugnacious, he sounded merely tired and much more like a man of nearly sixty. "There's no reason not to tell you about Palmer, though I can't imagine what good it will do you. Please, sit down."

Despite the chaos of the floor, it took only a few moments to clear two chairs. Ratcliffe and I sat down. Carleton retreated behind his desk and became pedantic.

"I assume," he said, "it is the safety of the swimming pool that concerns you?"

"Among other things," Ratcliffe said.

"Well, on that score I can reassure you. Stuart Palmer drowned because he was violating school rules. The boys are strictly forbidden to enter the pavilion unless escorted by a master."

Ratcliffe and I exchanged a look, both of us remembering how frequently—and how easily—that rule had been flouted in our school days, particularly by upperclassmen, and Ratcliffe said, "Suppose you simply tell us what happened."

"I can only tell you the events as they were reconstructed at the inquest," Carleton said stiffly.

"Of course," Ratcliffe murmured, as smooth and gracious as any prosecuting attorney.

I startled myself by asking, "Was Palmer of your year?"

"No. A year ahead," Carleton said with a slight resurgence of his customary glower. "You want the story or not? I have other things to do, you understand . . . "

"We are listening," Ratcliffe said.

"It was a Sunday," said Carleton, bringing out a pipe and beginning the slow, ineffectual search for tobacco pouch and matches so characteristic of pipe smokers, particularly when they want to buy time. I winced—I hate pipe smoke—but held my tongue. I did not want to derail Carleton's story, fiction though Ratcliffe and I both already suspected it was going to be.

"Then, as now," Carleton continued, "the pavilion is closed on Sundays, so there were no witnesses to say how Palmer got in there in the first place."

I remembered my dream: the pounding footsteps, the baying pursuers.

"Somehow or another he came to fall in. Probably skylarking about." He paused and added heavily, "Palmer was a facetious child. And since there was no one within earshot and since Palmer could not swim, he drowned. I pray God it was quick."

You know exactly how long it took, I thought. You stood there and watched. But still I did not speak.

"He was missed at the roll-call for dinner. It took some time to determine that he was not in the School, and longer still to find him. By then he had been dead several hours. That's the story, gentlemen.

A pointless, senseless, stupid tragedy. Boys are frequently thoughtless. It is only by God's mercy that the consequences are generally less final."

It was a chilling way to view the subject, even without my deep-seated conviction that Carleton was lying. But he had finally gotten his pipe to draw and was rapidly barricading himself behind a wall of smoke. It was clear we would get no more out of him. Ratcliffe thanked him for his time and we made our departure.

At the door, I paused and turned back. "Mr. Carleton, did you have a brother?"

"A brother?" He stared at me through his veiling pipe smoke, his owl-eyes round and blank. "I did have an elder brother, but he's been dead for thirty years. Why do you ask?"

"No reason," I said. "Thank you." And I shut the door.

Ratcliffe all but pounced on me. "What did you think?"

"One of us must be lying. Or . . . or deranged."

We started back the way we had come.

"Of course he was lying," Ratcliffe said impatiently. "But do you think he was the boy who was in your dream?"

"I . . . I don't think so. That is, I'm not sure. He *did* have an older brother, so—"

"Did he?" Ratcliffe said, and I imagined he got that same bright intentness in his eyes when he was fitting fragments into a reconstruction of a vase or an inscription. "Let's go look for Carleton Major."

I realized after a moment that I had stopped walking and had to trot to catch up with him. "Look for . . . what do you mean?"

He grinned at me, delighted with himself. "I'm willing to bet the pictures that adorned the library in our day are still there. Come on."

The library was—in a grandiose phrase I remembered hearing the current headmaster use in his speech the night before—the memory of the school. It was the repository of all the artifacts and memorabilia that such a school inevitably generates, including photographs and daguerreotypes commemorating every imaginable event, going all the way back to the school's founding. The first headmaster had been a fanatic and a pioneer of photography.

It took some searching to find what we wanted, the cleverly paired group portraits of each class, entering and graduating, each portrait with its carefully written label. We started at the beginning and worked forward, staring at row after row of round, alien faces.

The faces from my dream jumped out at me unexpectedly, even though I had been looking for them. "There," I said, my voice an uneven croak. "This boy and the one next to him. Carleton and Grimes."

Ratcliffe craned to look at them. "Nasty, smirking pair of codfish. Yes, here we are. 'V. Carleton' and 'N. Grimes.'"

He did not sound at all surprised, and I said before I could stop myself, "You believed me."

"Of course I believed you."

"Why?"

"Because you obviously weren't lying."

"But . . . I, er . . . "

He took pity on me. "Peter Ludgate—do you remember him?"

"The artist?" He, too, had been a member of our class, a shy, dreamy-eyed boy as awkward and silent as myself. We had frequently been in the library at the same time, peacefully unspeaking for hours, until either someone else came in or the librarian made us leave.

"Yes. His wife's always after him to come to these things—potential patrons and so on. Peter came once. After the first night, he insisted on leaving by the earliest possible train, and he hasn't been back since, despite everything Eleanor can say to him. He won't talk about why, but the image of the drowned child has become a recurrent theme in his work."

"You seriously think . . . "

"I think the coincidence is suggestive. And I don't think it's co-incidence. Now, do you recognize any of these other horrid specimens?"

I looked again at Grimes and Carleton's year, and then at the three years following. "There's Mr. Carleton," I said after a moment. He was as owl-eyed and scowling a child as he was an adult. "And I think . . . " I pointed to another boy in the younger Carleton's year, and then two in the year behind V. Carleton and N. Grimes. "I think these are the others."

"Six of them," Ratcliffe said and sighed. "Like many predators, boys hunt in packs." He found their names and noted them down on the back of an envelope. In the meantime, I found myself, without wanting to, searching for Stuart Palmer. I did not know what he had looked like, so had to scan the list of names the year before Mr. Carleton's for "S. Palmer," and then count over in the row of blank-faced first year boys until I found him. He was a thin, ferret-faced child, his mouth hanging slightly open; I could almost imagine the adenoidal wheeze of his breathing. In my head, I heard the terrified, panting sobs of the last breaths he had ever taken.

Ratcliffe said, startling me out of my morbid contemplation, "I think we've learned about all we can here. Booth?"

" . . . Yes. Yes, of course."

"Don't brood," Ratcliffe said, almost gently.

"I, er . . . that is, no."

"Good." He led the way out of the library, talking briskly and cheerfully over his shoulder as he went. "It shouldn't take more than a few minutes to find out if any of these boys are listed in the alumni records. Then we can—"

He pushed open the library doors, straight into cries of "Ratty!" "Where have you been?" "Come on! Lunch!"

Ratcliffe twisted around to look for me, but his friends were boisterous and had clearly been indulging in pre-luncheon cocktails. All he managed was the single word "Later!" before he was swept out of sight.

I walked alone to the dining hall, where in the teeming confusion I found myself wedged in next to Barnabas Wilcox, a fate which in my 'teens I would have considered worse than death. Now it was merely strange and insuperably awkward. Wilcox attempted to make polite adult conversation, asking me about my work, but after a brief, limping exchange, it was clear that without hatred we had nothing in common, and he turned his attention to his other neighbor. I ate silently and quickly and thought bleakly of Ratcliffe's remark that boys hunted in packs. That was how Palmer had seen his pursuers, his murderers, and I had a faint nagging feeling that if I could follow that thought far enough, it could make clear to me some of the things about which Carleton had been lying. But every time I tried, I came back to Palmer's last, dark, wavering view of the boys who had watched him die, and I could go no farther.

By the time I was finished eating, the conversation at the table had turned to the infamous and scandalous among our fellow alumni. I did not wish to listen to gossip, and they were all as enthralled as Scheherazade's sultan. I got up quietly and left.

I had somehow lost my typewritten schedule and, emboldened by Ratcliffe's example, I did not care. I had never played truant as a child; it was in some strange way exhilarating now to cut behind the school chapel and walk across the quadrangle, knowing that wherever I was supposed to be and whatever I was supposed to be doing, it was not here and it was not this.

I wandered in pleasant aimlessness for some time, enjoying the Brockstone campus as I never had as a child, glorying in my much-belated delinquency. But eventually—and, I suppose, inevitably—I found myself outside the swimming pavilion.

It had been refurbished since my graduation: a new coat of paint, dazzlingly white in the summer sunshine, modern and well-hung doors. But the changes were not enough to free it from the dark tints of my dream.

I should have turned away, gone back to the School and the safety of the schedule. But instead I walked up and tried the doors. They were unlocked, and I slipped into the pavilion.

It was dark inside, and the air was heavy with water. I should have left, and I knew it, but I crossed the atrium, cut through the students' changing room—the same dull tile in desperate need of regrouting that I remembered—and emerged into the great echoing vault that housed the swimming pool itself.

There were electric lights now. I pressed the switch and watched them flare into life along the walls. The pool lay blue and serene, as if it were as natural as a lake. In the glare of electricity, it looked nothing like the pool I remembered, nothing like the pool in my dream.

I suppose it was that which made me foolhardy enough to advance to the edge of the pool. I stood and looked at the water and waited madly to hear voices yelling behind me, to feel myself suddenly propelled by nothing into the water. I felt recklessly defiant, as if I had drunk champagne instead of water with lunch, and ready to face down any number of bullying ghosts.

They did not come, of course, and I was about to turn away and forsake my foolishness when I realized something *was* happening. At first it was just a disturbance in the water, an isolated eddy. But as I watched, it increased in size and intensity until there was a great cloudy roiling in the middle of the pool. And from it, with a frantic splash and a half-choked scream, emerged a boy's head and flailing arms.

A voice beside me called, "What's the matter, Palmer? Can't you swim?" and laughter, like the cries of hyenas, echoed through the pavilion.

Without turning my head, I knew the voice had been Grimes's. But the laughter had been everyone's, even my own. I wondered if I was going insane; inside my head I could hear myself screaming like poor Palmer—and surely whatever he had deserved it had not been this—but it was as if that screaming voice had been locked in a cellar. The denizens of the house could hear it, but they did not care.

And then, suddenly—so suddenly that I staggered and almost fell into the pool after all—it was gone. The turbulence, the drowning boy, the pack of predators along the side . . . the pack of which I had been a member.

I left the pavilion through the faculty changing room, taking no chances with what might be lingering, haunting, on the student side.

I walked for hours after that, though I have only the barest memory of where I went. I was horrified—mesmerized—by what had happened in the pavilion, but I realized very quickly after the initial shock had worn off, that as with my dream, there was a significant sense in which I had not been myself. I did not know what Grimes had sounded like; I had no idea whether Palmer had "deserved" anything or not, although I was inclined to doubt it. Those thoughts, and that strange, hysterical entrancement, had belonged to someone else, someone I was now willing to wager was Frederick Carleton. I had neither proof nor explanation, only that mad inner surety that I suspect is characteristic of all those who hear voices in an empty room, whether those voices be spectral or merely delusional.

As the shadows began to lengthen toward dusk, I realized I needed to talk to Ratcliffe. I had the knowledge, but I did not know what, if anything, I ought to do about it. It was certainly pointless to attempt to try Carleton for Stuart Palmer's murder when the evidence was only my dreams and megrims. And remembering what it had felt like to be Carleton, even briefly, I did not think that cold, blind, judicial Justice could make sense of Palmer's death.

But beyond that I could not go. I was too close, caught in the oscillation of terror between Palmer and Carleton, both of whom were drowning, albeit in water only one of them would die of.

I walked back to the School and straight into the convivial press of cocktail hour. Noise and light and the heat of crowding bodies struck me together like a stunning blow. If it had not been for my need to talk to Ratcliffe, I would have turned tail and fled. But I knew better than to imagine I could face the rising night of Brockstone without some kind of human contact and support, so I fought my way grimly through the throng, and at last ran Ratcliffe to earth in one of the window embrasures. Surrounded by his friends.

I pulled up short, cursing myself for an idiot. I had come so completely to think of Ratcliffe as an ally that I had forgotten he was not like me. He was not here under duress. He had been remarkably patient, giving up half his Saturday to my disordered imaginings, and I had no right to expect any more of him or to attempt to drag him away from his friends.

I was about to turn away when the image of Palmer's flailing hands burned across my mind like a comet. I wondered if Carleton was haunted by that same image and imagined what it would be like to be presented with that every time I closed my eyes, every night for the next forty years.

The ancient Greeks had a word, κάθαρσις, the exact translation of which is still hotly debated among classicists. At that moment it seemed to me no more elusive or troublesome than the word "justice." I was not sure if either could be achieved. But I understood now why the Grail Knights had continued with their quest, even knowing it was hopeless, doomed, futile. Some things demand that you search for them, even though you will not find them.

It was a pretty flight of fancy, imagining myself as a Grail Knight, but not enough to disguise the iron-cold meaning beneath it: I still had to talk to Ratcliffe.

I had been in this situation a thousand times. I could feel it ahead of me like the steps of a ritual: my advance, clumsier and more ungainly than ever; the polite, mocking silence as they waited for me to speak; my voice, stammering incoherencies; a pause, like the moment before the marksman fires; and then the dismissal, cool and stinging, leaving me with nothing to do except stumble away again, praying that they would contain their laughter until I was out of earshot. That was how it always went.

I took a deep breath in a vain effort to steady myself and started forward.

Ratcliffe looked up at my approach and, unbelievably, smiled and rose to greet me.

"Booth! Where have you been?"

" . . . I, er . . . "

"Charlie, you remember Booth, don't you? Mr. Booth, Mr. Cressingham. Mr. Cressingham, Mr. Booth."

Mechanically, I shook hands with Charles Cressingham, who looked as if he had swallowed a live spider. "Ratcliffe, I need to talk to you."

"Do you?" His bright eyes summed me up, seeming to recognize that indeed I did. "All right. Excuse us a moment, gentlemen, if you would." And he steered me away through the crowd, leaving his friends goggling after us like a collection of frogs.

Once out of the atrium, Ratcliffe simply picked the nearest classroom. When we were in school, it had been the domain of the terrifying Herr Brueckner, who taught history and German. Now Ratcliffe propped himself against the desk with insouciant *lèse-majesté*, and waved at me to speak.

I told him as quickly and clearly as I could of what had befallen me in the swimming pavilion. I fear I was neither particularly clear nor particularly quick, but he heard me out in patient silence. When I had at last stammered to a halt, he considered a moment longer and then said, "What do you wish to do?"

"What do *I* wish to do?"

"Is it such an odd question? They are your dreams, your visions. Surely the decision must be yours, as well."

"But I don't *know* what to do!" I cried and realized too late that it had become a wail.

"Well, let us consider your options. You can do nothing—"

"No. I can't."

"There. You see? Or you can go to the police." His quirked eyebrows and ironic tone indicated that he knew the feckless lunacy of that idea as well as I did. "Or you could, I don't know, hire a medium to speak to the departed spirit of Stuart Palmer. Or," and he raised one finger for emphasis, "you could talk to Frederick Carleton again."

"But—"

"You said you *were* him in your second vision. And he is both alive and here, as the other members of that group are not—least of all Stuart Palmer, God rest his soul. I agree that this is not a situation covered by the etiquette manuals and it is difficult to know how to proceed, but if there are any indications at all to be gleaned, they are pointing you at Frederick Carleton."

"Yes," I agreed dismally.

"Look. Come and have dinner, and then afterwards we can go up and beard the lion in his den."

"We?"

"Good Lord, yes! You don't think I'd bow out *now*, do you?"

"I didn't . . . that is . . . "

"I'll come with you," Ratcliffe said. "Now come and eat."

Dinner was surprisingly pleasant. Ratcliffe's friends did not know what to make of his sponsorship of me, but he said something about archaeology and museums, and they fell over themselves in their anxiety not to learn anything more. When none of them was watching, Ratcliffe winked at me.

I was left politely alone—which is a very different thing from being ignored. They looked at me if their remarks were generally addressed, including me in the social life of the table, but they did not demand a response or ask me questions. They seemed like a litter of half-grown puppies, good-natured, clumsy, and anxious to please, and I found it difficult to remember that they were all within a year or two of my own age. I realized somewhere in the salad course that they valued Ratcliffe's good opinion very highly. I listened attentively to their conversation and remembered not a word of it five minutes after we had risen from the table.

They were headed in pursuit of after-dinner drinks, and Ratcliffe had some difficulty in extracting himself from their conviviality. But he persevered and in the end prevailed, and he and I made our way to the masters' wing. We did not speak; Ratcliffe seemed to understand that I could not speak lightly, as his friends did, and that the subject of our excursion was something about which I was on the verge of being unable to speak at all.

As he had that morning, he led me with assurance. My perplexity must have shown on my face, for he grinned as he opened the door at the top of the fourth staircase we had climbed and said, "My father's on the Board, but he sends me to be his proxy if I happen to be in the country for the annual meeting. I try not to be, but I've still been taken over the school in loving, excruciating detail three times in the last ten years. I know where *everything* is."

"Is that why you're so . . . concerned?"

"No, not a bit of it. Can't resist a mystery, that's all. And here we are." He knocked with brisk authority on Frederick Carleton's door.

The door was opened remarkably quickly, almost as if Carleton had been waiting for us. He was still fully dressed, even down to the undisturbed knot in his tie.

"What do you want?" he said, words and scowl hostile, but his voice was tired.

"May we come in?" Ratcliffe said.

"I suppose." Carleton stood aside.

It was the first time I had ever been inside a master's chambers. Though far larger than any living space I had had as a student, Carleton's rooms were dark and depressing, and the oppressive wood-work made me not at all certain that the masters had gotten the better end of the deal.

Carleton slumped into a battered armchair and waved an apa-thetic hand at the Chesterfield, which itself had seen better days. Ratcliffe and I sat down, and Carleton repeated dully, "What do you want?"

Ratcliffe looked at me, and I realized, my heart sinking, that he was right. He had played my Virgil all day, but he could not take this final step for me.

"Er," I said. "Mr. Carleton, I need to tell you about a dream I had last night, and something that happened to me this afternoon."

He sat, inert as stone, while I fumbled and stammered my way through a description of what I had witnessed from two angles; when I had finished, he said, still in that flat, monotonous voice, "What do you want me to do?"

"Beg pardon?"

That seemed to rouse him; there was more than a hint of a defiant snarl in his voice when he said, "What do you want me to *do*? Turn myself in to the police? Write a confession to the headmaster? Take flowers to Palmer's wretched grave? *What*? What can I possibly do that will make the slightest difference?"

"Tell me what happened."

"I beg your pardon," he said with a savage parody of courtesy. "I thought that was what you had just told me."

"No," I said. "The rest of it."

For the first time, Carleton looked frightened. "I don't know what you mean," he said, but he and I both knew he was lying.

"Tell me *how* it happened. Tell me what Grimes and your brother wanted. I know you didn't want Palmer to die."

"No," he said slowly. "No, I didn't. Not really." He sat up straighter, as if he had come to a decision and in so doing had been relieved of a burden. When he spoke again, his voice was quicker, sharper. I imagined that was what he sounded like when he was teaching.

"You have to understand that none of us liked Palmer. Things would never have gone even half as far as they did if Palmer hadn't been what he was."

"Which was?" Ratcliffe asked.

"I have boys like him in my classes now," Carleton said, so distantly that if he had not been answering Ratcliffe's question, I would have thought he had not heard it. "Smart boys, sharp boys, but they won't learn the rules. Can't keep their mouths shut. Can't see that it all applies to *them*."

"Oh," I said involuntarily. There had been boys like that in my year; though none of them had been as relentless as Barnabas Wilcox, they had been among my most inventive tormentors—when they were not being tormented by other boys themselves.

Carleton nodded at me. "Palmer was a natural target. And Victor was looking for one."

"Your brother?"

"Yes. My elder brother, Victor, and his dear friend Norman Grimes." Carleton's face twisted, and it was a moment before he continued: "I don't know how much of it was deliberate—by which I mean I don't know how much they intended, and how much of it they simply let happen. Victor and I never talked about it, and I was grateful when he died because it meant I never had to ask."

He stood up abruptly. "I need a drink. If you want to get me fired, go ahead and tell Jernigan. That'll get me fired faster than you can say *Mene, Mene, Tekel, Upharsin*."

Ratcliffe and I looked at each other and said nothing as Carleton disappeared into what was presumably his bedroom. He returned with a tumbler three-quarters full of scotch, sat down, and took a large gulp. Then he continued with his story.

"Palmer had crossed Victor. I don't know how. We younger boys didn't ask questions—we knew what the rules were if we wanted to be 'friends' with Victor and Grimes." He invested the word *friends* with heavy sarcasm; what he really meant, of course, was *slaves*. "It was worst for Teddy Thorpe and me; we were only allowed to be part of the pack because I was Victor's younger brother and Teddy was my best friend."

"'Pack'?" Ratcliffe said.

"I've never been able to think of a better word," Carleton said. "We weren't a group of friends. We were like a pack of wolves. Or jackals. Victor was the leader, and Grimes was his lieutenant, and the other four of us skirmished and suffered and cowered and crawled behind them. It gave me and Teddy cachet with the other first-years, and kept us both from being trampled underfoot. I know now that it wasn't worth it, but I didn't know that when I was eleven. At least, not before Palmer."

He took another mouthful of scotch. "Grimes's father was a devoted follower of the philosophy of Herbert Spencer."

"Social Darwinism," Ratcliffe said grimly.

"Exactly. I don't know how much of what Grimes said was what his father actually believed and how much of it was his misunderstanding . . . never having had the misfortune of meeting Grimes Senior I can happily form no opinion of his intellectual capacity. But Grimes had taken it to mean that bullying wasn't bullying; it was admirable work done in the name of advancing the species. Come to think of it, I don't know if Grimes actually believed that himself, or if he just found it convenient. I don't know if Victor believed it either, but he certainly liked it. That's what they used to shout when they had us ganging up, six on one, on some poor boy who'd gotten better marks than Grimes or made Victor look stupid in Latin: 'Survival of the fittest!'"

"Palmer," Ratcliffe said.

"Yes, Palmer. He had crossed Victor. I don't know what he did. All I know is that that Sunday, Victor and Grimes told us we were going out to 'get' Palmer." He sighed heavily, sinking deeper into his chair. "He ran. That was his first mistake. They tell you never to run away from wild animals, and I know why. Because the longer we chased him, the more serious it got. I don't think I can explain it properly, although goodness knows I've made this speech in my head several thousand times since then. But, at first, we were just going to beat him up, or tear his clothes off and make him walk back to the School naked, or something like that. Some stupid humiliation, the sort that gets served out a dozen times a day in any school you care to name. But he ran. And we chased him, and well, after you've been chasing after someone for half-an-hour, you can't just punch him and yell 'Tag you're it!' and run away. Whatever you do has to be worth the effort he's put into trying to escape it. Do you see?"

I am not sure either of us did, but Carleton was no longer paying any particular attention to us. He paused only long enough to drink some more scotch. His words were coming faster now, as if the story was developing some inner urgency of its own. "You know what happened. We chased him into the pavilion; someone shoved him into the pool. And I know it sounds nonsensical, but I can't tell you which one of us it was. I don't *think* it was me, but some days I'm not even sure of that. And then we all stood there and watched him drown."

The silence was heavy and brackish, like the water in my dream. Carleton finished his scotch and said, "I can't explain it. Except that I knew then and know now, as clearly as I will ever know anything, that if any of us—Wrexton, Griffith, Teddy, me—if any of us had tried to help Palmer, or tried to run for help, Victor and Grimes would have thrown *us* in. If they'd had to, they would have held us under. And they didn't have to because we were . . . we were caught. Not by them, or not exactly. By something . . . " He made a despairing gesture with his hands. "Something deeper, darker. Something worse than those two stupid sixteen-year-old boys—although they were bad enough, and I did not weep at Victor's funeral. We watched Palmer drown and we laughed."

He looked at his glass, as if surprised to discover it held no more scotch. "Afterwards, when we'd left the pavilion, Victor and Grimes told us not to say anything. We didn't, and it never occurred to any of the masters, or the coroner, or *anyone*, that we might have had something to do with it. I don't believe it ever crossed anyone's mind that it might not have been an accident."

He stood up, and Ratcliffe and I stood up with him. "Swimming was made compulsory the next year," Carleton said, setting his glass down on the mantelpiece and beginning to herd us, like a surly old collie with two stupid sheep, towards the door. "Every day for six years, I had to swim in that pool and not think about Palmer drowning. When I had nightmares—and both Teddy and I did, although I don't know about the others—I had to lie there, sleepless and sweating until dawn, and not make a sound, waiting for Palmer's cold, wet, dead hand to touch my face. I know that I am damned. I have been damned since I was eleven years old, and Hell has not waited for my death. What more do you want of me?"

"We want nothing of you," I said.

He stopped where he was, staring at us. Ratcliffe opened the door and waved me through. In the hall, I turned. Ratcliffe was still standing in the doorway, looking at Carleton, who was still staring at us as if had never seen anything so strange in all his life. Ratcliffe said levelly, "Despair is also a mortal sin," and came out, shutting the door behind him.

In unspoken accord, we said nothing as we retraced our route through the masters' wing. On the other side of the enormous double doors, Ratcliffe looked at me and said, "Are you going to be able to sleep tonight?"

"No," I said, startled into honesty.

"Neither am I. If I drive you back to the city, will you promise never to tell Starkweather?"

"I promise."

"Good. Let's get out of here."

Scarcely half-an-hour later, we departed from Brockstone School; Ratcliffe had left a glib, facilely apologetic explanation with one of his many friends. The moon, almost at the full, was hanging in the sky like a lamp set to guide lost travelers. Ratcliffe said nothing until we had passed the school gates; then he said abruptly, "Will you go back?"

"No."

"No," he echoed. He drove silently and extremely fast for three-quarters of an hour, then asked, just as abruptly, "Do you think you'll have that dream again?"

"No," I said. "I think . . . I think it belongs to the school. I think that's why Carleton had to go back. He's the only one left, you know."

"He is? Did you look at the alumni records?"

"No. I looked at the five black-bordered photographs on his wall."

Silence caught us then, and held us, through the hours of darkness as Ratcliffe drove toward the city and the moon.

THE INHERITANCE OF BARNABAS WILCOX

Some four months after I attended the fifteen-year reunion at Brock-stone School, I received a letter from Barnabas Wilcox. I was puzzled, for there was no love lost between Wilcox and me, but instead of doing the sensible thing and throwing the letter unopened on the fire, I read it.

> Dear Booth (Wilcox wrote):
> I'm writing to you because you know all about old books. The case is that I have recently inherited a house in the country from my Uncle Lucius, and there's a stipulation in his will that his library catalogue should be made up-to-date. Would you care to come down with me this weekend and take a look at it? I don't know anyone else who would even know where to begin.
> Yrs,

And then an involved squiggle in which a "B" and a "W" were dimly perceptible.

It took no great leap of intuition to guess that Wilcox's "Uncle Lucius" had to be the noted antiquary Lucius Preston Wilcox, and that lure overcame my dislike of Wilcox. Friday I took a half-day, packed my bag, and met Wilcox on the platform at quarter of three. He was a big, square, red-faced man, with thick, blunt-fingered hands and smallish, squinty hazel eyes. Despite my white hair, he looked easily ten years older than I; when we shook hands, I smelled liquor on his breath.

"How are you, Booth?" he said when we were settled in our compartment. "It's good of you to come."

"I, er," I said. " . . . I like libraries."

"Well, old Uncle Loosh should keep you happy then. I remember, my brother and I used to think the books had to be fake, he had so many."

I recollected in time that Wilcox's brother had died in the war, and asked instead, "When did your uncle die? I don't remember reading an obituary."

"Daft old coot. He wouldn't have one written. It was the first stipulation in his will, and he'd told his lawyer and his housekeeper and everybody about it. And, after all, there's no law that says you have to publish one. It's just that people usually do. But Uncle Loosh was crazy."

" . . . Crazy?"

"He got into some weird things. He used to write me these long letters saying he'd figured out how to cheat death and was going to live forever. I couldn't understand half of what he said."

"That's not a very pleasant occupation."

"Uncle Loosh wasn't a very pleasant person. I can't think why he left everything to me. We didn't get along."

The train began to move. With a muttered apology, Wilcox dug some papers out of his attaché case and settled in to work. I stared out the window and watched as the train left the city behind.

The estate of Wilcox's uncle was called Hollyhill and was accurately named in both respects. The house stood on a prominence among the farms and woods of the gently rolling countryside, and was surrounded by as thriving a stand of holly trees as I had ever seen.

"I shall have those cut down first thing," Wilcox said as we turned through the gates. "I don't know what Uncle Loosh was thinking of, letting them grow like that."

In the rearview mirror, I caught the eyes of the driver; his name was Esau Flood, and he had been Mr. Preston Wilcox's groundskeeper. He was small, very tan, with a head of thick white hair. His eyes were gray and reminded me strongly of the sort of smooth, round pebbles one finds in a swiftly-moving stream. He said, "Mr. Preston Wilcox was very fond of the holly, sir."

"That doesn't surprise me," Wilcox said disagreeably. "I'm not."

"I'm sure not, sir," said Flood, too politely.

The house itself was remarkably unattractive, with an aggressively square façade and windows that seemed too small for the proportions. Inside, I was oppressed to discover that the entire house was paneled with dark-varnished oak, and that the windows gave as little light as one would expect. They had uncommonly thick curtains. Wilcox seemed uncomfortable as well; he said several times over dinner that he did not know why his uncle had left him the place, and he was not sure but that the best thing to do would be to sell it—"not that I could find a buyer," he added.

"It might be more pleasant without the, er, the paneling."

"Oh, but that paneling's valuable. They don't make stuff like that any more."

"Yes, but it's quite dark."

"Better lights would solve that," he said, staring up at the chandelier with disapprobation. "Well, *that* I can take care of tomorrow. I fancy I'll have to leave you on your own most of the day, Booth. There's quite a list of things that need buying, and for some reason Flood hasn't done any of it."

"Perhaps," I said, because I did not want to be a witness to what already seemed like an alarming escalation of hostilities between Wilcox and Flood, "perhaps he didn't like to do anything without . . . that is, without asking you first."

"Good God, it takes no more than common sense to see that I shan't kick over buying enough plaster to repair a great gaping hole in the cellar wall!" Wilcox stared at me; for a moment he was the bully I remembered from Brockstone. Then he said, more mildly, "I daresay you're right. Flood and I have rubbed each other the wrong way a bit, but we'll get along all right soon enough. I know Uncle Loosh couldn't speak highly enough of him."

I managed to mutter something about "time," and Wilcox turned the conversation to bridge, of which he appeared to be an addict. I do not play myself, disliking any form of activity which requires a partner, but Wilcox needed no encouragement to discourse at length.

After dinner, he said, "D'you want to look at the library now?"

"I, er . . . yes, while you're here to . . . "

He rolled his eyes. "Come on, then."

The doors to the library—vast, carved things like cathedral doors—were locked. While Wilcox, grumbling, sorted through his key-ring, I examined the carvings. They were crude, almost primitive, in design and execution, and their crudeness bothered me because I could not quite tell what the reliefs were meant to represent. There were trees—I was sure of that—and there was one figure, always holding a box and thus easy to identify, that seemed quite reliably to be human, but the rest of it was disturbingly muddled, so that I could not determine whether the other shapes were persecuting the human shape or obeying its commands.

"Ha!" said Wilcox and unlocked the doors.

In the library, at last, we found a well-lit and comfortably appointed room. It was quite large, large enough that it disrupted the severely square proportions of the house by jutting out into the back garden. Although the windows were still small and mean, in the library it seemed almost reasonable that they should be so, since every inch of wall space, including both above and below the windows, was taken up with bookshelves, themselves crammed with books. Where the shelves were deep enough and the books small enough, the books had been double-stacked; everywhere, books had been shoved sideways on top of the rows, and there were stacks on the floor in front of the bookcases, stacks on the desk, stacks on the two small tables—so that the impression was less of a collection and more of an explosion of books.

"Good God," Wilcox said faintly.

After a moment, I said, "You mentioned a catalogue. Do you know . . . er, can you find it?"

"I don't know," Wilcox said, staring around helplessly. "I just know it's mentioned in the will."

"Flood might . . . "

"Or the lawyer, Dropcloth or whatever his name is. But I'll ask Flood." There was a bell-pull, conveniently situated by the desk; Wilcox pulled it briskly.

Flood appeared in the doorway, and I thought again how round and flat his eyes seemed. Wilcox put his question, and Flood said, "Oh, yes, sir. I believe you'll find the catalogue in Mr. Preston Wilcox's desk. He was making notes just before his last illness." Flood did not come into the library; it struck me, perhaps unjustly, that he regarded the massed books with some distaste. Wilcox started opening desk drawers and said, "Thank you, Flood, that was all I wanted," without looking up.

"Yes, sir. Good night, sir," said Flood, and I did not like the expression in those round, flat eyes. He vanished as silently as he had appeared.

"How long was he, er, with your uncle?"

"Flood? Ages and ages. I remember him from when I was a boy, looking just as he does now. Why?"

" . . . No reason. He just . . . that is, I don't . . . "

"He gives you the creeps," Wilcox said, resorting to the lowest and deepest desk drawer, which seemed to be crammed to the brim with paper. "He does me, too. I don't expect I'll keep him on. Get my own people in. New blood and all that."

" . . . Yes," I said, although I found myself wishing he had not used the word "blood," and then did not know why it bothered me.

"This must be it," Wilcox said; he dragged a leather-bound ledger from the bottom of the drawer, sending sheets of paper flying in a kind of fountain. "Blast. Here, you take a look at this, and I'll get this stuff back in the drawer." He shoved the catalogue into my hands.

Lucius Preston Wilcox's rigidly legible handwriting marched across the pages of his catalogue like a conquering army. I noted the careful descriptions of the books, including provenances and conditions, and then, obedient to the signs of Wilcox's growing impatience, allowed myself to be herded out of the library and up to bed.

I slept badly that night. In itself, that was not surprising. I am an insomniac—I rarely sleep more than six hours a night, frequently no more than four, sometimes not at all—and I am always nervous in strange bedrooms.

I had not expected to sleep at all, had come prepared with a book on forgers' techniques. But my eyes grew heavy, and finally the book slipped out of my fingers entirely, and I found myself in a dream.

Even at the time, I knew it was a dream, which was some comfort. I was dreaming of being a boy again, thirteen or fourteen, the age at which I had most hated Barnabas Wilcox. I was standing on a staircase; in the dream, it was the main staircase at Brockstone School, but I recognized it as the staircase here at Hollyhill, the one I had just climbed in Wilcox's company on the way to our respective rooms. I was on the landing, by the newel-post, and two boys came running past me down the stairs. I recognized one as Wilcox and tensed, clutching the bannister. But they did not notice me; I wondered hopefully if I was invisible.

I followed them downstairs, where they had been caught by a master and were being scolded for something. He was an old man, with bright, piercing eyes. The dream insisted that he was Dr. Smayle, the Greek master, but I kept thinking that he was really someone else, although I did not know whom.

"Useless the both of you!" he was saying. "Senseless as stones. Can't lift your heads above the animal reek of the world, can you, lads?"

"But, sir," said Wilcox, "Tony's dead."

At that I recognized the other boy as Wilcox's older brother, the one who had died in the war.

"Makes no difference," said the old man. "Alive or dead, you just can't *see*. Your friend would be more use than you are. What's your name, boy?"

Then I'm not invisible, I thought sadly, and said, "Booth."

"Booth?" said Wilcox, twisting around to look at me, his face sneering. "What are *you* doing here?"

"You brought him, you lunk," the old man said. He wasn't Dr. Smayle now, and he never had been. "Brought him right into the middle of something you don't have the motherwit to understand." I fell back a pace under the hammerfall of his eyes. They were not Dr. Smayle's kind blue eyes; they were black and hard. "Booth, you said your name is. Stay in the library, Booth. Don't let Barney drag you out."

"That's right," said Wilcox. "Don't come out of the library, or I'll make you sorry."

The dream changed then, became a different dream, a dream of Wilcox chasing me through Brockstone School, Wilcox and his thuggish friends. I ran until I woke up.

At breakfast, Wilcox looked as haggard as I felt. He did not look like the Wilcox of my dream, but I still felt edgy, as if the fourteen-year-old boys we had been were watching us, each horrified at the perceived betrayal in our eating breakfast together. I was grateful that he did not speak.

He disappeared promptly after breakfast, with a mutter about "business." I went into the library and settled down to work.

There was no great difficulty. The catalogue was carefully kept and accurate in all its details. My worst trouble was in finding each volume; the shelves looked to have undergone at least two partial reorganizations, so that the volumes wedged in sideways might as easily be among Mr. Preston Wilcox's first purchases as among his last. I ended up making stacks of my own on his desk, and it was inevitable that around two o'clock that afternoon I knocked one stack over, sending books sliding across the desk and onto the floor.

I gave a yelp of dismay and dove after them. Happily, none had been damaged; it was as I was crawling out from beneath the desk, having retrieved the last of them (*Life among the Anthropophagi of the South Pacific*), that the corner of a piece of paper caught my eye.

I realized that it had to be one of the papers Wilcox had dropped the night before. It had slid all the way under the bottom drawer, so that no one who did not crawl entirely beneath the desk, as I had done, would ever see it. I put *Life among the Anthropophagi* on the desk and went back after the paper.

It was a page of notes, clearly belonging to Mr. Preston Wilcox. I recognized the handwriting from the catalogue, and the contents matched up with Wilcox's description of his uncle's obsessions. Elliptical and oblique, they were notes to jog the old man's memory, not to enlighten anyone else. There were references to the holly trees, and to something he called "the Guide" and something else he called "the Vessel." It did not make sense to me, but I was troubled by a feeling that it *ought* to, that I had seen something like this somewhere before. But every time I tried to track that feeling down, I found myself remembering my dream of the previous night—Wilcox chasing me through endless hallways, calling me "freak" and "coward" and worse things. In the end, I put the paper on the desk and returned to the catalogue.

When Wilcox returned, he came to the library and apologized for being so late. Startled, I looked at my watch and saw that it was past eight o'clock.

Wilcox laughed, not pleasantly to my ear. "Same old Booth. Come on and eat."

I went to turn the lamp off before I followed him, and the paper on the desk caught my eye. "Oh! I found this under the desk."

I handed it to him. He glanced at it, said, "More of Uncle Loosh's nonsense, looks like to me. Thanks." He stuffed it in his pocket, and we left the room.

Dinner consisted of sandwiches and soup. Wilcox was restless, fidgeting even as he ate, getting up periodically to stride over to the windows and stare out at the darkness. Finally, I said, "Is something the matter?"

"I'm having those damn trees down tomorrow!"

"Oh," I said, not usefully.

"I'm sorry. They get on my nerves, and it seems like every time I turn around, there's Flood telling me how much Uncle Loosh loved the hollies. All the more reason they should go."

"There was, er . . . there was something about them on that paper I found."

He raised his eyebrows in a disagreeable sneer, but did not comment.

"It looks like . . . however he thought he was going to, er, cheat death, it looks like the hollies . . . "

Wilcox stared at me, his brows drawing down in an ugly, brooding expression. Then, all at once, he burst out laughing. "My God, Booth, don't tell me you believe in that nonsense!"

I felt my face flood red; I could not answer him.

"I bet you do!" Wilcox hooted with laughter. "You're as crazy as Uncle Loosh!"

I stood up, said, "Good night, Wilcox," with what vestiges of dignity I could, and walked out of the room. I would have liked to return to work in the library, but I was afraid Wilcox would find me there. I went up to my bedroom and locked the door. I could leave tomorrow afternoon—maybe even tomorrow morning. I could ask Flood about trains before breakfast.

I did not expect to sleep at all, but I changed into my pajamas and climbed into bed. If nothing else, I could read comfortably. About half an hour later, I heard Wilcox come upstairs. His footsteps stopped outside my door, but he did not knock or speak. I was just as glad.

I read long enough to quiet my nerves. When I looked at the clock, it was five minutes past midnight, and the house was perfectly still. No one would notice or care if I went back down to the library for a couple of hours. I would feel better about leaving—less like I was running away—if I had at least completed the task Wilcox had asked me here to perform.

I got up, put my book carefully back in my valise, and put on my dressing gown, already rehearsing my story should I run into Flood or Wilcox. I needed something to read—what better reason to be found creeping downstairs to the library in the middle of the night?

But the house might as well have been deserted, for all the signs of life it showed. I made it to the library without incident and shut the doors carefully behind me before I turned on the light. In that single moment of darkness, I suffered the horrible conviction that there was someone sitting behind the desk, but when I turned on the light, no one was there.

I worked peacefully for almost five hours, slowly restoring order to the chaos of Mr. Preston Wilcox's library. The darkness beyond the windows was softening to gray, the sun's first rays reaching up above the brooding hollies, when I pulled a book out of the lowest shelf of the bookcase behind the desk and with it fell a second book, which flipped itself open to its title page.

I stared at that second book for a long time, perfectly still, just as I would have stared at a tarantula that might or might not have been dead. The book was not listed in Mr. Preston Wilcox's catalogue. I had only ever seen a copy once before. But now I knew why those notes referring to "the Guide" and "the Vessel" had looked familiar. It was *The Book of Whispers*—not the nineteenth-century fake, but the genuine edition from 1605. I could not bring myself to touch it.

And while I was standing there, staring at that small, fragile volume, I heard Wilcox coming down the stairs. I clutched my dressing gown closed at the neck. I could not let him see me like this: in my pajamas with my hair uncombed and my face stubbled. He would never believe me then, and the matter had suddenly become much larger than our enmity, preserved like an ant in amber, and my wounded pride.

Then I thought, He'll go in to breakfast. I can get upstairs and get decent without him seeing me.

At the same moment at which I remembered it was only a quarter after five, far too early for breakfast, I heard the front door slam. I knew then, and the knowledge made me cold. He intended to have those hollies down today; he was going out to look at them, to plan his attack.

I had seen *The Book of Whispers*; I knew what was waiting for him among the holly trees.

"Wilcox!" I shouted uselessly and plunged for the door.

The door would not open. I tugged and rattled, but the latch stayed jammed. The first part of my dream from Friday night came back; I remembered the old man saying, "Stay in the library."

But whether I liked Wilcox or not, I could not leave him to his fate, to the terrible thing Lucius Preston Wilcox intended.

"Flood!" I shouted and then caught myself; Flood had his own role to play among the holly trees. I shouted for the housekeeper instead, Mrs. Grant, and pounded on the door in between my frantic assaults on the doorknob. I could feel the old man's black eyes watching me from behind the desk. I did not turn around, afraid that I would find the feeling to be more than just nerves.

The library was not far from the kitchen, and Mrs. Grant got up at dawn to bake the day's bread. Although it felt like hours, it was no more than ten minutes—maybe only five—before I heard her on the other side of the door, saying, "What on Earth—?"

"The door's stuck!"

"Stuck? It's never been stuck before."

For her, the door swung smoothly open. I wasted no time in explanations, apologies, or curses, but bolted past her. The front door did not resist me; I threw it open just in time to see Wilcox disappear into the close-serried ranks of holly.

"*Wilcox!*" I shouted and started running.

I lost both my carpet slippers within ten feet, but ran on regardless. Stones and sticks and shed holly leaves hurt my feet, but there was still a chance. If I could get to the hollies, get Wilcox out of the hollies . . .

I reached the trees, ducked between them as Wilcox had, and came face to face with Flood.

"Where's Mr. Wilcox?"

"Mr. Wilcox has met with an accident," he said smoothly, well-rehearsed, "but I think—"

"Let it go, Flood."

Those smooth, perfect pebbles stared at me.

"Let *him* go."

"I don't understand you, Mr. Booth."

"You're the Guide, aren't you? And poor Wilcox is the Vessel. I found the book."

His face twisted; I remembered how he had stood in the doorway of the library, refusing to come in. And I remembered the carvings on the library doors; that thing I had taken for a box could just as easily be a book. I wondered, distractedly, my hackles rising, just what Flood had been before Mr. Preston Wilcox had used the book to command him.

"I'm sorry, Mr. Booth," he said. "I think you misunderstood me. Mr. Wilcox—"

"What on Earth are you doing out here, Booth?"

I whipped around, my heart hammering in my throat. Wilcox was approaching through the trees.

"Wilcox?" I said weakly.

"Good God, man, you look like you've seen a ghost. What's the matter?"

"N-nothing." I could not stop staring at him, his ruddy face and aggressively square body, his rumpled hair and— "What happened to your hand?"

Flood said, "I was trying to tell you, Mr. Booth. Mr. Wilcox met with an accident."

"Bumping around like a bull in a china shop," Wilcox said cheerfully. "Fell over and bashed my hand on some damn rock. I was just going back to the house for some meurochrome. Come on, and we'll get Mrs. Grant to make you some tea."

"All right," I said, numb and bewildered, and we started back toward Hollyhill. I could feel embarrassment rising, washing over me like a tide. "I'm done in the library, and I, er . . . that is, is there a morning train?"

"Ten o'clock," Wilcox said. "Capital work, old man. I'll have Flood drive you. Oh, and Flood!"

As he glanced over his shoulder at Flood, I saw his eyes plainly in the clarifying dawn light. They were Wilcox's little, sandy-lashed eyes, but surely Wilcox's eyes had been hazel, not that obsidian-hard black.

"Tell the men not to bother about the hollies," Wilcox said. "They're starting to grow on me."

I left by the ten o'clock train. Flood and I said nothing to each other. What could we say? We both knew what had happened; we both knew that no one would believe me if I tried to tell them the truth, and even if I were believed, there was nothing that anyone could do. After he let me out at the station, I saw him hiss at me like a cat through the windshield before the car pulled away.

I have not heard from Wilcox since.

ELEGY FOR A DEMON LOVER

I first saw him at the corner of Atwood and Haye.

It was dusk; I was on my way home from the museum, standing at the crosswalk waiting for the light to change. Even now, I do not know what made me look up. I only know that I did look, and I saw him. He was standing on the opposite corner, a tall, slender figure in a gray overcoat. His hair was a shock of gold over his pale face, and even at that distance I could see the brilliance of his blue eyes. I looked away at once.

The light changed. I stepped down into the street. I had no intention whatsoever of looking at him again, but as I neared the middle of the street, my eyes rose of their own accord. He was perhaps five feet away, and he was staring at me. He walked like a conqueror, like a lion. He could not have been more than twenty-two or twenty-three. His eyes were not merely vivid blue; they were intense, blazing, as if they were lit from within, as if this young man was burning with a flame that no one else could feel. His mouth was twisted in a mocking smile. He had known that I would look. I looked away at once, my face reddening, and then we were past each other.

I went home. I locked the door behind me and then circled the apartment, nervously checking the windows, the door to my postage-stamp balcony. But when I asked myself, I did not know what I was nervous of. It is a wonder I did not burn myself badly as I made dinner, for all the time I was listening, although I did not know for what. I ate without tasting anything, and as I washed the dishes my mind was so far away that I was washing the same saucepan for the third time before I noticed what I was doing. And all the time I was listening without knowing what I listened for and fearing when I did not know what there was to fear.

I did not attempt to go to bed that night. I picked a book at random from the shelves and stayed reading by the fire. Eventually, I did sleep, although I only realized it when I woke, my head thick and my neck stiff, to the knowledge that I had been dreaming of his blue eyes and beautiful, arrogant face. I looked at the book, lying open on my lap like a dead bird, and discovered that I had spent the dark hours staring at the pages of Wells-Burton's *Demonologica* without taking in a single letter of its dry, disturbing text.

It was four in the morning. I put the *Demonologica* back on the shelf, showered, shaved, and changed my clothes. I met no one on my way to the Parrington, and I did not see the blond man, not even in the darkest shadows where my nerves insisted he must be standing, watching me. I was so overwrought by the time I reached the museum that it took me three tries to open the door and two to lock it again when I was safely inside. I do not know why or how I knew that the blond man would not find me inside the museum, but I did know it; the knowledge was at once reassuring and disappointing.

I was distracted all day, without quite knowing why, unable to concentrate on anything. The people I talked to in the course of my duties looked at me strangely. Mr. Lucent asked if I was ill, and I did not quite know how to answer him. I did not feel ill, but I did not feel normal; from the look on his face, I knew that the febrile shimmer I sensed in my blood must somehow be showing through.

As I knew he would be, the young man was waiting for me on the steps of the museum when I came out at sundown. It was he, indisputably, the man who had stared at me in the cross-walk the day before, the man whose face had haunted my thin dreams. He was leaning against one of the great stone sphinxes that flanked the portico and smoking a narrow, foreign cigarette. There was no scent of smoke, although I could see it wreathing his head, only the sweet, strong scent of viburnum. His blue eyes were full of fire and darkness.

I knew that I should walk past him, go down the stairs and into the city, to a theater or a restaurant or even the house of my former guardians. I knew that, but I could not do it. I stayed where I was, as if I had been turned to stone, a new column for the portico, ugly and graceless.

He dropped his cigarette and ground it out with his left foot. He looked at me, his eyebrows raised in inquiry. "Are you Lot's wife, that you can only stare at me and not speak? What is your name?" His voice was warm and rich and smooth, like the scent of viburnum that surrounded him. He had a trace of an accent, though I could not place it.

I opened my mouth; the hinges of my jaw seemed corroded with rust. "Kyle Murchison Booth." My voice was deeper than his, husky and rasping, like the caw of a crow.

"Kyle," he said and smiled. I stood transfixed; no one had ever smiled at me like that in my life. "My name is Ivo Balthasar, and I hope you do not intend to stand here all night."

We went out to dinner. Ivo said he was a stranger to the city, but I knew most of the restaurants near the Parrington, and I took him to the best of them, a bistro run by a fat, cheerful Parisian. We talked through dinner; Ivo did not seem annoyed by my stammering inarticulateness, and he listened to what I told him without the faintest hint of boredom or impatience. When at one point I apologized for talking too much, he said, "Don't be silly. I think your problem is that you don't talk enough." I found myself telling him things I had never told anyone else, things about my parents, about the Siddonses, about prep school and college, even about my friend Blaine, who was dead. Ivo sat and listened, the look in his blue eyes enrapt, and I knew, though I could hardly believe it, that he was not bored or uninterested, that to him I mattered as I had never mattered to anyone in my life.

We walked back to my apartment through the dark, deserted streets, Ivo making me laugh with the story of a strange thing that had happened to him in Cairo. He seemed to have traveled everywhere, despite his youth; I had never been farther than two hundred miles from the house in which I had been born, and I could have listened to his stories of London and Berlin, Johannesburg and Moscow and Beijing, for the rest of my life.

He came upstairs with me when we reached my building; I unlocked my door and stepped inside, then looked back at him.

He was standing in the hallway, watching me. "Well, Kyle, aren't you going to invite me in?"

A blush scalded my cheekbones; his smile told me he had noticed. "Please," I said, " . . . come in."

"Thank you," he murmured and stepped past me into the apartment.

Cat-like, he insisted on exploring every nook and cranny, the kitchen, living room, bedroom, bathroom, study, even the closets and the narrow stair that twisted up to the attic. He admired the prints on the walls, the rugs on the floor. I stood in the living room, once I had hung up our overcoats, and waited for him to come back to me, aware of something fluttering in the pit of my stomach like a bird. Eventually he returned, his blue eyes sparkling.

"This is very nice, Kyle," he said, "but it seems so cold."

"Cold?"

He came up to me, tilting his head back slightly to look me in the eyes; he was tall, but I was taller, as I was taller than almost everyone, all knees and elbows and clumsiness. "Have you ever loved anyone in these rooms?"

I could not meet his eyes. "I . . . I don't know what you mean."

"No?" His tone was gently teasing, and I knew he could see the blush that made my skin feel as if it were burning. He raised his hand; his nails were like a woman's, long and sharp and slightly hooked. I flinched from his touch.

"Kyle," he said. The scent of viburnum was very strong. "Do you think I intend to hurt you?"

"I don't . . . I don't know what you want."

He laughed, and although his laugh was as beautiful as his voice, something in it disturbed me, some hint of a wolf's howl, or of the cry of a loon. Then he was speaking again; I could not help but listen. "And here I thought I had been as transparent as glass. Kyle." He touched my face; I could feel the heat of his fingers, and this time I did not flinch away, although I was trembling. "I want to make love to you. Will you let me?"

I did not know how to answer him; I could not imagine words either to reject or accept. As if I were reaching out to put my fingers into flame, I looked up into his face. There was no mockery there, no sign that this was some huge and elaborate joke at my expense. He was waiting for my answer, the hard lines of his face softened, his blue eyes containing nothing but warmth and something that almost seemed to be anxiety.

I said, a stupid, senseless non-sequitur: "No one calls me Kyle."

But Ivo did not snort with laughter, or sigh with impatience; he did not turn and walk back out into the darkness. He said, "Then I think it's high time someone did." His smile was sweet and warm, like the lifting of a burden. "Kyle. Come to me." I felt the hardness of his nails at the back of my neck as he gently pulled my head down so that his mouth could meet mine. His lips were soft, his teeth wickedly sharp behind them.

After a moment he released me, moving back a little so he could look me in the eyes. "Kyle, are you a virgin?"

Of course I was. I had never before met anyone who would look twice at me. My heart was clamoring in my chest as if I had been running, and I looked away from him.

"Beloved," Ivo said, "there is no shame, only an undiscovered country to explore. Come." His hands slid down gently to where my hands hung stiff and icy at my sides. The heat of his flesh was like fire. He took my hands and stepped slowly backwards, leading me step by halting step into the bedroom.

My life became bifurcated. From eight to five I was the museum's Mr. Booth, following the rounds of my duties as I always had, and I did not think of Ivo at all, except to remember to keep my cuffs carefully buttoned, so that the long welts left by his nails would not be noticed. And even that caution was queerly divorced from Ivo himself; it was simply something I knew I had to be careful about, without knowing or caring why.

At five, I went home and became Ivo's Kyle. I do not know what Ivo did while I was at work; he was always there, waiting, when I returned. The apartment became filled with the scent of viburnum and the darker scent of sex. I trusted Ivo as blindly as a child; he taught me pleasure and pain and the shadowed places in-between. It ceased to matter that I was ten years or more older than he; his knowledge and experience were more than I could have gathered in three lifetimes. I asked him no questions about himself; he told me stories of his travels but nothing more personal. There was only the slender beauty of his body, the flawless marble whiteness of his skin, the pleasures which he taught me to give as well as receive.

I had always been an insomniac; now I slept only when I had to, both of us loath to lose the beauties we could share. Moreover, when I did sleep, my dreams were bad and ugly. I dreamed of humiliation and shame and guilt; words like *monstrosity* and *abomination* shouted themselves through my dreaming mind, and when I woke, my eyes would be raw with unshed tears.

After one such dream—I had lost all track of the calendar, so I do not know how long Ivo had been there, how long I had known him—I rolled over, away from the moonlight streaming between the slats of the Venetian blinds. My eyes opened as my head came down on the pillow again, and I startled back so violently I nearly fell off the bed.

Ivo was lying there, perfectly still, his face as serene as a statue's, his eyes open, fixed, and brilliant with moonlight. He looked as if he had been lying there for hours, just watching me sleep.

"Ivo?"

His face did not change, but he said, "Kyle?" his voice as warm and caressing as ever.

"Are you . . . that is . . ." I could not articulate what was bothering me, and so fell silent. I did not know why he frightened me, lying there so still and quiet, except that he did not seem to be blinking. I realized that though I had seen Ivo close his eyes, I had never noticed him blink.

"Is all well with you, beloved? Another bad dream?" He did not move, and I could not, lying there, our faces inches apart, staring.

"Yes," I said. I did not lie to Ivo, although I would have to anyone else. I was staring, transfixed, at the opalescent brilliance of his eyes in the moonlight.

He moved then, one hand reaching forward to caress my hip. "Do you wish to sleep again?"

All at once, out of my fear and the memories of my dreams, I blurted, "Ivo, are you all right?"

"Of course," he said, his lips curving in a smile, although still he did not blink. "I am here with you, Kyle. How could I be otherwise?" His hand moved, and my breath caught in my throat.

I forgot my questions, forgot my fear. But as we moved closer together, the moonlight still lighting his eyes like lamps, I saw something I had never seen before, although I could not count the hours I had spent staring into Ivo's eyes: his pupils were vertically slit, like a cat's.

I could not think about Ivo. I discovered this only slowly, out of a nagging, angering sense that there was something I was missing, some blind spot in my mind. At the museum my thoughts would slide away from him, and I would only remember two or three hours later that I had been trying to put together the things I had observed. And then it would be another two or three hours before I remembered remembering that. At home, when Ivo was there, I could not think at all, mesmerized by his brilliant eyes, the scent of viburnum that surrounded him, the burning warmth of his skin. It was as if I had been divided in two. One part of me knew about Ivo; the other part was capable of rational thought. I could not bring the two together.

But I was more and more aware that something was wrong. In the washroom at the museum, when I rolled up my cuffs to wash my hands, I would look at the angry welts on my forearms, and I would not know how I had come by them. At home, it was part of my life that Ivo was always watching me, unblinking, the slits of his pupils expanding and contracting as a cat's do when it considers whether or not to pounce on its prey. And although I still wanted his touch, wanted the kaleidoscopic passion that only he could give me, at the same time I was coming to fear his hands, their heat and sharpness, as I feared his mouth and the roughness of his tongue.

Then, one night, Ivo burned me. It was not anything he meant to do—that, I still believe—merely that he caught my wrist, and I screamed at his touch.

He jerked his hand away, his eyes wide. "Kyle?"

I was staring at my left wrist, at the already blistering imprint, terribly distinct, of his fingers: the index, middle, and ring fingers clutching across the back of my arm, the little finger stretching down toward my elbow, the mark of his thumb resting across the vulnerable blue veins on the inside of my wrist.

I looked up at him. I had never seen fear on Ivo's face, and I hated the way it made him look. He said, his voice barely a whisper, "Oh,

Kyle, I am so sorry. Oh, my beloved, I never meant to hurt you. Here, come with me. I know what to do."

I let him lead me to the bathroom, let him wash the burn with cold water—his hands now barely warmer than mine—let him smear it with some ointment that he got out of his overcoat, a crumpled tin tube without a label. He wrapped my arm then, carefully, lovingly, in strips torn from an old shirt of mine. I was aware, all the while, of his eyes returning again and again to my face, of the anxiety he could not conceal. Finally, when he was done, he released me and stepped back, his gaze fixed on my face with such a naked look of pleading that I could not meet his eyes.

The pain had cleared my head; at least for this moment, I could both be with Ivo and think about him. I said, "What are you?"

"Kyle, beloved, please." He tried to smile. "I love you. Isn't that enough?"

"What are you, Ivo?"

I saw then that he would not answer me. Before he could choose his lie, I turned and walked past him, out of the bathroom, through the bedroom, out into the living room, buttoning my shirt with stiff, trembling fingers as I went.

"Kyle?" He followed me. I realized that I could hear the click of his toenails on the parquet floor, like a dog's. "Kyle? Where are you going? What are you doing?"

I found my shoes, my coat, my keys. "I need to think," I said, without turning back to look at him, and I left.

I walked for hours through the empty, night-haggard streets of the city. I neither noticed nor cared where I went, and if I had happened to fall in the river, I would have been glad of it. Perhaps because it was night, I found that I could remember Ivo, could piece together isolated, stranded thoughts that I had been having and forgetting for weeks: his eyes; his nails and teeth; the fact that I had never seen him either blink or sleep; the scent of viburnum that always surrounded him; the heat that he could only imperfectly control; the way he watched me, as if I were the only thing in the world that existed; the way I had become—I flinched from the word, but I knew it for truth—addicted to him. I remembered that after the first time I had seen him, my hands had dragged down the *Demonologica* from my shelves. And I knew.

Had I, I wondered, ever not known?

I stopped at last, in one of the city's many small parks; I sat on a bench and wept as I had not wept since I had been caned at the age of thirteen for mourning my mother. It felt as if, not only my heart, but my mind and soul and spirit were broken, lying in shattered pieces around my untied shoes. For a long time it did not seem to me as if I would ever find the strength or the courage to leave this bench, and it did not seem that there would be any point in any action I could take after I stood up. There was no point in anything.

But I knew what had to be done. I had read Wells-Burton and everything he had to say on the subject of incubi. The fact that I would rather have ripped my own heart out of my chest and left it for the crows was not relevant. I reached down with fingers that felt like dry twigs and tied my shoes; then I stood up and walked home.

Ivo was waiting in the living room. He had been crying; his eyes looked raw and hollow. "Kyle!" he said, coming toward me. "Kyle, you came—"

"You aren't here, Ivo," I said, hanging up my coat. "You never have been."

He stopped where he was, his hands still outstretched, his eyes widening with horror. "Kyle, what are you talking about? Kyle, don't you—"

"I know what you are, Ivo. *You aren't here.*"

I walked through into the bedroom. He trailed after me. "Kyle, please, what are you saying? You know I love you. You know I'd do anything for you."

"You aren't here," I said again. It was almost four o'clock. I took off my clothes, put on the pajamas I had not worn since I had invited

Ivo into my apartment and my life. I dragged the covers back and lay down on the bed, on my back, as stiff and comfortless as a medieval Christ. I stared at the ceiling. I could hear Ivo crying, but he did not come near me.

We stayed that way until seven o'clock, when I got up. I showered, shaved, dressed. My burns were already healing, thanks to Ivo's ointment, but I could see that the scars were going to remain with me for the rest of my life, as sharp and pitiless as a morgue photograph.

Ivo followed me from room to room, weeping. His control had slipped further during the night; his eyes were inhuman, without whites, the unearthly blue of marsh fire. His hair looked less like hair now, more like an animal's rich pelt. He did not try to speak to me, but I left without making any move toward the kitchen. I could buy something to eat later, if I had to, though I could not imagine being hungry.

As I was opening the door, I said again, "You aren't here, Ivo."

In the museum, in the daylight, I did not remember him. I did not know why I felt so ill and strained, why, on my lunch break, I slipped down to the basement and wept for half an hour, huddled for comfort against a bad Roman copy of a Greek nude. I did not remember him until I opened my door to the scent of viburnum.

"Kyle, please, I'll do anything you want, I'll be anything you need me to be. I don't care what it is, if it's wicked or depraved or perverted, *please*, I'll do it, I'll do anything, just don't do this to me. Kyle, please."

He was not as solid as he had been; I could see the wall through him, and his voice was faint. Only his eyes were still vivid, still fully present, and the terror and wretchedness and need in them tore at me like cruel teeth. For he did love me; to him I was the world. The fact that his love would infallibly kill me, leeching my essence away to feed his, as his previous lovers had fed him, was no desire of his. And when he had killed me, he would go on to his next hapless victim, his prey, whom he would love and destroy just as he loved and was destroying me.

"You aren't here, Ivo," I said.

He was weaker. Light hurt him now. I turned on the lights in every room in the apartment, pretending that I could not hear his cries of pain, driving him eventually into the bedroom closet, where he huddled like a beaten child, sobbing, only half-visible against my suits. I stayed in the living room that night, sitting with Wells-Burton's *Demonologica* by the fire, as I had sat on that other night, the night after he had chosen me, staring at the engraving that illustrated the chapter on incubi and succubi: a smiling youth with the teeth of a beast.

By morning, the scent of viburnum was fainter. I made myself ready for the day. When I looked in the mirror to shave, I could see him reflected behind me, a smear of gold, a smudge of blue against the white wall. I knew that if I concentrated I would be able to hear him, that by now all he would be able to say was my name. I did not try to hear him; I was trying with all my might to forget him, to bring that daylight oblivion into the night kingdom where once Ivo had ruled.

When I left, I said again, "You aren't here, Ivo," and this time I could feel the silence that answered my words, as if what I had said were true. When I returned that night, I could not smell viburnum.

That was effectively the end of it. There were still nights when I would wake in the middle of the night to the faint sweetness of viburnum, a feeling that there was almost weight on the mattress next to me, and I would have to get up, stumbling through the rooms of my apartment to turn on the lights. But as time passed those nights came farther and farther apart, and within six months they had ceased entirely. Ivo was truly gone, and now I cannot remember, even in the darkness, exactly what he looked like or how his voice sounded. Even in dreams, I cannot see him clearly, and although I know that is for the best, I know I do not want him back, yet I still miss him. I will always miss him—although I know that soon I will forget him entirely—for he was the only one I have ever known who loved me for what I am.

THE WALL OF CLOUDS

It was the head docent, Miss Chatteris, who found me. Coming to the Parrington very early one morning in mid-April, she observed a light burning in my office. Although that was not unusual—I was notorious throughout the museum for the odd hours I kept—it inspired her, she said later, to peek in and see if I could spare her a moment. I cannot imagine what she wanted to talk to me about; probably it was no more than nosiness.

She did not knock—either through her innate tactlessness or a cunning suspicion that I would not answer her—simply opened the door and walked in. And there she found me, lying crumpled on the floor in a dead faint.

It remains anyone's guess how long I had been lying there. My own memories seem to stop nearly a week prior to Miss Chatteris's discovery, with a hideous nightmare involving the Resurrection Hill Cemetery and the museum's vast, green, leather-bound *Catalogue of Books*; between that nightmare and coming back to myself on the couch in the Curators' Lounge with Dr. Archambault leaning over me, there is nothing. I cannot even remember that I remember nothing; there is only a kind of soft blackness, such as one might recall after a dreamless sleep.

Dr. Archambault said, "You are very ill, Mr. Booth."

I said, "I can't be. Our History of the Book exhibit opens less than a week from now." I do remember saying that, but as if it were a line delivered in a play of which I was merely a spectator. They do not feel like my words, and in the ears of my memory it does not sound like my voice which says them.

"And its success will be a great comfort at your funeral, I am sure," Dr. Archambault said. He left me then, with Miss Chatteris to sit by me. I was too ill to mind. When he came back, he and Dr. Starkweather, the museum director, had worked things out to their mutual satisfaction. Mr. Lucent would take over my duties, and I would go for an extended stay to an excellent convalescent hotel in Herrenmouth—having, as apparently everyone in the museum knew, no one to look after me. My protests were feeble, and Dr. Archambault did not listen to them. He drove me back to my apartment, packed a bag for me, and by midday had put me onto the Herrenmouth train with a promise that someone from the hotel would be at the station to meet me. He was a well-organized autocrat, and I had by then begun to be glad of it. My head was pounding, and all of my joints felt as though they had been wrapped around with lead. I was dimly aware that Dr. Archambault was right; I was ill, and I must have been ill for days without knowing it. I slumped into the corner of the compartment and, without intending to, fell into a doze.

I have never been one of those people who can drop off in a public place as easily as they can in their own beds. My friend Blaine had been able to, and it had always been a skill I envied. Even now, when I could not have stayed awake if I had wished it, I did not entirely fall asleep. When the door to the compartment opened, I heard it, and I heard the ensuing conversation. Weakly and dully, I wanted to drag myself back into the waking world, but that was as beyond my powers as flying to the moon. I could only stay where I was, an inert, helpless audience.

A female voice said, "What about this compartment, Auntie? It's nearly empty."

Another female voice, old and pretending to be feeble, said, "I don't know. There's a man in that corner."

"He's an old man, Auntie, and he's asleep. He won't bother us."

"I won't have anyone getting fresh with me."

"Oh, I'm sure he won't. He's all wrapped up, like he's ill. It would be funny if we were all going to the same place."

"Hilarious."

"Auntie, *please*. There aren't any empty compartments, and this one old man isn't going to bother anybody."

There was a long, thorny silence. "Very well."

I could not pry my eyelids open, but I heard them come in, the rustle of their dresses and the thumps and bangs of what seemed a quite extraordinary amount of luggage. The younger voice cajoled and pleaded; the old voice snapped and grumbled and refused to be placated. The two of them were in fact going to the same hotel that I was, the Hotel Chrysalis. The old voice seemed to fancy herself a great invalid, and the Hotel Chrysalis had hot springs that were supposed to be a sovereign cure. The younger voice was relentlessly optimistic about their beneficent qualities, and I wondered just what it was that bound her to her aunt.

The train pulled out of the station. Dr. Archambault had told me it was two hours to Herrenmouth; there was nothing either to do or to fear until we arrived there, and the steady vibration of the train was comforting, soporific. I fell into a deeper sleep, and so I do not know what occupation the two women found to beguile the time.

I was brought awake by a voice, a man's this time, saying, "Mr. Booth? Is there a Mr. Booth in this compartment?"

"*I* am Mrs. Terpenning," said the old voice magnificently.

"My orders are to meet a Mr. Booth," the man said.

I opened my eyes and managed to wave feebly.

"Mr. Booth?" He was a middle-aged man, brown and square and competent. "I'm Parris. Mr. Marten sent me to meet you."

"Mr. *Marten*?" the old voice said; I turned my head and got my first look at the two women. Mrs. Terpenning was a vulture-like dowager, not quite as ancient as I had expected. Rings encrusted every finger, and she wore a stiff black dress with a huge cameo at the throat. She was clearly the sort of woman who referred to her husband, when he came up in conversation, as "Mr. Terpenning." She horrified me.

The other woman looked nothing like her aunt. She was thirtyish, plump and small-boned, with fair hair and pale blue eyes. I suppose she was pretty. Her dress was dark green and shabby, and she wore no jewelry at all. Her eyes widened as she got her first good look at my face; if I could have found a way to reassure her that she was not the first person to make a wrong assumption about my age based on my white hair, I would have. But even if I had been well, I would not have known what to say.

"Can you stand up, Mr. Booth?" Parris said.

I rose, slowly and totteringly, losing my grip on Dr. Archambault's blanket as I did, and then stood, my feet entangled in plaid wool, unable either to move forward or to bend down to rescue the blanket. I could feel my knees shaking, and I knew how close I was to fainting again.

"Here, Mr. Booth." Parris offered me his arm. I clutched it. He seemed able to take my weight, and after a moment the compartment stopped swaying.

"Could you pick up the blanket, miss?" he said to the younger woman.

"Rosemary," Mrs. Terpenning said, "I forbid—"

The younger woman was already down on her knees, unwinding the blanket from my feet. Her hands were quick and deft. She was blushing when she rose again, and she pushed the blanket towards us without looking either Parris or myself in the face.

"Thank you, miss," Parris said, and tucked the blanket under his free arm. "The porter will get your bag, Mr. Booth. Come this way."

The world was starting to swim about me; I followed the pressure of Parris's arm and prayed that I would neither walk into anything nor fall down. After an interminable nightmare of stairs and shoving crowds, Parris said, "Here's the car, Mr. Booth," and I was able at last to sit down again. I shut my eyes and waited for the brazen gongs in my head to stop swinging.

Parris evaporated for a time; I was half-asleep when he swung the driver's-side door closed and said, "All set, Mr. Booth."

I could not find my tongue or lips or teeth to say, thank you. Oh I am ill, a dismal little voice moaned, away back in my head. Parris started the car, and the vibrations roared up through my spine into my skull; I felt as if they were going to shake something loose. Dr. Archambault's blanket was somehow over me again; I clutched at it and hoped faintly that it was not far to the Hotel Chrysalis.

I retain nothing of my first entrance to the hotel except a vast, vague impression of grayness. I think that it was beginning to rain as Parris extracted me from the car, and that the tall gray forbidding façade of the hotel became confused in my increasingly blurred and dizzy perceptions with the louring darkness of the sky. All I know is that the hotel seemed to stretch up forever.

The wall of clouds, I thought, and then I believe I fainted again.

For two weeks, I lay in a bedroom on the third floor of the Hotel Chrysalis, with at first no awareness of and then no interest in my surroundings. My dreams were rich and thin with fever, and they returned again and again to the book I had read as a child, in which the princess had lived in a castle surrounded by a wall of clouds. My father had given me the book, one of the few gifts I could remember receiving from him, and I had read it more times than I could count. The Siddonses, my guardians after my parents' deaths, had not approved of reading novels, and Mrs. Siddons had taken the book away from me; I had never dared to ask her what she had done with it. My dreams resurrected the book vividly in all its details: the loneliness of the princess, the cruelty of the giant who held her captive, the bravery and perseverance of the man who rescued her. One of the things I had liked best about the book was that the hero was a scholar, not a prince or a great warrior or anything of that sort. I dreamed of his quest endlessly and would wake weak and shaking in the night with the giant's laughter echoing in my ears.

Since I did not die, I eventually became better. The disease ran its course; having reached nadir, I gradually became stronger and more alert. I began to be able to look around my room, and I discovered letters from Dr. Archambault and Dr. Starkweather on my bedside table. A hideous bouquet of lilies squatted on the table by the window, sent by Miss Chatteris in proxy for all the docents. There was nothing from the Siddonses; I hoped that no one had told them I was ill.

Dr. Starkweather's letter was merely a formal reassurance that the museum could get along without me until I was well enough to return. From Dr. Archambault's letter—and from the grave, awed expression of the young woman who was my nurse—I gathered that no one had fully realized how ill I was until the second night after my arrival at the hotel, when my fever had reached 105°. *I would have insisted on your going to a hospital,* Dr. Archambault wrote, *your wishes and Dr. Starkweather's to the contrary, had I believed the problem to be anything greater than an influenza from which, it seemed to me at the time, you were already recovering.* I could not remember rejecting a hospital, but I have always loathed them, since the long months of my father's last illness, and it remains my abiding conviction that had I been trapped in a hospital, I would have died. Once I was strong enough, I wrote back to Dr. Archambault, a brief and rather shakily-penned note, reassuring him as to the excellence of the care I had received at the Hotel Chrysalis and my belief that he had done the right thing.

The nurse said simply, "We thought you were a goner, Mr. Booth, but you pulled through all right." She was a plain-faced girl, but vibrantly healthy. Her name was Molly Sefton. I do not think I would have liked her under any other set of circumstances, but as her patient, I loved her unreservedly, as a small child may love a favorite teacher.

She watched over me with a kind sternness, brooking no nonsense from anyone, including the manager of the hotel. He wished to come and express his personal gratification at my recovery, but Molly would have none of it. "There'll be time enough for that later," she said, plumping my pillows fiercely. "I won't have you being harassed by men as ought to know better." She herself was magnificently, restfully incurious; she did not ask about my work or my family or even about the old burn scars that made a mess of my left forearm. Molly's only interest was in my recovery, and in that arena her questions were probing and her judgments acute. Even Dr. Bollivar, the hotel doctor, did not interfere with Molly's decisions. As I later discovered, Dr. Bollivar spent most of his time, when not tending to the patients who genuinely needed his care, playing least-in-view with the hypochondriacs; once I was well enough to sit up and take notice, I almost never saw him again. He trusted Molly implicitly, and I think he was right to do so.

It was Molly who decided, two weeks and four days after my arrival at the Hotel Chrysalis, that I was ready to leave my room and take the afternoon sun on the hotel's back terrace.

"I won't leave you out there long, Mr. Booth," she said, "but it ain't good for you to stay breathing this old stale air all the time. So you come on with me and don't fret."

"But I don't know anyone," I said, clutching feebly at her as she helped me stand up.

"Well, they can introduce themselves if they want to," she said. "There ain't no monsters hereabouts, Mr. Booth. They're all nice folks."

I was unconvinced and uncomforted, but by that time Molly had started for the door, and it was either go with her or collapse to the floor where I was. My legs were terribly weak and wobbly; I felt as ungainly and defenseless as a newborn giraffe struggling to learn how to manage its knees.

My room had not been remarkable for personality, having sturdy, functional furniture, and walls of a clean, white, pleasing coolness. I was therefore entirely unprepared for the hallways of the hotel, with their brooding gas fixtures and glowering mahogany paneling. The carpets were all of a queer Indian design, like paisley seen in a fever-dream, and I kept having the impression that the shapes were moving just outside the edges of my peripheral vision. I clung to Molly's arm, and though I was nearly a foot taller than she, she seemed to find no difficulty in holding me up.

The hotel's back terrace was not really very far from my room, although that afternoon the pilgrimage felt like walking the Great Wall of China from one end to the other. We walked to the end of the hallway, where Molly summoned the elevator, a wrought-iron cage that I hated on sight.

"Come along, Mr. Booth," Molly said. I wanted to balk, but I did not have the strength. If Molly had led me into the jaws of hell, I would have had no choice but to follow her, and really, I told myself sternly, this elevator is *not* the jaws of hell, and Molly would not expect me to get into it if there were any danger. My clutch on her arm may have tightened slightly, but other than that I controlled myself and neither screamed nor fainted nor wept, though I hated the elevator no less from the inside than I had from the outside. I did not mind enclosed spaces particularly, but there was something about that elevator which felt unclean, like invisible bloodstains.

We emerged on the ground floor in good order, although Molly was essentially carrying me. The floor here was a parquet in dark and light woods, an interlocked pattern of squares that was elegant but dizzying. "Come on, Mr. Booth," Molly said and lugged me, ungainly and useless as a bundle of wet sheets, down the hall and out a pair of french doors, onto the terrace of the Hotel Chrysalis.

The terrace was a long granite-flagged affair, with a low balustrade stretching its entire length; decorative urns stood at the corners and flanked the three steps down into the garden proper. There were a number of deck chairs set about in twos and threes; Molly guided me to the nearest and almost literally dropped me onto it, not by intent but because my legs could not take the descent slowly.

"You all right, Mr. Booth?" she said.

"Yes," I said, although my heart was thudding up in my throat and I felt as if my head were a balloon filled with helium.

"Here." She helped me swing my legs up onto the chair. "I'll go get you a blanket." Because she was an essentially humorless young woman, she did not add, *Don't go anywhere.*

I lay back in the deck chair and shut my eyes, hearing my heart pounding in my ears and wishing feebly to be well. Molly returned quickly with a huge knitted blanket, the size to keep a giant warm, in which she proceeded to festoon me like an obscure and elaborate parcel. I was grateful for the warmth; although the day was a nice one, the breeze blowing seemed like ice against my skin.

"Now, I'll be back in half an hour, Mr. Booth," Molly said. "You just lie quiet and enjoy the sun."

"Thank you, Molly," I said and shut my eyes again.

I may have dozed; I do not know. I think that there was a gap of time before I heard a voice whispering, "That's the man from 315, the one who's been so sick."

Oh God, I thought and did not reveal by so much as a twitch that I was awake.

"I had no idea he was so old," another voice said.

"Rosemary Hunter says he's not. She says that he's a young man, really. It's just that his hair is white."

"Do you suppose the illness did it? Mr. Marten says he's never seen a man so ill."

"It's happened before. Why, I remember my Aunt Seraphina—my mother's eldest sister—she had a nervous breakdown when her first husband died, and her hair went white as white. All in a week, my mother said."

"That's nothing. The wife of my grandmother's brother, my Great-Aunt Lucille, a year after my great-uncle died, she dreamed that she saw him and he told her he knew she'd poisoned him. When she woke up in the morning her hair, that'd been black as pitch the night before, was pure white, except for one streak of black right down the middle of her head."

"*Had* she?"

"Had she what?"

"Poisoned him."

"Well, I don't know. My grandmother always said there was never a man who deserved it more. And he did die uncommon quick and uncommon painful. The doctor wanted to do an autopsy, but Great-Aunt Lucille's father wouldn't hear of it, and he was the judge."

"Oh my."

"She had to leave town, of course."

"Well *naturally*. People are so unkind. When my cousin Mattie had her trouble, there was nothing more rude than the way people spoke to her in the street. You'd think it wasn't in the Declaration of Independence that somebody's innocent until proven guilty. And they never proved that Mattie did *anything*."

"Mmm, I'm not sure that *is* in the Declaration."

"Well, it's *somewhere*. They had no right to say those cruel things about Mattie."

"People never have the right to be cruel, but I can't say as how that ever stops them. Not unless someone else stops them first. My sister Susannah's husband was a dreadful cruel man, but she stopped *him* all right."

I could not stand it any longer, more and more convinced that they were playing some strange, warped joke on me. I shifted position conspicuously and opened my eyes.

"He's *awake*."

"We'd best introduce ourselves then. No sense in rudeness."

I heard the clicking of heels, like the tapping of tiny hooves, and there appeared in front of me two tiny, withered crones. I thought I had to be dreaming still, for they were identical, dressed in the same dark red, with small, black, cunning eyes in their pale, wrinkled faces. They looked as if they put up their silvery-white hair in its coiled braids using each other as a mirror, and they wore long, dangling earrings of marcasite and jet.

"I'm Doris," said one.

"I'm Kerenhappuch," said the other, "but most folks call me Carrie, and I hope you will, too."

"Kyle Murchison Booth," I said faintly; even if I were dreaming—which seemed less and less likely all the time—that was no excuse to be rude. "Do you live at the hotel?"

"Oh yes," said Doris.

"For years and years," said Carrie. "We came here for a bit of a rest after my youngest grandniece Cecilia got married, and we liked it so much we've just never left." This was evidently a joke of long standing, for they both tittered, a thin, brittle sound like sparrows arguing.

"We just take little trips," Doris said.

"For weddings."

"And christenings."

"And funerals."

They cocked their heads, Carrie to the left, Doris to the right. "It's nice to see you out taking the air, Mr. Booth," said Doris.

"Everyone's been ever so worried," Carrie said. "Mr. Marten was quite gray with thinking that someone might die in his hotel. Not that it hasn't happened before, of course."

"Oh gracious no. Why there was that nice Mr. Ampleforth, just last year."

"And the woman who came here after her baby was born—was that two years ago, Doris, or three?"

"I don't remember, but anyone could see she was dying from the moment she got here. I've never seen a face so white."

"You'd think from the way her husband carried on that someone here had murdered her."

"Oh, I don't hold that against him. The poor man was half-distracted with grief, and that's apt to make anybody a bit wild. You wouldn't believe the things my aunt Charlotte's husband did when she died, but then he insisted first to last, right up to the moment they had him committed, that she wasn't really dead. I'm afraid he wasn't very stable, poor man."

"But I do think people shouldn't be encouraged to give way to their grief. I mean, my father's sister Lavinia, when her husband died, and their son with him, she got up the next day and went right on taking care of her two little girls like nothing had happened. I do think she cried at the funeral though."

"And that's no more than natural, and I'm sure there's not a soul in the world could object to it. My dearest school friend, Millicent Carter, when she died her husband didn't so much as shed a tear at the service, and it came out not two months later that he'd smothered her himself. I don't stand with hard-heartedness and never have."

If they were joking, it was clearly a charade that they had been carrying on for years and was nothing to do with me. While that was at least some comfort, the two old ladies were frightening me, and I felt the same relief at hearing Molly Sefton's voice as one feels at seeing the first light of dawn after a night of nightmares.

"Miss Doris, Miss Carrie."

"Hello, Molly," the old ladies chirped in unison.

"It's time for Mr. Booth to go back to his room," Molly said.

"Oh what a pity," one of them said, but I had lost track of which one was which.

"We've been having such a nice conversation," said the other.

"Such a polite young man."

"You don't often meet someone these days who *listens* well."

"Be that as it may, he's got to rest," Molly said. "Are you ready to get up, Mr. Booth?"

"Yes, I think so," I said.

"Well, we'll leave you to it," said Carrie or Doris.

"But we'll hope to see you again soon, Mr. Booth," said Doris or Carrie. "It's always nice to see new faces and talk to new people." Mercifully, they pattered away.

"They're nice ladies, Miss Doris and Miss Carrie," Molly said as she hauled me out of the chair.

"They seemed very, er, talkative. Is there any particular reason they're here, Molly?"

"Reason? I don't quite know what you mean, Mr. Booth."

"Well," I said, floundering, "that is, this is a convalescent hotel, and they don't seem . . . *physically* ill, so I wondered . . . "

"They like the company. And they're quite wealthy ladies, I believe. Now here's the elevator, Mr. Booth, and we'll have you back to your room in a brace of shakes. I think the fresh air did you good."

"Yes, Molly," I said, and I was so relieved to get back to my familiar room and the soft warmth of my bed, that I put Doris and Carrie out of my mind. But I heard them twittering all night long in my dreams.

Over the next several days, Molly continued stubbornly with her program of getting me fresh air, and I was passed under review by all the population of the Hotel Chrysalis that was not actually bed-ridden. Aside from Doris and Carrie, I was introduced to Madame Vlaranskaya, an emigrée lady at the hotel on account of "nerves"; Mr. Ormont, a harmless, portly gentleman who happened to be a poet of no small skill and reputation—also here for "nerves"; Major Berinford, an exceedingly ancient gentleman whose vital forces had apparently been sustained for the last decade by the Chrysalis waters alone; Mrs. Stepney and Mrs. Langtry, invalids of vague but convincing symptoms; and of course I renewed my acquaintance with Mrs. Terpenning and her niece. There were other inhabitants, whom I saw on the terrace or in the halls, but they did not introduce themselves to me, and I did not seek out their company. There was nothing I could do to prevent Mrs. Langtry or Major Berinford from settling down next to me and telling me lengthy stories about campaigns (the Major) or children (Mrs. Langtry), but insofar as I could avoid social interaction, I did.

Molly thought this was unhealthy, and she encouraged me relentlessly as I grew stronger to "enjoy" myself, by which she apparently meant joining one of the interminable games of bridge in the Small Library or the equally interminable conversations in the conservatory or the Brocade Room. I did not know how to tell her that there would be no way in which I could enjoy myself less, and so I simply disobeyed her, with the same guilty feelings with which I had disobeyed my mother and my nurse as a child. Once I was on my feet again, I spent as much time walking in the gardens as I could, an activity which was at least *less* disobedient than hiding in my room.

The gardens of the Hotel Chrysalis were extensive. Directly west of the hotel and about a tenth of a mile away were the hot springs, which had their own enormous and marvelous building, like a vast, fossilized Victorian greenhouse. The path from hotel to chalybeate was broad and paved in mellow red sandstone, for the better progress of the halt and the lame. I took that path once daily myself, both because Molly had an unswerving belief in the sovereign powers of the springs and because I felt a need to propitiate Mr. Marten. I knew that he approved of people taking the waters.

The water of the Chrysalis springs was not unspeakably vile. It tasted strongly of metal, and I found it unpleasantly warm, but compared to Mrs. Stepney's stories of the waters she had drunk in

England and Switzerland and in other parts of the United States, I was aware that I was getting off lightly. But still I drank off my draft as quickly as possible and lingered no longer in the Chalybeate than was strictly necessary.

For most of the day I could avoid other people. I was not the only person who walked in the gardens, but the gardens were extensive enough and their paths torturous enough that it was no great feat to avoid the other walkers. I glimpsed Dr. Bollivar occasionally in the distance, but he avoided me as assiduously as I avoided him. I did frequently encounter Miss Hunter, coming down a path as I was coming up, standing in an arbor as I passed, seated in contemplation of the lily pond around which I liked to walk. She would say, "Hello, Mr. Booth," in her soft polite voice, and I would answer, "Hello, Miss Hunter," and hold my breath against the possibility that she would wish to converse until I was safely out of earshot. But it seemed that all she wished was to escape Mrs. Terpenning, for she never made any further conversational gambits.

The worst torment were the meals. Mr. Marten believed in communal dining, with small gracious tables reminiscent of the first class dining room on a ocean liner. At lunch people were allowed to sit where they chose, and by coming early I could claim one of the small, dim tables along the wall, where I was unlikely to accumulate companions. When I did, they tended to be persons as adverse to conversation as myself, and we could proceed with our meal in harmonious silence.

Dinners were infinitely worse. At dinner, Mr. Marten produced his elegant place cards and assigned us places with the arbitrary ruthlessness of a dictator. I was swept from the Scylla of Doris and Carrie one night to the Charybdis of Mrs. Terpenning the next. I preferred Doris and Carrie, for they were perfectly happy to do all of the talking themselves, their voices weaving in and out like a large and complicated tapestry of malevolence that they had been working on for decades. Mrs. Terpenning insisted on trying to "bring me out." She put questions, about my parents, about my schooling, about my employment. I answered in desperate monosyllables and mumbles, and after a night or two she gave me up as a bad job and turned her greedy eyes elsewhere.

For Mrs. Terpenning collected people. I witnessed her casting her barbed nets toward Madame Vlaranskaya and Mr. Ormont, but the most blatant example was her niece, Miss Hunter. I heard about Miss Hunter's history at interminable length one evening, while Miss Hunter sat and pushed infinitesimal amounts of chicken around on her plate, her soft pale face becoming redder and redder. Once started, Mrs. Terpenning's monologues were like juggernauts; trying to stop them would only get you flattened.

Miss Hunter was Mrs. Terpenning's niece merely by marriage, the only child of Mr. Terpenning's only sister. Lydia Terpenning Hunter had apparently been one of those fragile, exquisite beauties like an overblown rose. She had been a poet—Mrs. Terpenning seemed to imagine that this put her herself on a footing of equality and intimacy with Mr. Ormont, whose manners were too good to permit him to repudiate that suggestion with the loathing it deserved. Lydia Terpenning had taken intellectual society by storm at the age of nineteen; she had enjoyed a meteoric courtship with the brave and dashing Captain Cornelius Hunter. They had married; Lydia had borne her child and died of it; Captain Hunter had, in the most romantic way possible, renounced all civilized pleasures and gone off to Africa to hunt big game, where he had been killed by a lioness when his daughter was five.

The combined Terpenning-Hunter fortune was considerable, but Captain Hunter had, with execrable judgment, placed his finances in the hands of his dearest friend, one Captain Warren Starling, in trust for Miss Hunter, and Captain Starling had contrived to lose it all. I could not tell from Mrs. Terpenning's dark and delphic conversation exactly what the wretched Starling had done, and I did not like to ask for clarification. Regardless, Miss Hunter was left a pauper at the age of twelve; her kind and generous uncle had taken her into his household. He had died scarcely a year later, and Mrs. Terpenning, knowing that "it was what Mr. Terpenning would want," had continued to allow the child to make her home with her, asking in return for the money lavished on her education, her clothes, and all her other expenses, only that she keep a poor, lonely old lady company until such time as she should find a husband. For which last phrase, read "forever." I felt desperately sorry for Miss Hunter.

It was a day or two after that ghastly dinner that Mr. Marten came to me with a proposal. He caught me on my way out of the dining room after lunch and said, "Mr. Booth, I understand that you are a curator of some kind."

"Yes," I said, wondering, a little uneasily, where this was going. "I work for the Parrington."

"Yes, yes, of course, but I thought I understood from Major Berinford that your specialty is documents."

"Yes," I said, amazed and flattered that Major Berinford had noticed.

"Then I was wondering . . . you see, the Hotel Chrysalis has a long and most distinguished history, and I have always wanted to put together a book—or at least a pamphlet—but all the documents are simply shelved, higgledy-piggledy, if you'll pardon the expression, in the Greater Library. I've never been able to make heads or tails of them. But if, perhaps . . . I don't like to bother you when you've been so ill . . ."

"No, no bother," I said, scarcely able to believe my good fortune. "That is, I'd like to see them."

He beamed at me. "Splendid! I shall give you the key, and you must feel free to come and go as you wish. There is no . . . I don't want you to feel that there is any *obligation* involved."

"No, I understand," I said. "But really, I'd like to."

"You are most kind," said Mr. Marten and led me back into the staff's part of the hotel. The Greater Library turned out to be a room I had often wondered about during my peregrinations through the gardens; it was a long, two-story peninsula, jutting out from the hotel into the rose garden. It had looked to me like a chapel, and I had wondered a little nervously about what religion might be practiced in it and whether I might be proselytized to attend services as I was proselytized to play bridge. But it turned out to be the religion I loved and understood, the religion of books. The shelves stretched up to the ceiling on all sides, with a one story pier down the middle of the room. There was a balcony at that height running all the way around, and there were two bridges, one a quarter of the way down the room's length, and another three-quarters, so you could walk from one side of the upper shelves to the other without having to descend and ascend the torturous stairs. The second story was punctuated periodically with windows, like a clerestory, and some skilled artist had installed stained glass in every other window, depicting the life of King Arthur. A room more clearly meant to delight the heart of a bibliophile I could not imagine.

The collection itself was excellent, though I did no more than browse occasionally through its shelves. Someone in the hotel's history had been a collector of skill, means, and perseverance; the temptation to abscond quietly with a volume or two was extreme, and I recommended Mr. Marten strongly that he have a catalogue made and appraised. He seemed a little surprised; his energies and passions were devoted to the running of the hotel, not contemplation of its books.

The documents pertaining to the history of the Hotel Chrysalis, as Mr. Marten had warned me, existed in a state devoid of order or pattern on the two sets of shelves immediately flanking the door. I spent that first day, from lunch until dinner, simply exploring, trying to make sense of what had been saved, and when, and why. I would have gone back after dinner, but Molly caught me and insisted that I join the company in the conservatory. "It's them nasty old books made you sick in the first place," she said, and since I did not know what had made me ill, I could not argue with her effectively.

The conservatory, unlike the other rooms at the guests' disposal, did have some advantages, namely the philodendrons that grew to enormous height and amplitude. It was possible to disappear almost entirely into their foliage; I could sit and be safely unnoticed for hours. I made my way to my favorite coign of obscurity and sat. I *was* tired, a headache beginning to push at my temples, and I thought, though reluctantly, that Molly was right. I was not yet well, and I would have to pace myself carefully, lest I throw myself into a relapse. I did not believe that my books had made me ill, but I was not fool enough to ignore the signs of fatigue in my mind and body. I leaned back in the chair and closed my eyes.

Nearby, Madame Vlaranskaya, Mrs. Terpenning, Mrs. Langtry, and a newcomer, a Mrs. Whittaker, were discussing illnesses with the passion that only dedicated invalids can bring to the job. I had heard installments of that conversation, with a variety of celebrants, twenty times since coming to the hotel and had even come to find it queerly soothing. No longer deathly ill, I could not fall asleep in the public forum of the conservatory, even screened by philodendrons as I was, but I sank into a kind of reverie, imagining that the women talking were participating in the one great conversation of the Hotel Chrysalis, a dialogue echoing from decade to decade down the hotel's long history, in which individual speakers might come and go, appear and vanish, be heard and fall silent, but the conversation itself never paused in its ceaseless murmuring and muttering, the catalogue of symptoms like Homer's Catalogue of Ships, the tales of doctors' kindnesses, nurses' cruelties, miraculous recoveries and sadly unexpected deaths—a vast and powerful river which neither time nor death, nothing but the destruction of the hotel itself could dry up. And even then I imagined pale, sickly specters drifting through the ruins, so enrapt in their descriptions of pain that they would never notice that they had died or that the hotel itself lay open to the stars and rain, that the great edifice of their illness was constructed now of words alone and had no—

There was a crash like the war trumpets of Armageddon.

I came upright out of the chair so fast I nearly fell over and bolted out of the conservatory. I think that to my half-dreaming mind a noise that dire could only signal the destruction of the library. But when I came into the hall, I saw it was no such thing.

The hotel's main staircase was flanked by two massive stone urns, each large enough to conceal a child of five. There were Greek characters inscribed on each; on the right was ΤΙΜΟΣ, Honor, and on the left ΚΛΕΟΣ, Glory. Now ΚΛΕΟΣ lay on the floor, a huge chip out of its mouth, surrounded by a dismal knot of people, including Mr. Marten, Mrs. Stepney, and Miss Hunter, who, I gathered, had actually been coming down the stairs when the urn fell.

"It's a mercy you weren't killed," Mr. Marten was saying as I approached from one side and Major Berinford hobbled up from the other. "But what I don't understand is how it came to fall."

"I don't know," Miss Hunter said; between her shaking voice and paper-white face, she was clearly near fainting. "I was coming down the stairs, and it just *went*."

"I'm not blaming you for anything, dear girl," Mr. Marten said. "You couldn't have moved that thing even if you'd wished to. But I can't *imagine* . . . "

"Perhaps there was an earthquake," Mrs. Stepney suggested.

"*Rosemary*," came Mrs. Terpenning's voice from the conservatory door. "What have you done?"

"Nothing!" cried Miss Hunter, and, bursting into tears, she turned and ran back up the steps.

Much questioning and soul-searching among the staff and guests of the Hotel Chrysalis resulted in a tolerably exact timetable for the evening, but no clearer understanding of what had happened. At 8:03 p.m., immediately after dinner, Mrs. Terpenning had sent Miss Hunter upstairs to fetch her pills. This was attested by Madame Vlaranskaya, who had dined at their table and had much admired the generosity of aunt toward niece and the dutifulness of niece toward aunt. The two women—Mrs. Terpenning and Madame Vlaranskaya—had then accreted Mrs. Langtry and Mrs. Whittaker and gone into the conservatory. At the same time, Carrie, Doris, Mr. Ormont, and Mr. Grierson (another sufferer from "nerves," in this case meaning alcoholism) had gone into the game room, the room farthest from the front hall, to play bridge.

From 8:05 to 8:08, Molly Sefton and I had stood arguing beneath the ΚΛΕΟΣ urn. Then I had gone into the conservatory, and Molly had gone upstairs to check on one of her other patients. At 8:15, Major Berinford had crossed the front hall to the Small Library, where he joined Mrs. Stepney and two other women discussing the most recent developments in Russia. Most of the other guests had gone immediately upstairs to their rooms. No one reported noting anything odd about the ΚΛΕΟΣ urn. The staff were all accounted for, either in the kitchen cleaning up or in Mr. Marten's office discussing next month's budget.

At 8:25, Miss Hunter descended the stairs, and the urn toppled. When questioned by her aunt as to why it had taken her so unconscionably long to fetch three simple pills, Miss Hunter had explained that she had had a headache and had stopped to take some aspirin, for which (Mr. Marten interjected hastily) she could hardly be faulted.

The upshot of it all was that there were only ten minutes in which the urn had been unobserved between its not falling on Major Berinford or Mr. Ormont or me, and its swan dive before the horrified eyes of Miss Hunter. Even if that were time enough to shift the urn's balance sufficiently for it to fall—and even if one could somehow then keep it from falling until one was out of sight—even an able-bodied man could not have done it alone. Indeed, as the next day proved, it took three able-bodied men—Parris and two of the gardeners—the better part of an hour to hoist it back into place. No one could have done it; moreover, there seemed no reason why anyone would have wanted to do it. Reluctantly, in bafflement, Mr. Marten accepted Mrs. Stepney's earthquake theory, even though no one had felt a tremor and nothing else in the hotel had been disturbed. It remained a mystery.

Over the next week, the hotel continued to be plagued by falling objects. None was as spectacular as the urn, but we would come downstairs in the mornings to find pictures off the walls, books off the shelves. On Wednesday, eight packs of cards were scattered across the floor of the Small Library, and on Thursday, in the dining room, of the four settings at each table—laid out the night before in preparation for breakfast—one plate per table lay in shivered pieces on the floor. They looked as if they had been smashed by something heavy. People made nervous and unhappy jokes about poltergeists. As the week wore on, the nervousness increased and the joking decreased. By Saturday, people were starting to leave; Mr. Marten was close to a nervous breakdown.

By the next Tuesday, the residents of the hotel were reduced to eight in number, not counting Mr. Marten and his unwaveringly loyal staff: Mrs. Terpenning and Miss Hunter, Major Berinford, Madame Vlaranskaya, Mr. Ormont, Mrs. Whittaker, Carrie and Doris, and me. The neurasthenics and hysterics and pampered, discontented women had all taken themselves off. Those who remained gave various reasons for their stubbornness—I do not believe Carrie and Doris minded a bit—most of us, I think, had nowhere else to go.

Mrs. Whittaker pointed out, with great good sense, that no one had actually been harmed, and Major Berinford reiterated tirelessly that there would turn out to be a good scientific explanation for it all, and then the hotel's fair-weather friends would look a pack of fools.

I had been continuing my activities in the Greater Library, which seemed to be immune to the poltergeist's malice, and what I found there drove me, that Tuesday evening, to seek out Doris and Carrie. I could think of several things I would have preferred to do, including standing under the ΚΛΕΟΣ urn the next time it fell over, but I had been trained by my nature, by my professors, by my work, to pursue historical truth even into the mouth of a dragon, and I knew—I had known for days—that of all the people at the Hotel Chrysalis, Doris and Carrie were the two most likely to be able to answer the questions that nagged at me when I tried to sleep.

I found them in the Brocade Room, sitting by the fire and tatting lace, their thin twittering voices exploring the dreadful tragedies that had struck the family of Doris's second cousin Irene. They broke off when they saw me.

"Mr. Booth!" said Carrie. "Will you join us?"

"Thank you," I said and sat down. "I wanted to ask you something."

"Us?" said Doris.

"What about?" said Carrie.

"You've been here at the hotel longer than anyone else, haven't you?" I said.

"Oh, yes," said Doris.

"Probably," said Carrie. She was smarter than Doris and more watchful.

" . . . I wanted to ask you," I said, "how many people have died here that you know about? Died . . . oddly."

"Not like old Dr. Hastings and his heart attack, you mean," Carrie said.

"Yes, exactly."

"Well, let me see," Carrie said.

"There was Mr. Ampleforth," said Doris. "And Mr. Trask."

"Yes, and Mrs. Quincey and Mrs. Sharpe and Mrs. Leland—"

"Although that *might* have been suicide, which isn't that odd."

"Oh, Doris, honestly! Face down in the lily pond?"

"She might have done it herself," Doris said stubbornly.

"Mrs. Leland couldn't drag herself from the dining room to the conservatory without suffering vertigo and palpitations. And if she'd wanted to kill herself, she had all the veronal she needed right in her room. That's what Miss Elchester did when she committed suicide, although nobody ever did figure out why."

I sat and listened for more than an hour, while Carrie and Doris delved back through the hotel's dark history. After a while even Carrie forgot to be cautious, and they told me about the strange case of Mr. Sebastian Granger, who had hanged himself in the garden gazebo with a woman's long scarf. At least, everyone assumed he had done it himself, but since the gazebo floor had been spotlessly clean, despite the bog that a week's torrential rain had made of the path, there was no way to be sure. I knew, from my own researches, that Mr. Granger had died nearly a hundred years ago, but I did not say so, even when Doris gave me a vivid description of the gardeners bringing the body out—"Ooh, and the look on his face! It makes my blood run cold just thinking about it." I did not want them to suspect that I had guessed their secret, that they had been living here nearly as long as there had been any hotel to live in. I had found their signatures in one of the very early registers: "Doris Milverley" in a round, unformed, schoolgirl hand; "Kerenhappuch Soames" in a neat, crabbed copperplate. I wondered how many deaths they had been responsible for, particularly among the women suffering from postpartum depression who littered their conversation, but I knew—I could see in their bright amoral eyes—that their tolerance for me would come to an end far more quickly than I could find answers. I did not wish to make another of the company of the Hotel Chrysalis's unexplained deaths.

And then Carrie said, "Never mind the gazebo, Doris. What about the elevator?"

"The elevator?" I said, my voice squeaking a little.

"They should never have put it in," Doris said. "Nothing but trouble right from the first."

"It was a good idea," Carrie said. "I mean, with all the people here who can't manage the stairs. But Doris is right. They never could get it to run the way it ought, and then after the little girl died in it—what was her name, Doris?"

"Mary Anne Dennys."

"She was a nasty piece of work."

"Carrie!"

"She was, for all her poor mother thought the world of her. Spoiled rotten and *hard*. Supposed to be here to keep her mother company—what was it Mrs. Dennys was dying of?"

"Cancer."

"Thank you, yes, poor lady. And there's that awful little witch running away when Mrs. Dennys calls her and throwing tantrums in the dining room over a piece of burnt toast and being rude to everybody in sight. 'High-spirited,' her mama called her, but at ten that's not high spirits, that's willfulness. And I *still* think, Doris, that it was her killed those kittens."

"Now, Carrie, there was never any proof."

"Her hands were scratched, and a stone could have seen Mrs. Dennys was lying when she said Mary Anne had been with her all afternoon."

"How did she die?" I said, feeling the skin of my arms and back marbling with gooseflesh—knowing I did not want to hear their answer but compelled to ask all the same.

"No one quite knows," Carrie said. "It was odd, like you said you were asking after, Mr. Booth. She liked to break the elevator, did little Miss Dennys, and she was good at it, too."

"It was August," Doris said. "She and her mama had been here for nearly five months by then. She'd had lots of time to practice."

"Yes, and she knew that if she got herself stuck in it between floors, then it would mean a full afternoon's work for three or four men. She liked that, and they'd pull her out every time, her face wet with tears and promising she didn't know how she'd done it and she'd never do it again."

"That child couldn't keep a promise for love or money."

"She liked breaking things."

"Anyway, she got it stuck between the second and third floors on a Saturday afternoon. Screaming and carrying on she was, and her mother standing at the elevator doors on the third floor, calling down to her to be brave."

"Mrs. Dennys was white as a sheet. But, see, the only one who really understood how to make the elevator work was a young man named Colin Ricks. He was the hotel handyman—nice young man and clever with his hands. Collie Ricks loved that elevator like a baby, and he'd got to the point where he could get Mary Anne out of it in maybe an hour, although it'd take him another three to get it running again."

"He didn't like Mary Anne Dennys one little bit," Doris said.

"And who can blame him? But anyway, what Mary Anne didn't know, when she did whatever it was that she did to the elevator, was that it was Collie's afternoon off."

"He'd gone into Herrenmouth to play pool. So they had to send somebody into town after him, and they couldn't find him right away—"

"You've got it backwards again, Doris," Carrie said patiently, as if she had to correct Doris at this point every time they told the story. Possibly she did. "The trouble was that Collie *said* he was going to play pool, but he was really going to see Katy Dempsey, one of the local Jezebels. So they couldn't get ahold of Collie until he showed up at the pool hall, and by then Mary Anne had already been in that elevator for two hours."

"She'd quit screaming after the first three-quarters of an hour, although she was still shouting rude things up at her mama from time to time. It was about the time that Collie was getting back to the hotel that she called up and said she was frightened."

"Nobody believed her. By that time everyone in the hotel knew Mary Anne wasn't frightened of anything from a spanking to eternal damnation. But she said she was frightened, and she *sounded* frightened."

"Her mama asked her what she was frightened of, and she said she didn't know."

"Collie came up then, mad as a hornet, and he started in yelling at Mrs. Dennys about why couldn't she keep an eye on her hellborn brat and more of the same, with poor Mrs. Dennys getting paler and paler and shakier and shakier. And then Mary Anne started screaming."

"Really screaming."

"She wasn't faking. You can tell the difference, and nobody screams like that if they don't mean it. Collie took off like a rocket, racing up to the attic where all the machinery is, and he got that elevator unstuck in maybe half an hour."

"Mary Anne stopped screaming after ten minutes."

"She was dead when they opened the doors."

"No sign of what killed her."

"Just some scratches on her hands and face, and she might have got those trying to get out."

"They had an autopsy, and they didn't find a thing."

"One of the maids told me her brother worked for the county morgue, and he said the coroner said the little girl just plain died of fright."

"And me and Carrie, we've been wondering ever since what could have scared Mary Anne Dennys that bad."

"Hard as nails, that girl."

Carrie cocked her head. "Doris, I think we're frightening Mr. Booth."

"No, no," I said feebly.

"Just don't go in the elevator, and you're fine," Doris said. I could tell she meant to be comforting.

"How many others . . . "

"Oh, nobody like Mary Anne," Carrie said. "There have been a couple of heart attacks, I think, but nobody's died."

"Not since Mr. Nelson," Doris said.

"You're right, Doris. I was forgetting Mr. Nelson."

"He was here with his wife. He screamed, too, like Mary Anne."

"Stay out of the elevator," Carrie said.

"Thank you, I will," I said. And since they were frightening me and I was feeling shaky, I thanked them for their patience and crawled up to bed. I stood in front of my door for some minutes, looking down the hall toward the elevator, but nothing in the world could have made me go near it.

⊶

Wednesday morning in the garden, Mr. Ormont approached me. "Good morning, Mr. Booth."

"Good morning, Mr. Ormont," I said. He was fiftyish and stout, with exophthalmic blue eyes and white wispy hair. I had read his volumes of poetry—*The Velvet Phoenix*, *The Ambassador of Night*, *Roses for Horatio*—and admired them very deeply. The second or third time I had been placed next to him at dinner, I had worked up all my courage and told him so. He had seemed pleased, but that had been the extent of our conversation. I hoped he knew that I listened when he spoke about books with Mrs. Whittaker, but no matter how much I wanted to, I could not find the nerve to join in.

"May I walk with you?" he asked.

"Er . . . if you wish," I said.

We walked maybe thirty yards in silence before he said, "Mr. Marten tells me you've been archiving his records for him."

"I . . . I suppose so," I said. "I've been trying."

"Have you found anything of interest?"

"I . . . well, it depends on what you mean by 'interest.'"

"I have stayed here three times, and on each occasion, something odd has happened."

"Odd?" I said, thinking of Doris and Carrie's inexhaustible well of "oddness."

"Odd," said Mr. Ormont. He was looking at a topiary rabbit. "The first time, when I was a boy, I came here with my mother, who had been advised to see if the waters would do anything for her liver. They would not, and she died the next year. That was before Mr. Marten's time, of course. The place was run by a married couple. I have forgotten their names . . . "

"Victor and Selena Thackeray."

"Thank you, yes. I knew it was something like that, but I wanted to say Wordsworth. In any event, near the end of the month which we stayed, one of the chambermaids killed herself. Her name was Jemima Kell. She hanged herself in the conservatory and left a letter, which I heard about by hiding under one of the sofas in the parlor. In the letter she confessed that she had been, ahem, submitting to the virile affections of Mr. Thackeray for several months. She was afraid to leave the hotel, knowing that they wouldn't give her a character, but, she said, she couldn't bear Mrs. Thackeray coming to her bedroom at night to revile her. She'd been waiting and waiting to be turned off, and it wasn't happening, and she couldn't stand the waiting any longer, so she chose suicide instead. The odd part," and he turned his head to look at me, "is that Mrs. Thackeray had not the slightest idea that her husband was disporting himself with the maids. Not so much as an inkling. She left him that same night—or, rather, she was carried out the front door by her brother, herself being in strong hysterics."

He was waiting for a response. I said, "But if she didn't know . . . "

"Exactly. Who was whispering poison in Jemima Kell's ears? No one ever came forward, although of course I don't imagine that the culprit would."

"No," I said faintly, "I imagine not."

"The second time was only five years ago."

"What happened five years ago?" I had not found anything, except for a consumptive girl who seemed to have succumbed to her disease rather more swiftly than anyone had expected.

"Nothing too alarming—at least, no one died. It was just that I kept seeing a young man in the garden. I walked a great deal, as you do. And I would see a man, young, dark, always on a different path than mine, always heading off at an angle from where I was going. I never saw him near to, and I never got a good look at his face."

"And there were no dark young men staying at the hotel."

"Exactly. I have been looking for him this time, but I have not seen him."

" . . . Perhaps he found who he was looking for."

"Perhaps." He gave me a look like an owl's, the round eye under the steep, tufted eyebrow. "But you see, I am not the sort of man around whom supernatural events occur. Those two things, and now our poltergeist, are the only paranormal activity—if I have the phrase correct—that I have ever witnessed. And so the question has crossed my mind, is it perhaps something about the hotel?"

"Perhaps," I said unhappily.

"What have you found, Mr. Booth?"

"Odd things, Mr. Ormont." I paused, gathering my thoughts. "People tend to die here—I suppose, in a way, that isn't surprising, as this is a convalescent hotel. I almost . . . that is, I could easily have died here myself."

"But you didn't."

"No, and . . . and the people who do die here often aren't the people you'd expect. Carrie and Doris told me . . . there was a man named Ampleforth who died last year. I found his name in the register, and it said . . . that is, he was here for 'nerves.'"

"A convenient umbrella. I am here for 'nerves' myself."

"Yes, but it's not the sort of thing one dies of . . . generally."

"Not without some forethought, no."

It was a grim way of putting it. I said, "And that's what's odd. Mr. Ampleforth didn't commit suicide. He simply died."

"How simply?"

"They . . . they found him dead one morning when he didn't come down to breakfast. Mr. Marten kept the clippings of the inquest, and no apparent cause of death was found. They put 'heart failure.'"

"Which we all die of, yes, I see."

" . . . And Mr. Ampleforth isn't the only one. It gets harder as you go back to—to figure out whose deaths might be, er, odd. There's a suspicious number of women who checked in for postpartum depression and never checked out again. And then I found Marina Stedman." I didn't want to talk about Mary Anne Dennys and the elevator; I'd had nightmares about it all night.

"Something tells me I shall be sorry I asked, but who is Marina Stedman?"

"A lady who checked in and never checked out."

"Mr. Booth, you are becoming increasingly gnomic."

"I'm sorry. You see, she didn't check out, but she didn't die, either, at least . . . not that anyone knows. She just vanished."

"Vanished?"

"Into thin air. There's a long entry in the ledger—this was during the . . . the reign of Mr. Haverforth, who ran the hotel before the Thackerays. She liked to walk in the gardens, it says. One sunny afternoon, five people saw her walk into that gazebo—" I pointed; it was a pretty gothic curlicue in the middle of the roses, the same gazebo where Mr. Granger had been discovered, hanged with a woman's rose-patterned scarf that no one in the hotel had ever seen before— "and she never walked out."

"Oh, come now," said Mr. Ormont uneasily.

"There's only one door to the gazebo. An active and vigorous young woman—which Miss Stedman wasn't, being in the middle stages of dying of tuberculosis—a healthy young woman *might* have climbed out another way, but she couldn't have done so without . . . there would have been signs. And yet Miss Stedman walked into the gazebo at 3:33 p.m., by the watch of one Mr. Cypresson, who was testing the sundial, and at quarter of four, when one of her friends went to ask her if she wanted to join the group on the terrace for tea, she was nowhere to be found. They searched for her high and low, but they never found so much as a hair ribbon."

I stopped, nervously, realizing how much I had been talking. Mr. and Mrs. Siddons had always preferred me when I was silent, and Blaine had chided me sometimes about talking too much about boring things. But Mr. Ormont merely looked bleak and thoughtful.

"Vanished into thin air," he said.

He was listening and interested. I gathered my courage and plunged on: "And I've, er, there are several complaints from Mrs. Thackeray to the agency she used to hire maids. She says that she's tired of them sending out morbidly imaginative girls who can't look into a teacup without seeing disaster. And the turnover rate for servants here has always been abnormally high."

"I am not comforted," Mr. Ormont said.

"I'm sorry."

"No, why should you be? But I had hoped *I* was being 'morbidly imaginative.' Poets tend that way, you know."

"I'm afraid this isn't your imagination. This hotel seems to be a very odd place." And then there were Carrie and Doris—but I knew that Mr. Ormont liked them.

"You're taking it very calmly."

I grimaced. "I have some experience of . . . oddness, and I feel a debt to Mr. Marten. But you aren't running either, Mr. Ormont."

"I'm with Mrs. Whittaker. It doesn't seem to me that this poltergeist is intent on hurting anyone. Its disturbances take place at night, when no one is around, and they really aren't more than petty destruction."

" . . . Except for the urn."

"Yes, I know. It could have fallen on Miss Hunter."

"Do you think she's in danger?" I said, since it was a thought that had occurred to me.

"I think she might be. That was why I wanted to talk to you. None of things which I have witnessed, you see, have done anyone any direct physical harm. I am afraid there can be no doubt that the unfortunate Jemima Kell hanged herself."

"I understand. You were looking to see if the pattern would hold."

"Yes, but I find that it does not. The story of Marina Stedman is most disturbing."

"Yes," I said. And the story of Mary Anne Dennys even more so, but I could not bring myself to speak of it. I knew my voice would shake.

"Have you found any other evidence of poltergeists?" Mr. Ormont asked.

"I wasn't looking particularly, and certainly no one left any records, as Mr. Haverforth did. . . . But I remember that in the books for the hotelkeeper before him, a Mr. Lazenby, there was a run of about six months with inordinately high purchases of china. I assumed he had been changing the pattern, but perhaps . . . perhaps that assumption was unwarranted."

"Perhaps." Mr. Ormont sighed deeply. "Food for thought, Mr. Booth. Food for thought."

The gong sounded for lunch, and we went in.

Friday night, I dreamed about Blaine. He had died three years previously, in one of those episodes of "oddness" I had mentioned to Mr. Ormont, and I had dreamed about him and his death on and off for months. But it had been nearly a year since the last dream, and even sleeping I was aware of that oh-God-not-again feeling with which we greet nightmares that have grown almost too familiar to be disturbing. Almost.

In my dream, I was walking back into the apartment we had shared as undergraduates, although I was thirty-five and myself. And there, as I had known he would be, was Augustus Blaine, sitting in the overstuffed armchair by the bay window; he was still twenty—an undergraduate with the world in the palm of his hand— except for his eyes, which were the eyes of the man he had been when he died.

"Hello, Booth," Blaine said. "Do you want to sit down?"

"No, I don't think so. I can't stay long."

"Do you know what the wall of clouds is, Booth?"

"The . . . it's something out of a book I read as a child."

"That's what you *think* it is." Blaine winked at me grotesquely, his fresh, youthful face contorting around his ravaged, staring eyes. "Try again."

"I don't understand you."

"Boothie, Boothie." He shook his head, more in sorrow than in anger. "Come on. I know you're not that dumb. What's the wall of clouds?"

"It's what imprisons the maiden."

"That's better! That's almost right. But you're still not *thinking*."

"I don't know what you want!"

"I don't want anything, Booth my boy. This is just a dream."

As he said it, I woke up. I lay there for a moment, my heart hammering at my ribs, afraid—as I was always afraid when I woke from dreams of Blaine—to sit up or roll over or even open my eyes, lest I should find myself staring at Blaine's shape in the darkness of my room. As I was lying there, my hands clenched together beneath my pillow, I heard a noise.

It was a noise I had grown accustomed to in the weeks of my illness. One of the boards in the passage creaked when weight was put on it, more or less loudly depending on the weight and vigor of the person involved. This time, it was barely a gasp; if I had not been straining my ears, praying not to hear any noise that would signal Blaine's presence, I might not have heard it at all.

I was not afraid of anything outside my room, although it would later occur to me how exquisitely stupid that was. I got up and grabbed my dressing gown without a second thought for Blaine, and opened my door just in time to see a dim shape drifting around the corner at the end of the hall. By the long hair, I knew it was a woman. I remembered Mr. Haverforth's account of Marina Stedman's disappearance, and this woman was headed for the stairs, not the elevator, so I followed her.

There was only one way she could go without the telltale rattle and click of a door-latch, so I followed the corridor around to the stairs and down. There was no sign of the woman in the front hall, and I was standing, wondering which way to go, when I heard a crash like the fall of the Tower of Babel from the conservatory. In the daylight, I would have hesitated. In the middle of the night, dreamlike and brave, I ran to the conservatory door and looked in.

I believe I had been entertaining some confused notion that our poltergeist was not a poltergeist at all, but a purely material being intent on mischief. That idea was dispelled immediately.

The woman, a pale shape in the moonlit dimness, was standing motionless in the middle of the room. All around her potted plants were whirling like moons circling a planet. The crash I had heard had been one of the monstrous philodendrons; as I watched, another tipped and strewed its length across the floor. The woman was perfectly motionless, and she was nowhere near them. She was smallish and fair; of all the women in the hotel, there was only one she could be.

"Miss Hunter!" I said. And then, although I had never used her Christian name before, "Rosemary!"

Her eyes flew open. The pots crashed down around her, and she screamed, her hands going up to clutch at her face. I heard the breath she pulled in, like the prelude to a sob, and she cried out, "Oh God, where am I? What's going on?"

"I think you've had a bad dream, Miss Hunter," I said. "Are you all right?"

"Mr. Booth? What are you doing down here? What am *I* doing down here?"

"I heard . . . that is, I followed you. I think you were sleepwalking. It's . . . it's all right."

"But . . . " She was looking around, her eyes dark pits above her white, clutching fingers. "Oh, *no*. Did I do this?"

"Miss Hunter—"

"I did, didn't I?" She began to laugh, the pealing chimes of hysteria. "I'm the poltergeist! I broke the plates! I tipped the urn! I only wish it had smashed Aunt Erda!" And then she was sobbing in earnest, her hands covering her face, standing still in the midst of the wreckage.

I picked my way across to her, cautiously. "Miss Hunter," I said, "don't you—"

"Oh, can't you call me Rosemary?" Suddenly, she flung her arms around me, pressing her face into the front of my dressing gown. "If only you *knew*! I've been waiting and hoping, but you wouldn't say anything, and no one ever *does*! I feel like there's a wall around me, a wall nobody can see, and I can't break it down myself but if someone outside would just *push*!"

"The wall of clouds," I said without meaning to, putting one hand up awkwardly to pat her shoulder.

"Yes," she said, sobbing and laughing, her face still pressed against me. "That's exactly what it is, a wall of clouds. You try to push through it, and it's not where your hands are, it's everywhere else. Oh, I hate it, I hate it!"

"Miss Hunter," I said, trapped by the iron grip she had on my dressing gown, "why haven't you left your aunt?"

"I can't. I haven't any money, and she wouldn't let me. And no one will marry me. You won't marry me, will you?" She looked up at me then, her eyes huge and dark in her pinched face.

"I . . . I . . . Miss Hunter, I'm really not—"

"'Not the marrying kind,' I know. No man I meet ever is. It's because I haven't any money."

"I wouldn't care about that, but I couldn't . . . I just couldn't . . . "

"Of course not," she said bitterly. Behind her, I saw something move—the shards of terra cotta from the potted plants, starting to jerk and twist.

"Miss Hunter—"

"*Nobody loves me!*" she screamed at me, shoving me suddenly backwards. "*Nobody ever will! And it's all Aunt Erda's fault! Damn her! Damn her! Damn her!*" With each "damn," the pot shards leapt higher and higher, starting to spin around her, to form a miniature cyclone here in the middle of the desolated conservatory.

"*Rosemary, stop it!*" I shouted back at her, still too wrapped in dreams and moonlight to think of running.

She recoiled as if I had slapped her. The pot shards crashed to the floor again. We stood, staring at each other, both of us panting for breath. I did not know how to help her; I was not the hero for whom she waited, the man whose touch could dissolve the wall around her and set her free.

That was when I heard a noise, a noise I think I had been dreading, subconsciously, for days.

"I'm sorry, Mr. Booth," Miss Hunter said stiffly. "I've—"

"Hush! Do you hear it?"

"Hear what?"

"That's the elevator."

I glanced at her; her eyes were as big as bell wheels. "Aunt Erda!"

And just then, the noise of the elevator stopped.

"Oh God I think it's stuck," I said, and then we were both pelting down the corridor. Miss Hunter had somehow picked up on my urgency, for she asked no questions, merely ran after me until we came to the elevator doors. They were closed. Looking up at the sundial-style pointer, I saw that it had come to rest, with a kind of smug stolidity, between "2" and "1."

"What's she doing in the elevator?" I hissed at Miss Hunter.

"She must have been coming to look for me. She won't use the stairs on her own."

How like her, I thought savagely. "Go, run and wake . . . " I nearly said Collie Ricks, but he had left the employ of the hotel almost twenty years ago. "Go get Mr. Marten. Hurry!"

Miss Hunter shifted her weight, but her look was puzzled. "It's only a stuck elevator, Mr. Booth."

"No, it's not," I said, looking for a way to get the doors open. "*Go!*"

I glanced at her; even by the dim night-lighting of the hall, I could see the doubt in her eyes, the pull between her rational mind and whatever she had felt about the elevator on her own account. I had kept a nervous tally of the hotel guests who would use the elevator and those who would not, and I knew that Miss Hunter was among the Nots.

"This is no time to be reasonable," I said. "Please."

She went.

By the time she came back, I had managed to pry the doors open. Although even the shaft made the back of my neck prickle, I leaned in and shouted up, "Mrs. Terpenning?"

"Who's that?" a voice demanded from the elevator. She sounded irate; I hoped that was a good sign.

"It's just me, Mrs. Terpenning . . . er, Mr. Booth. Your niece has gone to get Mr. Marten, and we should . . . we should have you out of there in no time." It was the sort of comforting thing

Blaine would have said; he would have brought more conviction to it, too.

"What was she doing? What was she doing running around the hotel this time of night? And why were you with her?"

I knew I had to lie before I opened my mouth. "I think . . . we were both woken by a noise. I met her in the conservatory. The poltergeist has been busy again."

"Fool girl," Mrs. Terpenning muttered. I could not tell if I had been supposed to hear her or not.

The shaft was too dark, and I was too aware of the weight of the elevator over my head. I backed away again and found Miss Hunter beside me.

"Thank you," she whispered; then, more loudly, "Mr. Marten is fetching Parris. They'll be here in a minute." She leaned gingerly into the shaft. "Are you all right, Auntie?"

"No, of course not. What do you think you're doing, running around the hotel like a hoyden?"

Miss Hunter followed my lie. "I heard a noise, Auntie."

"And have you been hired by Pinkerton's, that you have to go snooping about?"

"No, Auntie."

Mr. Marten came trotting up, wearing an astounding peacock dressing gown. Parris was with him, in plain striped pajamas as sturdy and sensible as his person. Parris made his arcane investigations while Mr. Marten shouted reassurances up at Mrs. Terpenning—who shouted imprecations back down at him. We were joined by Carrie and Doris, in matching quilted bathrobes, and by Mr. Ormont, so there was a cloud of witnesses collected to hear Parris say, "It's the same old trouble, Mr. Marten. I'll go up to the attic."

"The same old trouble?" I said.

Mr. Marten shrugged crossly, like a wet cat. "The elevator has never been very reliable. Parris knows what to do."

A cricket-thin voice said at my elbow, "He's almost as good as Collie was."

I glanced down. It was Carrie, her long moonlight braids hanging over her shoulders like a schoolgirl's. Her black shoe-button eyes twinkled at me. "I saw you'd guessed," she said, her voice so low that no one but I could hear her. "But it's very unkind of you to be frightened of us, Mr. Booth. Doris and me, we wouldn't hurt a fly."

"I . . . I'm glad to hear it," I said; she patted my arm and moved back to Doris's side. I wondered if I believed her.

We were silent for a time, fifteen or twenty minutes. Mr. Marten made only one, feeble attempt to convince everyone to go back to bed; after that, he stood like the rest of us, uneasy, unspeaking.

Mrs. Terpenning's voice said sharply, echoing out of the shaft, "What was that?"

"What was what, Auntie?" Miss Hunter had gotten her mask back in place; no one would have guessed, seeing and hearing her, that it was her fury that lay at the root of all the destruction.

"That noise. What was it?"

"Probably just Parris up in the attic," Mr. Marten said.

But he was wrong. I knew it; Carrie and Doris knew it. Miss Hunter looked back at me, and I could see the same knowledge in her eyes. Even Mr. Ormont looked uneasy, and it was he who asked, "How long does it generally take?"

"Parris is very good. Half an hour or so."

"Hour and a half," said a creaky little whisper, but I could not tell if it was Doris or Carrie who spoke. Mr. Marten pretended not to hear.

"There it is again!" cried Mrs. Terpenning. None of us in the hallway could hear anything.

We waited in silence; it occurred to me how strange we would look to a late-arriving guest, all of us clumped anxiously around the gaping mouth of the elevator, like querents waiting for an oracle's response.

Fifty minutes after Parris had made his way up to the attic, Mrs. Terpenning cried, "Mr. Marten, are there *rats* in this hotel?"

"Good heavens, no!" Mr. Marten shouted up the shaft.

"I hear them! I hear them in the walls!"

"Mrs. Terpenning, that's just Parris working on the machinery. I assure you, there are no rats."

"I would never have come here if I'd known there were rats."

"Dear lady, there are no rats."

"Rosemary, we're leaving tomorrow. I will not stay in an unclean establishment."

"Yes, Auntie," Miss Hunter said reflexively. As Mr. Marten began shouting protestations up the shaft, she moved back to stand by me. "It isn't rats, is it?"

"It . . . I suppose it might be."

"But you don't believe it."

" . . . No. No, I don't."

Mr. Ormont joined us. "What do you think it is?"

"I don't know," I said, perfectly truthfully. "But Carrie and Doris told me . . . told me stories about this elevator. I don't think it's rats."

We fell silent again. Mr. Marten and Mrs. Terpenning argued themselves to a standstill. Fifty minutes became an hour, became an hour and ten minutes.

Mrs. Terpenning screamed. As Carrie had said of Mary Anne Dennys, no one would scream like that who did not mean it. "Things in the walls! I can see them! There are things in the walls! No! No!" We could hear banging noises, as if she was throwing herself against the sides of the elevator. She was still screaming, though I could no longer make out any words.

All of us had drawn away from the shaft, so that we were standing in a huddle, like sheep in the rain, against the far wall. Miss Hunter's hands were pressed against her face; even Carrie and Doris had the wide-eyed, solemn look of children who hear their parents fighting.

After five minutes, the screaming stopped. Miss Hunter's breath hitched in, like a sob. Ten minutes after that, the elevator whirred back into life, and the cage descended to the ground floor.

Parris was there almost as soon as the elevator was, his face white under the smears of oil and grease. It was he who opened the inner gate; none of the rest of us seemed to be able to move. Erda Terpenning fell forward into his arms; even before Parris checked her pulse, I knew that she was dead.

Somewhere around dawn, sitting in the Brocade Room with Carrie and Doris and Mr. Ormont, I fell into a thin, miserable doze, my phobia about sleeping in public broken at last.

Blaine said, "You are a coward, Booth. You always have been."

The dream was of my hotel room, with its white walls and functional furniture. Blaine was standing just inside the door, where Molly Sefton had been standing the first time I had been strong enough to ask her name.

I was lying on the bed, as weak and comfortless as if I were in the depths of the fever again. "Blaine," I said.

"There's evil here in this hotel," Blaine said. "You know it, and you won't do anything about it."

"What can I do?" I said, twisting and thrashing futilely in search of a more comfortable position. "I have no proof of anything."

"You could help Rosemary Hunter," Blaine said.

"No!" It was almost a shriek, though I did not feel as if I had the strength for anything more than a whisper.

"I didn't say 'marry her,' twit. I said, '*help* her.' What's the wall of clouds, Booth?"

"It's what imprisons the maiden," I said, as I had said the last time he had asked me that question.

"Who's the maiden, Booth?"

I woke up then, my heart hammering in my ears, to find myself slumped sideways in the armchair, alone in the Brocade Room. Someone had put an afghan over me. I stayed there, staring into the fire, pleating the afghan nervously between my fingers, and wondering: who was imprisoned by the wall of clouds?

Rosemary Hunter?

Or me?

It was that dream which prompted me to seek her out before I left. I had had an unpleasant and inconclusive interview with Mr. Marten beforehand, trying to tell him what I had found in my researches. He had not wanted to believe me; in fact, I was fairly sure he had not believed me. He and Major Berinford and Mrs. Whittaker were busy papering over Mrs. Terpenning's death with rationality and logic. Dr. Bollivar had signed the death certificate: heart failure.

Mr. Ormont knew better; he was already gone, and I thought that he would not be returning to the Hotel Chrysalis for a fourth time. I myself wished to leave and never see this place again, but I had to talk to Miss Hunter first.

I found her by the lily pond, sitting on her favorite bench and staring at the water. She looked up at my approach and smiled; it was a wan but valiant effort.

"May I . . . may I sit with you, Miss Hunter?"

After the first start, she hid her surprise well. "Of course, Mr. Booth," She moved over, and I sat down.

"I'm sorry," I said. "About your aunt."

"I wanted her dead. I did. You know that. But not like *that*."

"Of course not."

"Mr. Marten is very apologetic, but . . . you know, he says it was claustrophobia and a weak heart. He won't admit there's anything wrong. With the elevator, I mean."

" . . . No, he wouldn't. He can't."

"He's offered to let me stay here as long as I like, on the house. But I'm going to leave as soon as—as soon as things are settled."

"What will you do?"

"I don't know. She left me all her money, so I suppose I can do anything I want."

She sounded dreadfully forlorn about it, and I said, more forcefully than I had meant to, "Then *do*."

"Do what?"

"Do anything you want. Don't wait for someone to do it for you."

"Mr. Booth—"

"No, please, hear me out," I said, Blaine's accusations of cowardice ringing somewhere inside my head. "That's what you were doing, you were waiting for someone else to rescue you. But it doesn't work. It can't work. If anyone's going to rescue you, it has to be yourself. Otherwise you'll just end up another mean-spirited old woman."

"Like Aunt Erda."

" . . . I didn't mean it like that."

"I did." She touched my hand; I was not ready for it, and I flinched.

I looked away, at the lily pond. I could feel her looking at me, could feel the way that what she saw was changing, as she ceased to see herself as a captive princess, ceased to see me as the hero come to rescue her. After a long, meditative silence, she said, "I'm sorry."

She did not say for what, and I did not ask her.

We sat for another few minutes, in a more comfortable silence, and then she said, "I think I'll travel. I spent five years studying French. It seems a pity not to get any good out of it." She stood up; I stood up with her.

She extended her hand. "Thank you. For not rescuing me."

I looked into her face. She was smiling, lines of character suddenly showing themselves around her eyes and mouth, making her less pretty but far more vital.

"I . . . er, that is . . . I suppose you're welcome." She laughed, and we shook hands, and she made her way back toward the hotel.

I took one last walk around the gardens, for love of their beauty, and then went back to the hotel myself. I collected my bag, said good-bye to Molly Sefton, and walked down the staircase for the last time between TIMOΣ and chipped ΚΛΕΟΣ. Doris and Carrie were waiting for me in the front hall.

"Miss Soames," I said, setting my bag down. "Miss Milverley."

"Beautiful manners," Doris said.

"We're sorry you're leaving, Mr. Booth," Carrie said. "You were lovely to talk to."

"Thank you," I said.

"You don't want to go worrying about things," Doris said.

"It'll blow over. It always does."

"People forget so quick."

"Not like us."

"*We* remember."

"In another week, it'll be just another old lady with a heart attack," Carrie said. "People will come back, and everything will be fine."

"Everything?" I said.

In unison, they shrugged.

"More or less," Carrie said.

"It *is* a convalescent hotel."

"People do die here."

"That's why we stay."

"Doris! Honestly! You couldn't hold your tongue if your mouth was glued shut."

"Sorry, Carrie."

"And now you've got nice Mr. Booth thinking we're murderesses or vampires or something. We aren't anything of the sort, Mr. Booth."

"No," I said. "I know that." I knew what they were. I knew, because I'd asked Mr. Marten what would happen to Mrs. Terpenning's body, that Doris and Carrie generally laid out anyone who died in the hotel, and that had been the last piece of the puzzle. Not predators, but scavengers. The word "ghoul" is not a pretty one, and I preferred not to use it to their faces.

"*Such* a nice boy," Doris said.

"Will it really, er, blow over?" I asked.

"It always does," Carrie said. "I think it's something about the hotel. People just forget."

"Like little Pentecost forgot about us."

"He was such a sweet little boy. You'd never have thought he'd grow up to write such wicked poems." From which I deduced that Carrie had read at least part of *Roses for Horatio.*

"But he forgot us."

"People forget the nasty things."

"Maybe it's the water," Doris said brightly, and Carrie gave her a pained look.

"Someday, I suppose," Carrie said, "we'll get a manager as bright as you, and he'll put it all together, and then Doris and me will have to find a new home. But it hasn't happened yet."

"No," I said, thinking of Mr. Marten's nervous indignation at what I had tried to tell him. I picked up my bag and then set it down again. " . . . Will you do one thing for me?"

"Of course," Doris said.

"We'd be glad to," Carrie said.

"The elevator," I said. "Can you get him to tear it out?"

Doris looked at Carrie. Carrie said, "We can try. He's not so fond of the elevator, Mr. Marten."

"Not like Mr. Haverforth was."

"And it really *isn't* safe."

"Nasty old thing. Always breaking."

"Parris hates it. We'll talk to Parris."

I heard the car on the gravel of the drive and picked up my bag. "Thank you, ladies."

"You're welcome, Mr. Booth," Doris said.

"Don't come back," Carrie said.

I looked back at her. Her small bright eyes were perfectly serious, and I wondered, with a shudder, how much more Carrie and Doris could have told me about the hotel if I had known how to ask.

"No," I said. "I'll remember."

She nodded, and then they pattered out after me to stand on the porch and wave their handkerchiefs until the car turned the corner of the drive, and the great cloudy-gray wall of the Hotel Chrysalis was lost from sight.

THE GREEN GLASS PAPERWEIGHT

When he died, Eleazar Siddons named me as one of the executors of his will. This responsibility was both unlooked-for and unwanted; he had been my guardian from the time I was twelve, and I had hated him as much as he had hated me.

My co-executor was Mr. Siddons' godson, a blank-faced, decent man named Henry Levington-Price. After the funeral, when that fat basilisk, the widow, had been carried off to the house of her spinster cousins, Mr. Levington-Price and I met the lawyer, Mr. Eversleigh, at the Siddonses' house.

Mr. Eversleigh was the son of the Eversleigh who had been the lawyer of both Mr. Siddons and my father. I had chosen when I reached my majority to place my affairs in the hands of another firm, so I had never met the younger Mr. Eversleigh, but I recognized him instantly. He was an eerily accurate replica of his father, even down to the narrow, gold-rimmed spectacles and the three-strand comb-over. I told myself vehemently that it was silly to be afraid that I would walk back into my childhood and followed Mr. Eversleigh and Mr. Levington-Price into the study.

The room looked exactly as it had looked when I had left the Siddons house for good at the age of eighteen, as if the intervening years had never happened, as if my escape had been nothing but a dream. It still seemed to me that at any moment the door might open and Mr. Siddons come in, his mouth as vicious as a snapping turtle's, the cane he favored switching back and forth at his side. I reminded myself that I had just seen him buried and set myself to listen to the lawyer.

The will was a simple document. The bulk of the estate went to Mrs. Siddons, with small bequests to Mr. Siddons' two goddaughters, a larger bequest to Henry Levington-Price, and "'to Kyle Murchison Booth, by whom I did my duty during his minority—'"

Mr. Eversleigh broke off with a cough and gave me an uncomfortable look over the tops of his glasses.

"Go on," I said. "I . . . I know how Mr. Siddons felt about me."

"'I bequeath his choice of one object from my house, its value not to exceed fifty dollars, and the choice to be approved by my wife, Hermione Eldred Siddons, and my godson, Henry Levington-Price—so that he may remember me.'"

There was a short, appalled silence.

"It would have been less insulting to leave you nothing at all," said Mr. Levington-Price.

I pinched the bridge of my nose. "That, er, that was the point."

I knew the incident to which Mr. Siddons had been referring. When I was fourteen, I had come back from my prep school for the summer to discover that the Siddonses had sold my parents' house. It had been the last time I had sought a confrontation with Mr. Siddons, and in my memory I could hear my own voice, shrill with indignation, "You didn't even leave me anything to remember them by!" and see the vicious, self-righteous thinning of Mr. Siddons' lips. The caning he had given me had left me unable to sit down for a week. I supposed I was pleased, in a vindictive way which horrified me, that the memory had rankled him so badly.

The lawyer said, "That's it for the substance of the will," and read off the closing legal formulas.

It took perhaps two hours for Mr. Levington-Price and me to finish our obligations. When we were done, and Mr. Levington-Price had generously arranged with Mr. Eversleigh that if anything else came up, I should not be bothered with it, they both looked at me uneasily, and Mr. Levington-Price said, "Do you want to choose your bequest now, Mr. Booth? I'm glad to wait, I'm sure."

I was about to say, No, thank you, I want nothing from this house, when I remembered that several of my parents' belongings had mysteriously ended up in the Siddonses' possession. I said, " . . . Thank you. You're very, er, kind."

"It's no trouble," Mr. Levington-Price said. He grimaced and added, "I'm not looking forward to facing Mrs. Siddons." Politely, Mr. Eversleigh pretended not to hear.

We began a slow, methodical parapeteisis through the house. I felt like the foulest kind of vulture, peering at the Siddonses' furnishings, wondering how much they were worth and if they had belonged in my parents' house before. I was and am sure that invoking such a feeling, a beslimed sense of moral uncleanliness, was precisely the reason that Mr. Siddons put that clause in his will. He had never forgiven me for suggesting that he partook of the sin of avarice.

I was disturbed to discover how few things I could identify positively as having belonged to my parents. Everything in the house was familiar, but I had lived there for six years—and had done my best since then to forget the house, my guardians, even my parents, whose deaths had felt so powerfully like betrayal. And those few things—the vanity with the beveled mirror, the original John Singleton Copley, the set of Sèvres china—were all worth far more than fifty dollars.

I came to the front parlor in this state of gloom, Mr. Levington-Price and Mr. Eversleigh lingering tactfully at the door, and began to investigate the drawers of the Chippendale secretary—which, since Mrs. Siddons did no writing, served only for ornament. One drawer stuck. I tugged at it; it shot open and stuck again with what seemed like almost sentient malice, hurling the single item within to the very front of the drawer. I recoiled so hard that I nearly fell over backwards, catching myself at the last moment on my right hand and twisting my ankle painfully.

"Mr. Booth?" said Mr. Levington-Price.

"I'm all right," I said, a purely reflexive lie.

Inside the drawer, the green glass paperweight stared at me balefully.

I had found the green glass paperweight very shortly after I had come to live with the Siddonses. They took no pleasure in my company, and, although they had not exactly encouraged me to spend most of my time in the disused rooms on the third floor, they had certainly placed no hindrance in the way of my doing so.

A week or so after my thirteenth birthday, in a shabby, miserable sitting room whose windows looked out on nothing but brick walls, I opened the drawer of a three-legged end table and found the green glass paperweight inside. It was of a size to fit comfortably in the palm of my hand—at thirteen I was already gangly and awkward, and my hands were as big as some adults'—its texture smooth and ridged at the same time and infinitely pleasing. It was heavy for its size, as if it were stone rather than glass. In color it was a pale green; it would be wrong to call it "milky," because that suggests opacity, and the green glass paperweight was luminously translucent. I used to stare into it for hours, imagining that if I just looked hard enough, I would find it to be truly transparent. But it was never quite—except for once, and that might have been a dream.

I had already learned that the Siddonses classified as "stealing" touching anything that did not belong to me, so I put the paperweight back in its drawer before I left the room. But I remembered how it had felt in my hand, and I crept back up to that third-floor sitting room several times in the next two weeks, to sit in the dust, cradling the paperweight in my hands, staring into it and pretending that it was a magician's crystal ball. After a caning from Mr. Siddons—he seemed to believe that I was clumsy on purpose, and if I was just punished enough, I would stop being intransigent and stop breaking things—I decided that I did not care if they punished me for stealing. I took the paperweight to my bedroom, and that night I lay in bed, its hard, cold smoothness cupped in my palms, and imagined that if I looked into it, I would see Mr. Siddons being eaten by Apollyon. The fantasy made me feel better; it was the first time I had been punished by the Siddonses that I had not cried myself to sleep.

I was sent to Brockstone School that spring term; I had not attended in the fall because of my father's slow dying, and the Siddonses did not want to wait until the next school year began. The schoolwork was no difficulty; even coming in half a year behind, I was well ahead of my classmates. But I made no friends, being too shy to venture an approach to anyone and everyone else having found their particular friends months ago. The boys began to say that I was peculiar and stand-offish, and I was an easy target for bullies. When I was sent back to the Siddons house for the summer, I wrapped my hands around the green glass paperweight and imagined my tormentors being burned in the fiery furnace that did not touch Shadrach, Meshach, and Abednego.

Mostly, though, I used the paperweight as a means of catharsis for my hatred of the Siddonses. Every time Mr. Siddons caned me, every time Mrs. Siddons said to one of the ladies who visited her that I was "backwards" or "disturbed," I would go up to my room and lock the door—although I was not supposed to—and sit on the bed with my back against the wall, the paperweight cradled in my hands. I stared into the paperweight's cool depths and thought about Mrs. Siddons being eaten by dogs, like Jezebel, or the earth opening beneath Mr. Siddons' feet and swallowing him whole.

I came to imagine myself as putting my anger in the paperweight, along with all the horrible things I thought and did not say. I had never been a voluble child, but it was in my early teens that I began to stammer and pause—or even stop dead in the middle of what I was saying—to be unable to get through a sentence before the person to whom I spoke impatiently finished it for me. Everything I said in the Siddonses' hearing was offensive; I could not express an opinion, state a fact, or ask someone to pass the butter without Mrs. Siddons remarking that in her day children were brought up to be nicely spoken and she couldn't imagine what my poor mother (with the word "crazy" never spoken but always implied) had been thinking. Or if Charybdis was sleeping, Scylla would bark that there was no need to

mumble, and weren't they teaching me how to behave like a gentleman at that damned expensive school? And if I said nothing, one or
the other of them would fix me with a petrifying stare and demand
to know what I was thinking. They did not trust my silence.

All this I poured into the green glass paperweight. And gradually, as time dragged on and my life did not change, it came to seem
to me that the paperweight was responding. It never warmed, no
matter how long I held it, but I began to see—or to imagine that I
saw—flashes of light deep within it, and it began, contradictorily,
to seem to admit less light into its depths, as if it were clouding up
from within.

I should have been scared. Twenty-one years later, I *was* scared,
staring at that thing in the drawer and remembering the dream
that—perhaps—had not been a dream. But I had been barely adolescent, friendless, grieving still, trapped under the authority of people
who hated me. I continued my orgies of hatred, pouring anger and
venom and vengeance into the paperweight, and the paperweight
continued to suck those things out of me. By August of the year I
was fourteen, I cannot remember ever being angry except when the
paperweight was in my hands. Without it, I became passive, meek,
infinitely apologetic; holding it, I raged and seethed and hated, as
if I were a cup running over with poison. If Mr. Siddons' sin was
avarice, then mine was surely wrath.

And then, in the last week of August, the last week before I had
to return to Brockstone School, I had the dream.

But it was not a dream. I had told myself, day after day until I
finally forgot about it, that it was a dream, but now, crouching awkwardly on my heels in the Siddonses' front parlor, I knew it had not
been a dream. And I had known it was not a dream at the time. I
had been wide awake.

It had been late. I had heard the Siddonses come upstairs, sepa-
rately, first her heavy and ominous tread, then his light, swift stride,
like the tapping of an insect against a window pane. When I was

sure they were both asleep, I sat up in bed again, found the paperweight in the dark by feel, and surrendered myself to my fury.

After a time, I became perfectly sure that the paperweight was glowing. I bent over it, closer, and the clouds within it parted, and I saw, clear as daylight, trapped within the paperweight's green shell, the image of myself: a skinny, gawky boy with untidy brown hair, his ankles and wrists protruding from his pajamas, sitting cross-legged on his bed in the dark, hunched over something in his hands which glowed green.

As I watched, the boy got out of bed, still clutching the paperweight in his left hand. He crept silently to the door, out into the hall, down the long, cold stairs. He moved smoothly despite the darkness; at the bottom of the stairs, he glanced over his shoulder, and I saw that his eyes glowed the same green as the paperweight. He went to Mr. Siddons' study, slipped a key out from under the blotter, and unlocked the bottom desk drawer. He took Mr. Siddons' loaded pistol out of the drawer and started back toward the door.

My hands spasmed, and I dropped the paperweight. The light died out of it instantly. My hands were cold, and my heartbeat was too fast, too painful. After a long moment, I fumbled my handkerchief off the bedside table and picked up the paperweight. It sat inert, a lump of glass. Without giving myself time to think about it—for if I had thought about it, I would surely have panicked and brought down disaster upon my head—I got out of bed, slipped out of my bedroom, and snuck back up to the third floor sitting room where I had found it. I put it back in the three-legged end table, still wrapped in my handkerchief, and crept back downstairs to bed. Two days later I returned to Brockstone School and began the process of convincing myself it had all been a dream. By the Christmas holidays, I had succeeded in forgetting about the paperweight entirely, and I had not thought about it again from that day to this.

"This," I said, and I barely recognized my own voice. "I take this as my bequest."

Mr. Levington-Price came with me to speak to Mrs. Siddons, since her approval, too, had to be secured. He saw how troubled I was, but he was compassionate and did not ask me to explain myself.

Mrs. Siddons was sitting in her cousins' front parlor, knitting. I could feel myself becoming mesmerized by her knitting needles, just as I had as a child. It took a real effort to drag my gaze away from them, and I made no effort to look her in the face.

"Hello, Aunt Hermione," said Mr. Levington-Price and leaned over dutifully to kiss her cheek, although I did not imagine that it gave either of them pleasure. "How are you doing?"

"I am well," she said. "Why is *he* here?"

"It's about Uncle Eleazar's bequest, Aunt Hermione," Mr. Levington-Price said, and I admired him, because he did not sound nervous. "Did he tell you?"

"Yes. Foolishness, I thought, but Mr. Siddons was like that. Generous to a fault."

I clenched my teeth and swallowed hard. I said, "Do you mind . . . that is, I thought . . . er . . . "

"You haven't changed in the slightest," she said, worlds of damnation in her voice. "What is it you want?"

I took the paperweight out of my pocket and unwrapped the handkerchief I had used to pick it up.

She leaned forward, peering at it short-sightedly. "That's Cousin Eunice's paperweight. Where on Earth did you find it?"

"It was in your secretary, Aunt Hermione," Mr. Levington-Price said hastily, having detected the note of accusation in her voice.

I said, "Who's, er, Cousin Eunice?"

"Mr. Siddons' cousin. She lived with his parents when we were first married. His mother's charity case, or so I always understood. She died of a heart-attack, thankfully before she became my problem."

My heart was thudding horribly against my ribs. I said, "Is it . . . is it all right?"

"Oh, it's fine with me. I believe Mr. Siddons' father used it for a few years after Cousin Eunice's death, but neither Mr. Siddons nor I ever cared for it."

I believe that she sensed somehow that the paperweight upset me, for she would never have given me anything she thought I wanted.

" . . . Thank you," I said and bolted out of the room. I was still struggling into my overcoat in the hall when Mr. Levington-Price came out.

"Mr. Booth," he said, "I don't wish to pry, but . . . what is the matter with that paperweight?"

I looked at him. He was decent and upright and would never understand what I had done with the green glass paperweight, but for that very reason his company might be a comfort.

I said, "Mr. Levington-Price, there is one thing I have to do. If I . . . if I tell you about the, er, the paperweight . . . will you accompany me?"

"Gladly," he said.

"Then, er, come."

We left the house of Mrs. Siddons' spinster cousins and walked until I was sure that Mrs. Siddons' terrible eyes could not see me.

"Now," I said. I took the paperweight out of my pocket, unwrapped it. I touched it with the tip of my left index finger.

A spark of green light shot into the depths of the paperweight; for a moment, I felt the full force of my raw, adolescent hatred. I jerked my finger away as if the paperweight had burned me—though of course it had not; it was as indifferently cold as ever.

"My God," said Mr. Levington-Price.

"Did you, er . . . "

"I felt . . . I don't know." His bland, good-natured face was creased with distress. "I felt as if I wanted to . . . to *kill* someone, and yet, I don't know who or why."

"Yes," I said, and standing there in the cold, the paperweight resting on my handkerchief in my palm, I told him about the paperweight, about what I had seen in it, what I had done with it.

He did not disbelieve me. I think that single surge of abyssal wrath, a feeling which Henry Levington-Price had surely never experienced before in his life, would have convinced him of far more extraordinary things. When I had finished, he was silent a moment, frowning, and said, "But you found it in Mrs. Siddons' secretary. How could it . . . ?"

"I don't know," I said. "Either Mr. Siddons found and moved it, or . . . or it moved itself."

"But—"

"He died of a heart attack. Where . . . where did they find him?

"In the front parlor. But you don't think . . . "

"Yes. I think he walked into a trap I set for him twenty-one years ago." I turned my hand over, letting the paperweight fall. For a moment, it shone in the dim November sunlight, as beautiful and perfect as if that were the moment for which it had been made, and then it hit the pavement and shattered. I ground the shards to splinters, then to dust, with the heel of my shoe.

Mr. Levington-Price was silent for a long moment, watching. Then he said, "You couldn't have known. No one could. It isn't even . . . "

I thought of the boy I had been, of his murderous, pent-up hatred, of his strange, silent, green glass maelstrom of wrath.

"No," I said. "I knew."

LISTENING TO BONE

In clement weather, I sometimes went to the Henry Davenport Public Zoological Gardens on my lunch break. The zoo was free to the public, and an hour spent watching the *credo quia impossibile* gaudery of the flamingoes or the bright-eyed inquisitiveness of the otters was more than worth the discomfort of the crowds. That particular early June day, I was standing by the elephant's cage when there was a tug at my sleeve and a high-pitched voice said, "This is my bone, and I want you to have it."

I do not like children. I do not know how to speak to them. They frightened and confused me when I was a child myself, and they frighten and confuse me now that I am an adult. I could not determine either the age or the sex of the child clutching my sleeve, but it was an unhealthy-looking creature, its skin almost gray in the bright summer sunlight; its pale curls were badly tangled, and although its clothes were clearly expensive and well-made, they were dirty and torn.

"I beg your pardon," I said, looking around frantically for an adult that might belong to this tatterdemalion.

"I want you to have my bone," the child said. Its blue eyes were as glassy as marbles—definitely not well, this child—but their stare was accusing. And the hand that wasn't gripping my sleeve was extended, grubby palm up, proffering a small, unremarkable bone.

"I, er . . . that's, er, very kind of you, but—"

"I *want* you to *have* it." Out-thrust lower lip, and one did not need to know anything about children to recognize the signs of an imminent temper tantrum. I looked around again, even more desperately, but still there was no sign of a parent in the offing.

"I, er . . . " But there was really nothing else I could do, not without creating a scene. "Thank you." And I let the creature give me its bone.

It was a mistake. I knew it as soon as those cold dirty fingers touched my skin. "Now you can help me," the child said. "I'm lost, and I want to go home."

"But I can't—" Automatically, I shoved the bone in my pocket. I wanted it not to be touching my skin, and I knew I could not simply drop it, not here with the child's blue eyes eviscerating me.

"I got away from the bad man, and I want to go home. But I'm lost, and you have to help me."

"I can't help you," I said to the child in a ludicrous imitation of firmness. "I have to get back to work. But if you're lost, you should, er, find a policeman. *He*'ll help you." I pulled free—with an effort, for its stick-like little fingers were remarkably strong—and fled, ig- nominiously routed. I did not care, so long as I could get away from those staring blue eyes and that piercing voice.

At the gate, I looked back, a foolish Orpheus. But the child was nowhere in sight. I hoped, somewhere between guilt and relief, that it was taking my advice.

***

When I came out of the Parrington that evening, the child was wait- ing for me at the foot of the stairs.

I went backwards against one of the flanking sphinxes, wish- ing its guardianship were more than symbolic. The child fixed me with its accusing blue stare and said, "I'm lost, and you have to help me."

It was also patently invisible to the other people going up and down the steps, to the people passing by on the sidewalks, and if it could track me from the zoo to the museum, it was not lost by any conventional definition of the word. Looking at it more carefully, in surrender to the fact that I could not pawn it off on a policeman or otherwise escape it, I saw the leaden tinge to its lips, saw that some of the smudges I had taken for dirt were actually bruises ringing its throat, and although it was standing beneath one of the tall lamps that guarded the stairs at the bottom as the sphinxes did at the top, it cast no shadow. The fixed blue eyes did not blink.

My bone, the child had said, and suddenly, horribly, I understood what it meant.

It took me three tries, but I managed to ask, "What is your name?"

It said only, as it had said before, "I got away from the bad man, and I want to go home. You have to help me go home." It started up the stairs, its clawed hands reaching.

My nerve broke; I bolted back into the museum, and the child did not follow.

All I had accomplished was to trap myself in the Parrington. I did not make the experiment of trying the back door, but retreated to my office to think.

Asking why the creature had chosen to give me its bone was pointless. My foolish and unwilling foray into necromancy had made me attractive to such things, as a magnet is attractive to iron. Whether the child could or wished to harm me was an equally futile line of inquiry, although one singularly difficult to dismiss from consideration.

The only proper question was: who was this child, and how could I help it?

I got away from the bad man, it had said. And it had appeared at the zoo. There was a faint sense of familiarity, an echo as of a story I had once known. Sharp voices murmuring in my guardians' parlor, a thin exhausted woman, always in black. "She used to be quite a beauty," Mrs. Siddons's flat gloating voice said in my memory. "Before her Trouble, of course."

A noise. I looked up—screamed, jerking back so violently that I overbalanced and fell. The child had found me again, its face pressed against the glass of the window, blue eyes goggling. There was no breath to mist the pane. I do not remember how I got into the hall, whether I crawled or ran, my mind yammering, Thank God I keep the window closed, thank God, thank God. I slammed the door shut, pressed myself against the opposite wall, the cool plaster making me aware of pain in my hip and shoulder. I had hit the floor hard and badly. But the fall seemed also to have jarred something looks, for I could now remember that woman's name: Rosalie Merton, born a Crowe, and if that was not proof that birth and breeding could not save one from grief and horror, then nothing was.

It was a relief to have something to do, even if it involved going into the stacks. The revenant pressed against my window like a ghastly moth was worse even than the causeless noises and capricious electricity of the Mathilda Rushton Parrington Memorial Library Annex, and I knew where to find what I sought: the wedding announcement of Rosalie Crowe and Harcourt Merton. Then, armed with that date, I plunged into the newspaper archives and secured a teetering armful of bound collections of the *Hub-Telegraph*, starting two years after the Crowe-Merton marriage and continuing through the tenth anniversary. I fled the stacks for the Archivists' Reading Room, which had no exterior windows and thus was safe.

I hoped.

There was not much information reported in the *Hub-Telegraph*. There never is. But I had long practice at reading between the lines, and the story came back to me with very little prompting.

Harcourt and Rosalie Merton had had one child, Gareth, who had been, due to the inability of Rosalie Crowe Merton's brothers to beget children on their wives, heir to both the Merton and the Crowe fortunes. One sunny June day when Gareth Merton was five—and I was not at all surprised when I saw the date: the dead are strongest on their anniversaries—his mother yielded to his pleading and allowed him to go to the Davenport Zoo as part of a small friend's birthday celebration.

That afternoon, Gareth Merton disappeared and was never seen alive again.

There had been the inevitable paraphernalia of sightings, ransom notes, imposters, clairvoyants. But the clairvoyants were frauds; the ransom notes were fakes; the sightings led nowhere. No one was ever arrested. Gareth Merton was presumed dead, and the fortunes to which he was heir were dismantled.

And now Gareth Merton wanted to go home.

"What am I supposed to do?" I said and flinched at the echoes of my voice from the marble walls. The Merton family had died out; the house that Gareth Merton had called home had burned down twenty years ago. Doubtless the Mertons were buried, like the Crowes and the Parringtons and the Booths, in Resurrection Hill Cemetery, but would the child consider that its home?

Somehow, wretchedly, I did not think so.

I am not given either to obscenities or to blasphemies, but at that moment I was sorely tempted, transfixed by a horrifying image of being accompanied by that loathsome, demanding creature everywhere I went for the rest of my life.

I slept that night, little and fitfully, on the couch in the staff lounge, blinds down, curtains drawn.

I could not stay in the Parrington forever; I was not convinced, in any event, that the revenant might not find its way in, given time. I washed as best I could in the men's lavatory, but I had slept in my clothes, and I looked it. At least it was unlikely anyone would notice white stubble on pale skin and realize I had not shaved.

I hoped.

I kept moving that morning, not sure whether I feared more being caught by the revenant or by the museum director. Fortunately, I saw neither of them, and there was a surprisingly large number of things I legitimately needed to do in various storerooms, card catalogues, and other nooks and crannies of the museum. I would have been rather pleased with myself if it had not been for the louring knowledge that I was merely delaying the inevitable. And that I still did not have any answers, or even any wild guesses.

At noon or thereabouts, Miss Coburn came upon me in the staff lounge, where I was gloomily contemplating a lunch of cold coffee and stale doughnuts. "Growing a beard, Mr. Booth?"

"What? Oh, er, no. I . . . "

"You look terrible. What's wrong?"

"I, er . . . "

"Spend your lunch money on books again?" she said, and I blushed at her teasing.

She relented, smiled. "I'd be happy to take you out for lunch, if you'd like."

"No, I, er . . . " But perhaps the revenant would not approach me if I had a companion. And I could trust Miss Coburn. "That is, thank you, Miss Coburn. I would be very grateful for your company. But I can, er, buy my own lunch."

"Then why . . . ?" She frowned at me. "Are you in trouble?"

"No. Yes . . . er. Maybe. Do you know anything about Gareth Merton?"

"Who?"

"The heir to the Crowe-Merton fortune."

"But there *is* no . . . Oh. You mean the little boy who disappeared."

I nodded. She tilted her head, frowning at me suspiciously. Miss Coburn had witnessed one of my previous encounters with the supernatural, and she was clearly putting the pieces together in her head. I nodded again.

"Let's go out to lunch," Miss Coburn said decisively.

She took me to a harborside restaurant, where we ate clam chowder and sourdough bread, and I told her what I could about Gareth Merton. Although there had been no sign of the revenant when we left the museum, I was careful to sit with my back to the window.

"But what do you think he wants you to do? Find his body?"

"No. That's the, er, bone."

Miss Coburn shuddered.

"Sorry. But it, er, it wants to go *home*. I just don't know where it thinks its home is."

"Home is where the heart is," Miss Coburn said.

"But where is that? It doesn't *have* a heart any longer. And there's no one left . . . the Mertons have died out, and the children who were Gareth Merton's friends wouldn't—"

"Wait," Miss Coburn said, frowning fiercely into her coffee. "Children . . . children . . . Aunt Ferdy said something once . . . There was an imposter, you know."

"Yes."

"And *he*'d remember Gareth Merton, I bet."

"But how on Earth am I supposed to find him?"

"You don't have to. You already know him. He's Mr. Garfield, the piano tuner."

The Parrington had two Blüthner concert grand pianos, which were used for fund-raising concerts and were hired punctually four times a year by a consortium of the city's piano teachers, who apparently wished to hold piano recitals in the most overpowering venue possible. And the man who tuned the Blüthners was Mervyn Garfield. As Miss Coburn had said, I knew him. I made a habit of slipping into the concert hall when he had finished tuning, so that I could listen to him play. I never said anything; I only wanted to hear the music that came pouring out from beneath his strong, square hands. I had never thought about what he was beside a piano tuner, never wondered what other lives he might have had.

"Do you know his address?" I asked Miss Coburn.

"No, but I can find out." She rose and, after a quick murmured exchange with the maître d', strode out of the main dining room. Without wanting to, I turned my head. The revenant was standing on the restaurant's patio, oblivious to the patrons seated around it, as they were oblivious to it. I saw its lips move: *I'm lost. I want to go home.*

And then Miss Coburn returned, and I turned back to the table hastily and gratefully.

"Is he . . . there?" Miss Coburn said, and I noticed she was being very careful not to look at the window.

"Yes. But I don't think you'll . . . that is, no one else seems to be able to see, er, him."

"Doesn't matter," she said with a shiver, and kept her face carefully averted. Illogically, I felt better for this small proof that she believed me.

She said briskly, "According to Aunt Ferdy, Mr. Garfield lives in a boarding house on Hamish Street. I wrote down the address." She tore a page from her memorandum book and handed it to me. "Are you going to go talk to Mr. Garfield?"

"I have to do *something*," I said, not turning around, not yielding to the force of the revenant's lightless blue eyes. "At least . . . at least he will remember."

"Yes," said Miss Coburn and signaled for the check, her eyes still avoiding the window as resolutely as if Gareth Merton were visible to her.

Hamish Street was one of a tangled skein of streets not old enough to have historical interest but too old to be fashionable. It was within walking distance of the Parrington if one did not mind a long walk—which, when faced with the horrors of the city's public transportation system, I embraced gratefully as the lesser of two evils.

The boarding house on Hamish Street was a massive, moldering Queen Anne, its porch railings leaning erratically out of true and its clapboards peeling leprously. I rang the bell with a sense of dread not entirely attributable to the revenant which had trailed me all the way from the restaurant and was now standing at the bottom of the porch steps, its dull blue eyes fixed on me. It had not attempted to approach me, although that might have been because I set a pace fast enough that it was difficult for the creature to keep up at all.

The door was opened by a small woman, bright-eyed and neat as a wren; I observed that whatever the state of the exterior of the house, the interior was spotless. "Can I help you?"

"I, er, I'd like to speak to Mr. Garfield, please. Is he in?"

"Is it about a piano?"

"No. It's, er, a personal matter."

She seemed surprised, but said, "Yes, sir. Just a minute, and I'll go to fetch him."

I waited in the hall, regarded somnolently by two enormous white cats on the stair-landing. It was more than a minute, but less than five, before I heard the landlady's voice " . . . and mind the cats on the landing," and Mr. Garfield's cane came into view, followed by Mr. Garfield himself. I noticed that the cane nudged the cats only very gently, and the cats, clearly resigned to the eccentric behavior of human beings, did not even twitch.

Mr. Garfield stopped two steps up and said, "Mrs. O'Mara said there was someone here to see me?"

"Er, yes," I said. "You don't know me, but my name is Kyle Murchison Booth—"

"At the museum?" Mr. Garfield had turned his head toward the sound of my voice, although his clouded eyes seemed to be gazing past my left shoulder.

" . . . Yes."

"But you wouldn't come about the Blüthners." He came down the last two steps, as if the mention of the pianos somehow established my bona fides.

"Er, no." I hesitated wretchedly, but there was no tactful way to introduce the subject, and I did not need to turn my head to know the revenant had come up onto the front porch. "I'm sorry, but I must ask you about Gareth Merton."

For a moment, Mr. Garfield seemed not to understand what I had said; then I watched in helpless dismay as his face crumpled, not like an adult's, but like a child's, the child both he and Gareth Merton had once been. He drew breath as if against a great weight and said, "You'd better come sit down."

I followed him into the parlor, chose a chair that put me with my back to the window and the dead, accusing eyes of the revenant. Mr. Garfield sat down and said sadly, "I thought people had forgotten about that."

"I, er . . . I was reminded."

He sighed, a noise like his heart tearing free inside his chest. "I love my work, Mr. Booth. I love my pianos and I love the fact that nobody ever notices me. I love being just Mr. Garfield, the blind piano-tuner. I don't want to be the Gareth Merton Imposter again."

"I won't bring your name into it," I said, hesitated, added, "The museum didn't send me. You won't, er . . . that is, you won't lose . . . the pianos won't . . . "

"I understand." He did not smile, but there was perhaps a little less grief in the lines of his face. "This is important to you."

"Yes. Er. I actually . . . that is, I'm not really interested in the, er, imposture."

"No?"

"No. I meant what I said. I need to know about Gareth Merton. There's no one else left to ask. And I . . . " Again, I could not help myself. I twisted to look out the window, and the revenant was there. I felt pinned between its glassy stare and Mr. Garfield's clouded sightlessness.

"Mr. Booth?"

"Mr. Garfield, I am truly sorry. But do you believe in ghosts?"

I could not believe I had said it. Both my hands were pressed to my mouth, as if it were not already too late to keep the words pent in.

But Mr. Garfield did not shout for Mrs. O'Mara to see the lunatic out. He said, "I've been blind for twenty years. I hear things. And even more so in my line of work. I could tell you stories about a Steinway on McClaren Avenue that would make your hair stand on end. And even before . . . " He sighed, folding his hands together on the head of his cane. "I don't remember much of anything before the day he said to me, 'You're Gareth Merton now,' and shoved me at the door of Mrs. Merton's house."

"He?"

"I'll get to that. I wasn't Gareth Merton, of course, and the lady knew it, although her husband took longer. I think Mr. Merton would have been happy enough to let me *be* Gareth Merton, as long as I could be raised up to do the right thing with all that money. But Mrs. Merton was having none of it. She was a kind lady, and a lovely one, but she would not lie, and she would not let her husband lie. And when she told me not to lie to her . . . well, I couldn't, that's all. Even though he said I had to. And I don't know if it was her, or him, or just something in me, but I've never been quite—never been quite in harmony with this world. It was a relief, actually, when the cataracts started to make everything go dim, because it meant I didn't have to try to believe what my eyes told me any longer. My ears and my hands. They don't lie to me, the same way I didn't lie to Mrs. Merton. And they tell me now that there's something on the porch, and it's something you don't like."

"Oh God," I said breathlessly.

"It's what drove you here, I'm guessing."

"Yes, sir," I said. "It's Gareth Merton. He says he's lost, and he wants to go home."

"Ah," said Mr. Garfield. "I'm sorry for you, Mr. Booth."

"I, er, I brought it on myself. Er, mostly. But thank you. Can you help me?"

"And this is where we get back to him." Although he said the pronoun with no particular emphasis, I realized that every time he used it, he meant the same person. The same man.

"I don't think he was my father," Mr. Garfield said. "Although he might have been. He had big, hard hands. He always smelled of blood, because he worked in a slaughterhouse and he wasn't too particular about soap. They asked me his name, but I never knew it. I don't know where he lived, or if I lived with him. He made me swear that I would never tell anyone I wasn't Gareth Merton, that I would never tell anyone about him, and that I would never forget what I owed him. He made me swear on Gareth Merton's body."

"And thus ensured," I said, very quietly, "that you would never forget Gareth Merton."

Mr. Garfield nodded once, convulsively. "I can no more forget him than my heart can forget to beat, though I never knew him when he was alive."

"He is not alive now," I said and did not—*did not*—look at the revenant standing on the porch. But I did not have to look at it to know it, to understand finally what it wanted.

"Mr. Booth?"

Gareth Merton had been a *cause célèbre* once, but that had been sixty years ago. Everyone who had known him, who could remember him, was dead—everyone except for a blind piano-tuner who had once been a *cause célèbre* himself. Language was ashes and mud in my mouth. "I'm sorry, but I think . . . "

"Yes?"

"I, er . . . I . . . I think you might be his home."

"I beg your pardon?" His head tilted as if that would help him to hear my meaning instead of just my flailing words.

"Gareth Merton wants to go home, Mr. Garfield. But his house burned down twenty years ago. His family is dead. A cemetery is not a home."

"And you think . . . "

"I think . . . that is, you're as close as he gets."

"Yes. And I . . . I have no home, either. 'Mervyn Garfield' isn't the name I was born with, you know. I don't know what is. I've thought sometimes that we both died that June, although I was brought back to life—a sort of life—and he was not."

"You understand," I said, relieved.

"Yes," he said. "I'm all that's left."

He held out his hand, and I gave him Gareth Merton's bone.

His head tilted, that posture of listening; after a long moment, he nodded. "It's all right, Mr. Booth. I hear him. I hear him just fine."

And when I turned to look out the window again, the revenant was gone.

ACKNOWLEDGMENTS

Many thanks to the editors in whose publications these stories first saw daylight, especially Barbara and Christopher Roden, and Steve Pasechnick.

Thanks also to Sonya Taaffe, without whose enthusiasm this collection would not exist. And to Sean Wallace, who listened to her.

"The Wall of Clouds" first appeared in *Alchemy* 1 (December 2003).

"Bringing Helena Back" first appeared in *All Hallows* 35 (February 2004).

"The Inheritance of Barnabas Wilcox" first appeared in *Lovecraft's Weird Mysteries* 7 (May 2004).

"The Green Glass Paperweight" first appeared in *Tales of the Unanticipated* 25 (August 2004).

"The Venebretti Necklace" first appeared in *Alchemy* 2 (September 2004).

"Wait for Me" first appeared in an online magazine, *Naked Snake Online* (September 2004), and was then on my website: www.sarahmonette.com.

"Elegy for a Demon Lover" first appeared in *Tales of the Unanticipated* 26 (October 2005), and was reprinted in *The Best of the Rest 4* (2006).

"Drowning Palmer" first appeared in *All Hallows* 41 (February 2006) and is being reprinted in *The Year's Best Fantasy* and *Horror XX* (2007).

"The Bone Key" first appeared in *Say . . . What's the Combination?* (May 2007).

"Listening to Bone" is appearing for the first time in this collection.